# FALLING INTO SENIOR YEAR

S. N. CHRISTENSEN

# CONTENTS

# AUTHOR'S NOTE

fALLINg into Senior Year is the second book in the fALLINg series and must be read after fALLINg into Summer. This book does not have a HEA, but the following book does.

Some content in this book may be triggering to some readers.

Trigger warnings include bullying, mention of rape, attempted suicide, suicide, and the use of drugs and alcohol.

# Chapter One

Three weeks into my senior year of high school and everything is going great. Too great. James and I decided to give what we have a try, which means we are exclusive. We didn't necessarily put the title of boyfriend and girlfriend on us, but I'm assuming that's what we are. We also haven't told anyone.

The long distance hasn't been much of an issue yet. He's only an hour or so away from home and we text every single day. He plans to drive home every other weekend to spend time with me and his family. I'm hoping to go there at least once a month. Having his own apartment outside of the college campus is beneficial, so I can stay at his place.

Next weekend is James' birthday, so I need to come up with a plan to surprise him. Ben and Jake's birthdays will be coming up in the new year, which I still find amazing that they are exactly two weeks apart in age. Ben and Jake, along with Bash and James. So, we will be celebrating Bash's birthday soon too.

"Who are you going to homecoming with?" Ashley places her food tray down on the lunch table, scooting in beside me on the bench.

"No one has asked me yet," I reply because I still haven't told her about James, who said he can't go anyway.

"I'm finding it hard to believe that no one has asked you yet. What about Jake?" Lauren comes and sits down next to Ashley.

"What about Jake?" Jake smiles as he puts his tray in front of me and sits.

Of course, Jake would be sitting with us today and come in on the conversation when we're talking about him. Ashley and Lauren usually sit with me at the lunch table. Sometimes Jake, Ben, and Alex will join us, but they are the most popular in the school, so they tend to sit with the other popular kids. It's just like the movies where everyone has their own tables, own seats, and own friends.

"We were asking Everly who she's going to homecoming with, and she said no one has asked her yet," Ashley tells Jake as if that will make him want to ask me.

Ashley knows that I'm in love with James, but I guess since she doesn't know I'm dating him, she thinks Jake and I would still be good together. I'm not sure why she thinks that, considering she was there for the downfall of us at the party last summer.

"Is that true?" Jake asks surprised.

"Yeah. I mean, I don't know anyone but you, Ben, and Alex at this school." I shrug my shoulders like it's no big deal.

"Do you want to go with me?" Jake asks with the biggest smile.

I know that he's trying to be sweet, but I'm not going to make him take me. "Jake, I'm certain you have someone you want to take to homecoming."

"Yeah, you," he says seriously, keeping that seductive smile on his face.

I laugh. "I appreciate the offer, but no. It's your last home-coming in high school, and I know you want to have a good night. After the dance, of course."

"Good point. I think we could have a great time during and after the dance, Everly." He winks at me.

I roll my eyes and continue to laugh. Ben and Alex make their way to our table and sit next to him.

"What's so funny?" Ben asks, as he takes a bite of his sand-wich.

"I asked Everly to homecoming, but she turned me down," Jake says with a fake pouty lip.

Everyone laughs except Lauren. It hasn't gone unnoticed that she has been quiet through this whole exchange.

"What about you Lauren? Are you going?" I ask her.

"No, I'm not," she says sadly.

"What? Why not?" I ask.

She looks at Ashley and then back down at her lunch tray. Clearly, she doesn't want to talk about it and Ashley knows. I'll have to ask her later. Alex changes the topic thankfully to football. Not that I'm a fan of football, but this conversation is getting awkward.

I feel my phone buzz and see a text from James.

James

I hear Jake is bothering you at lunch today.

Um what? How does he know that Jake is sitting with me at lunch today?

How do you know that?

James

Ben told me.

You have your brother spying on me?

James

Lol no. I texted him something and he mentioned you were eating lunch together.

Does he know about us?

James

Not yet.

Okay

It's true. I hate dances. The last couple of dances I went to was with Adam, and I don't want to even think about those. I won't lie that I'm a little envious of the girls who get to go with their boyfriends. I wish that James could come with me.

I feel my phone buzz again, but I ignore it. We only have a few more minutes of lunch, and I don't want to talk about this right now. I thought it didn't bother me that he doesn't want to tell anyone yet about us, but it does. I thought it was because it would make it harder to see each other if our parents knew since we would be in the same house, but I have a feeling that's not the case.

Jake pulls me out of my thoughts by kicking me under the table. I look up at him, and he raises his eyebrows at me. He can always tell when something is bothering me. I give him a smile to say I'm okay.

The bell rings, indicating the end of lunch. I throw my tray away and say goodbye to my friends. Jake catches up to me and puts his arms around my shoulders, walking me to our next class.

"Everything alright?" he asks.

"Yeah, why?"

"You just looked a little sad for a moment at lunch with whoever you were texting," he says, staring at me with concern.

"Oh, no. I was just thinking about something."

We reach the classroom, and he sits at the desk next to mine like he does in every class. Somehow, Jake has every class with me this semester, except one. I joked that he bribed the school to make the schedule like that, but I'm starting to wonder if he really did. Ben has one class with us, and Ashley and Lauren are in another class with us. I'm thankful to have friends in every class this year, except for one class. I also have a class with Alex.

When the school day ends, Ashley invites Lauren and me over to her house. Ashley drives us and Declan follows behind in his car. It's still odd to always have security around me, but thankfully, they allow me some privacy.

"So, what's it like having Declan around all the time?" Lauren asks.

"It's not so bad. You get used to it," I respond, shrugging my shoulders.

Ashley laughs. "I mean, I wouldn't mind having a hot older guy around me all the time, either."

Both Lauren and I laugh, too. For a while, I thought Ashley was crushing on Declan. I wouldn't blame her, though. He is pretty hot. Especially when we are training and he doesn't have a shirt on.

"How do you keep your hands to yourself?" Lauren asks seriously.

"Really? I mean, he's a lot older than me and that would just be weird. He's my bodyguard. Besides, I'm in love with someone..." I say, but immediately regret it.

"Yeah, we know. James. So, do you know if he feels the same way yet? Have you talked to him about it?" Ashley looks at me in the rearview mirror.

I look away and bite the inside of my cheek. Do I tell them? I know James doesn't want anyone to know right now, but would it be so bad to tell my best friends? They won't tell anyone. It's getting harder to keep this from them.

"Okay, you have to tell us. Clearly something happened," Lauren says, looking back at me now.

Crap. I'm horrible at keeping things to myself. I don't know how I've been able to for the past month. I mean, really, what could it hurt?

"Yeah, we talked about it. He likes me too. We're kind of just seeing where things go, so no one knows," I say, trying to downplay it.

"What?! Really? Have you two kissed?" Ashley asks, excitedly.

I feel the heat rise to my cheeks. If only she knew... "Yes."

"Oh my God, have you two had sex?! You have, haven't you?" she asks.

My heart jumps out of my chest. "What? Why would you say that?"

She laughs. "Well, for one you didn't deny it, so you have! But your face was bright red. When did this happen?"

I can't lie to her anymore. "Right before he left for college."

"Why haven't you told us?" Lauren asks like she's hurt.

"Like I said, we're just seeing where things go. I mean, it lasted all of like two days with Jake when we tried a relationship. We just don't want to make a big deal out of it, especially with our family..." I say, hoping that's the only reason James doesn't want to tell anyone.

When we get to Ashley's house, we immediately head to her bedroom. I know they want to have some more details about James and me, but I really don't want to talk more about him right now. I want to know what is going on with Lauren.

"Lauren, why aren't you going to homecoming?" I ask, hoping that she'll finally open up to me.

Lauren and I have become friends quickly, but she hasn't been as open about things with me as she is with Ashley.

She shrugs her shoulders. "My parents don't want me doing any of that this year. They said that I need to be serious about my marriage with Lorenzo."

I found out a couple of weeks ago that Lauren is supposed to be marrying a family friend named Lorenzo. I didn't know that arranged marriages were really a thing. I know that sometimes rich people try to match up their children, but this is a legit arranged marriage. Apparently, there is no getting out of it for her.

"So, you're not allowed to have fun this year? That's not really fair. What if we went together? Would your parents allow that?" I ask, hoping they might.

That wouldn't be so bad if we could go as friends, since neither of us could bring a date. It would be fun to go to the dance with just friends.

"I doubt it. My parents either would think that I'm meeting a guy there or that I've become lesbian. They are pretty strict about what I do right now. They are thinking about moving up the wedding to be during Christmas break," she explains.

I was taking a sip of water from my water bottle and spit it out all over Ashley. "I'm so sorry, Ashley." I wipe her shirt while turning back to Lauren. "Lauren, do you mean this Christmas break? Like as in two months from now?"

She nods, and her expression is not a happy one.

Dear God, what are her parents thinking? I know that she's technically eighteen, but she's still in high school. Lorenzo is a lot older than she is too, by nine years. He comes from a very wealthy family, and I know they want him to marry and have heirs. Is she going to be pregnant in high school? This is awful. Even if her parents have lost money and need help getting out of a debt, I can't believe they would just sell off their daughter like this.

"What does Brandon think about that?" I ask.

Her older brother has been against this whole thing from the beginning. He really cares about her, and I can't imagine him letting this happen without a fight.

"He's not too happy with my parents right now. He's still trying to convince them to call the whole thing off," Lauren answers.

"So, have you been on any more dates with him?" I ask, hoping that she has gotten to know him a little better.

She nods. "Yeah, we've been going out once a week now since everything is moving so fast." She doesn't offer any more information than that.

"Lauren, I need you to tell me everything. What is he like? I know he's attractive, but is he at least nice to you?" I ask, hoping that he is.

She doesn't answer and looks away from me. "Lauren, tell me," I say seriously.

She sighs. "He's okay, but he's controlling. He keeps telling me exactly how everything is going to be after we get married. I'm going to be a stay-at-home wife and mother. I'll attend functions with him, but I won't be able to go anywhere else really. He also has a temper..."

No. The way she said that last part is concerning. "Has he hurt you?"

She looks away again, and that's all I need to know. "What happened?" I demand.

Ashley has been eerily quiet throughout this entire conversation, and I know it's because she knows already. I don't like that they haven't told me any of this before. How can she be okay with this?

"He was just a little rough one time. I tried to walk away, and he grabbed me hard. It left a mark on my arm, but he's never hit me. There's just a lot of rumors about him... He's not a good man," she says it like she's scared of him.

"Lauren, there has to be a way out of this. Fine, if your parents won't end this, then maybe we can get you out of here. I have money and I'm sure Ashley can get some, too. We can get you out of town. We can..."

Lauren interrupts me. "No. There's not. I already thought about it. They would find me. He would find me. There's no escaping this."

I'm getting angry with this whole situation, but the way she said that makes me sad for her. She looks so hopeless. I've been noticing she seems depressed. I know these looks and feelings too well.

I put my hand on her shoulder. "It's going to be okay, Lauren. We're here for you and we will figure this out."

She gives me a weak smile. The same smile I again know too well. In her mind, there is no out, and this is what her life is going to be.

Ashley crawls under her bed and pulls a box out. She places it on the table and locks her door. "I feel like we need this today."

I have to say that I'm shocked when she opens the box and reveals what's inside. I did not expect her to have joints in there. She pulls one out and lights it, handing it to Lauren. She doesn't hesitate as she inhales. Ashley lights another and hands it to me. I take it but hesitate.

"Don't tell me you've never smoked pot before!" Ashley raises her eyebrows at me.

I laugh. "Nope, never. But I'm down."

I inhale and cough. They both laugh. I suppose it takes a moment to get used to it. Honestly, I have nothing against doing drugs. I just never had the means to get them or really wanted to. I had thought about it and about getting drunk, especially when Adam was forcing me to do things, but I never did. I didn't like the idea of feeling even more out of control in a situation I wasn't in control of in the first place.

We hung out for another hour before I needed to head home. I can't believe I've never smoked weed before. I feel so relaxed and just so... good. Lauren looks like she feels the same way. She looks much better than she did an hour ago. I stand up too fast, the dizziness hitting me as I stumble into Ashley's desk. My foot catches on Lauren's shoes, then a stuffed animal, and somehow I'm still tripping my way across the room, only managing to catch myself when I finally reach the door. We all laugh because I'm clumsy as it is, but apparently when I'm high, I'm even more clumsy. Maybe this isn't a good combination.

I say my goodbyes and head home. Once I get outside, I jump in the passenger seat in Declan's car.

"I'm ready to go home!" I say, maybe a little too giddy than I should've been.

He doesn't move, looks me over, and grins.

"Everly... Are you..." he looks back and forth between my eyes. "High?"

I laugh. "Whaattt? Nooo! Why would you think that?"

He smirks. "I could smell it on you the moment you got in the car, and you're acting high."

"Shit! Really? How do I get rid of the smell?" I ask like he should know.

He laughs again. "Go home and take a shower. You'll be fine."

I do as he suggests the moment I get back. I run upstairs as fast as I can to avoid everyone and immediately jump in the shower. The effects of the weed didn't last as long as I had hoped. I really like feeling relaxed and not caring about anything. I can see why people do it, and I really regret not doing it sooner. I have a feeling it won't be my last time.

# CHAPTER TWO

I lay in bed, staring at the ceiling while tapping my fingers on my leg. James was supposed to come home today, but it's already noon, and I haven't heard from him. I pick up my phone and decide to call him instead of text.

"Hello?" he answers on the third ring.

"Hey! I was wondering when you were going to be home?" I ask.

There's a slight pause before he says, "I'm sorry Everly. I thought I texted you. I had some things come up this weekend, so I don't think I'll make it home."

I can't help but feel disappointed. "Oh, okay. What about next weekend? It's your birthday on Friday. Do you think you'll come back to celebrate?"

"My buddies have something planned for me on Saturday, so probably not," he says with some sadness in his voice. At least he feels sad about it, I think.

"You're not able to come home the following weekend, either. So, what, it'll be like a month before I can see you again?" I ask as my heart sinks, thinking about it.

Once again, he pauses before answering. "Everly. I'm sorry. I told you this would be hard once I went back to college..."

He's right, he did. I can't get mad at him for it, but I do have a right to be upset.

"I know, and it's okay. Really. I just... never mind." I stop myself. It's probably best that I don't say anything.

"What?"

"Nothing," I say a little too fast.

"Everly. Tell me."

I sigh. "I'm okay with being apart for a bit, but... I have to know. What are we James? Are we boyfriend and girlfriend? I just... I don't like to think that with so much time between seeing you that you might be... with someone else. I know you said we're exclusive, but..."

"What? No Everly. I'm not going to be with someone else no matter how much time passes that I don't see you. Yes, you are my girlfriend. I only want you," he says sincerely.

I can't help but smile because that makes me feel better.

"Okay. Good," I say and there's silence between us again.

"I'll see what I can do to see you. I don't want to go a month without seeing you either," he says, breaking the silence.

This distance between us is getting harder than I thought it would be, but knowing how much he wants me too makes me feel better. We can do this.

"Okay," I say.

"Is something else bothering you?" he asks, because he knows me.

I sigh. "I was hoping you'd be home today so I could talk to you about it. I don't want to on the phone and you get mad at me."

"What is it?"

Ugh. I have to tell him. I can't keep secrets from him. "I just... I did something the other day, and I don't want to hide it from you."

He's silent, and I take that as he wants me to continue.

"I got high," I spit out so fast I'm not sure he could understand them.

"You what?" he asks, shocked.

"I was at Ashley's house and well... She had some weed and for the first time, I got high."

I feel like I should apologize to him, but I don't really know why I'd apologize. I'm not sorry that I did it or ashamed. I just wanted him to know. I feel like if he was doing drugs occasionally, I would want to know.

He laughs. "Okay, so you got high. What did you think?"

What? Really? This is not at all the reaction I expected. "Um... I kind of liked it. Except I'm apparently even more clumsy when I'm high."

He laughs again. "I don't see how you can get more clumsy than you are now. I'm not mad Everly. I'm surprised that it was your first time. Just be careful if you do it again, okay?"

"Shouldn't you be telling me not to do drugs?" I ask him.

"Do you want me to tell you not to do drugs?"

"Not really."

"Then I won't. I trust that you know what you're doing. I'd be a hypocrite because I've done them myself," he says.

I love he has that trust, and I don't know why I'm shocked to find out he has. Maybe it's because he always seems like he's in control.

"Do you still?" I ask, wondering if he has since getting back to college.

"Not really. It was more of a high school thing, but I did occasionally last year."

Good to know. We talk for a little longer, and our phone call is exactly what I needed. I miss him so much.

"I miss you, James," I say before saying goodbye.

"I miss you too," he says.

"I love you," I say while hovering over the end call button.

"I love you too, Everly. Goodbye."

I hang up the phone. I hate those prolonged goodbyes that people do. They are too sappy and honestly just make things worse when you do finally hang up. My heart did sink a little though once we ended our conversation. I don't know how I'm going to go a month without seeing him. He did say next week he had plans on Saturday, but he said nothing about Friday night. I think I know exactly what I'm going to do for his birthday on Friday.

My phone buzzes in my hand to find a group message from Ashley and Lauren.

Ashley has been begging to go dress shopping for home-coming and apparently, she decided, today is the day. If James was here, I would have said no, but since he's not, then it's the perfect time. I have to say I'm surprised Lauren is allowed to go, since she's on a tight leash now.

Declan and Barry sit in the front seat while I hop in the back. We picked up Ashley first and then Lauren. We're heading to the mall, so they will have to accompany us inside. I don't mind, and by the looks of it, neither does Ashley. She's been watching Declan drive the entire way.

We head into the dress store, while Declan and Barry stand at the entrance of the store. One is watching outside while the other is watching inside. It really makes me wonder if they believe that something could happen to me here.

My thoughts are torn away as Ashley comes running up to me with a dress. "You have to try this one on!"

I grab it from her and laugh. "You're joking, right? This is hideous!"

The dress is long and flowy with fake flowers and butterflies all over it. There are sparkles on the bottom of the dress, too. This is not at all my style, nor is it hers. I know she's just being cruel.

"That's the fun of it! We each have a hideous dress to try on. Go find me one!" Ashley says as she goes back to the racks.

I look around at all the dresses and found one that I think Ashley would hate. She finds one for Lauren. While searching for hideous dresses, I also find a few pretty ones that I'd like to actually try on for homecoming. I've been debating not going, but Lauren's parents finally caved and are letting her go. She's just not allowed to dance with anyone.

The first dresses we try on are the hideous ones. I look ridiculous, but Ashley looks decent in hers. She looks great in everything. We take a selfie, and I make them take a picture of just me so I can send it to James.

What do you think of this dress for homecoming? It's my favorite so far!

We all got a good laugh at the fact I tricked James into thinking I did really like the dress. Ashley ends up finding a beautiful, green, tight-fitting dress that goes down to her knees. It's sparkly just the way she likes it. My dress is also tight-fitting and shows off the little curves that I have perfectly. It's dark blue and also very sparkly. It looks like the night sky and that's probably why I like it so much. Lauren picks a pink flowy dress. It isn't sexy or revealing at all, just like her parents wanted. She still looks amazing in it. I can't wait for us to get ready together. I just wish James could come with me.

When we leave the dress store, I notice a lingerie store across the way.

"Can we stop in there real fast?" I nod toward the store and Ashley's face lights up.

"Ohhh, you want to get something sexy for James?" she asks, and I elbow her in the ribs.

Declan is standing right behind us, and I know that he heard. He's going to find out sooner or later that I'm dating James, but I don't want him to yet. I trust Declan with my life, just not my secrets anymore. We walk around the store, and Ashley keeps picking up items to show me that are way too mature for me. I know I've had sex, but I don't feel mature enough for these types of items. I'm pretty sure she's trying to get Declan's attention. I can't help but smile.

"What?" she asks.

"You really like Declan," I say it as a statement, not a question.

She blushes, shrugs her shoulders and says, "I guess he's hot."

Lauren and I both laugh. Lauren says, "You guess? Girl, you've been drooling over him all day."

"I have not!" Ashley wipes the side of her lip like she's checking if there really is drool on her mouth.

I feel uncomfortable walking around the store with Declan right now, so I quickly make a pick for Friday night. I think James is going to like these.

We get back in the car and go to drop Lauren off first because her parents didn't want her out long. I've only met her mom once, and she seems super strict. Lauren's brother is nice, and he really tries to look out for her. He's in college, though, so he's not home much to help.

When we pull up to Ashley's house, I reach into my purse and pull out a hundred-dollar bill. "Before I forget. For home-coming night for us all."

She knows what it's for as we talked about it yesterday. Since none of us have dates to homecoming, we figured we would spend the night at Ashley's house afterward and have a little fun. I gave her extra, of course, for the future.

Before she gets out of the car, Declan asks, "Do you want some help to the house with your bags?"

I cough at him offering to help her. I look over at her face and she's shocked and bright red.

"Sure," is all she gets out in a high-pitched voice.

I see a smirk on Declan's face. What is he doing?

He gets out and opens the door for her. Then he grabs her bags out of the trunk and walks her to the front door. I can see her say thank you and then she runs into the house. Declan comes back to the car and drives off.

"Declan, what was that?" I ask, confused at what just happened.

"What? I was being nice and helping your friend," he says.

I shake my head. "You know she has a crush on you. Don't make it worse."

He looks at me through the rear-view mirror like he's trying to decipher something. "Oh, does she? I didn't notice." He smirks.

I lean forward and smack his shoulder. "You are not that dense to not have noticed her flirting today."

He laughs and I still don't understand what his intentions were there. I know he doesn't like her. Not that she isn't gorgeous. Any guy would want her. It's just that Declan is much older, and I know he's not interested in high school girls in that way.

My phone buzzes and I know it was Ashley before I even pull up the text.

Ashley

> Um... Why did Declan help me in with my stuff?

> Really not sure. But you're hot so not surprising.

I don't know why I just said that. I mean, it's true, but I know Declan doesn't like her. Right? I keep staring up at the rearview mirror, catching Declan's gaze every now and then trying to figure him out. Yeah, I can't figure him out.

# Chapter Three

The weekend flew by fast, and I spent most of yesterday reading a book in bed. It's been a while since I've gotten into a good book. I used to read all the time when I was trying to escape my life, but now my life is going really well. Too good, I keep thinking to myself.

I head to my locker and notice a note taped to it. I look around to see if there is anyone watching me, but it doesn't look like it. I take it off and read it.

*I hope you haven't gotten too comfortable at school. We let you get settled and now it's time to shake things up a bit. You tried to ruin my life, now it's time to ruin yours. My friends will be in touch. Have a great year.*

I hold the note in my hand and stare at it for a minute, thinking that's definitely from Adam. I was hoping that I wouldn't be dealing with him anymore after my father said things were taken care of with him. Adam wasn't joking when he said he had friends at this school. What does that mean for me?

I shove the note in my pocket and try to forget about it. I open my locker, and something startles me as it comes flying out, hitting me in the stomach, and dripping down my shirt. There's a clinking sound as a red solo cup hits the floor and rolls away with a trail of red paint. I now have that paint on my shirt and down my pants. You're joking, right?

I feel a hand on my shoulder pulling me from my thoughts.

"Hey, what happened?" Ben is standing beside me, looking at the mess before him.

Jake comes up too. "What happened Everly?"

Wow, I can already feel the tears forming in my eyes. I'm not sure if it's because I know I'm going to have a miserable year at school because of Adam, again. Or if it's because I now have friends who care about me and are there for me. I'm pretty sure it's both.

"Nothing, just an accident," I say as I lean over to pick up the cup.

The note that was partially in my pocket falls onto the floor. Jake bends down to pick it up and reads it before I can grab it away from him.

"Is this from Adam?" he asks.

He knows it is and I know it is, but I shrug my shoulders anyway like I don't know.

"Fuck. Why won't that guy leave you alone?"

"He told me he has a lot of friends at this school and in the city," I say nonchalantly.

"You need to tell your security team," Ben says.

I don't say anything back and just nod. I'll tell them later. It's not a huge deal. It's just a note and some paint. I go to grab the spare clothes that I keep in my locker and notice they are missing.

"Seriously, they stole my clothes. I guess I'll be carrying everything around with me all year..." I try to stay calm.

I'm used to keeping my backpack with me because of last year too. I never trusted Adam and once Kayla stabbed me in the back, I didn't trust her or her friends, either. When you have money, it's easy to get whatever information you want, especially something as simple as a locker code. Who knows who all has my code now, so I won't be risking anything getting stolen or ruined. It makes it easier to get to class anyway when you have everything with you all the time.

"Let's get you cleaned up," Jake says, leading me toward the bathroom.

"I got it Jake, it's okay. Seriously, I'm fine," I force a smile on my face to convince him.

He lets me go in the bathroom alone to get cleaned up, which is a good thing because there are quite a few girls in here. I don't want him getting in trouble for entering the girls' bathroom, even if he's just trying to help me. All the girls are staring at me while I try to clean the paint up. They start whispering and I'm not sure if it's my paranoia or what, but I'm pretty sure they're talking about me. So much for staying invisible this year.

The paint did not come out of my clothes, but I at least got it off, so it won't drip anywhere or spread to anything if I rub against something. When I look toward my locker, the mess is cleaned up off the floor, and I can only assume Ben did that for me. I will have to thank him later. Jake is waiting outside the bathroom and places his arm around my waist as we walk to our first class together.

"Are you okay?" Jake asks, concerned.

"I'm fine Jake. This is nothing but a small prank."

He doesn't look convinced, but he drops it.

The rest of the day went smoothly, but I'm not going to lie that I was looking over my shoulder all day. I was trying to keep an eye out on who was watching me so I could figure out who might be in this with Adam. I could go to administration, and they could look at the cameras, but I really don't want to get them involved. I just want to stay invisible.

My phone rings on the way home from school, and I look at the caller ID to find James calling.

"Hello?" I answer.

"Hey, how was today?" he asks.

"It was fine. How was your day?" That was such an automatic response.

He's silent for a moment. "Everly, I know what happened today."

I sigh. "Who told you?"

"Ben."

I laugh. "Why is Ben telling you about everything that happens at school with me?"

"Because I asked him to," he says this like it's normal.

"Okay... Why did you ask him to? Don't you think he might guess that we're together?" I ask, while picking at the paint on my pants.

"Maybe," he says.

I sigh again. "James... Why don't you want them to know?"

"Look, you can tell them if you really want to. I don't mind them knowing we're together."

That's not convincing. "Okay, I will tell them. But I want to know why you've kept it a secret for so long."

This time he sighs. "Because... I don't want Jake trying to steal you from me."

Well, that is not at all what I was expecting.

"What? Why would you say that?" I ask, and it comes out in a whisper.

"Because he still likes you, Everly. If he knows that we're together, he's going to try to get you back. If he thinks you're not with anyone, then he will feel comfortable where you guys are currently in your relationship," he says like he had really thought this through.

"I don't understand why you think that. Jake and I are just friends, and he knows that," I say, trying to sound convincing.

"I know that because I felt the same way when you started dating Jake. That's just how guys like us are," he says like that's all the explanation I need.

"Well, you are missing one key point here, James," I speak a little more harshly than I mean to.

"What?" he asks.

"I love you, not Jake. So even if he tries something, I'm going to remind him of that. Do you trust me?"

The pause before he answers is concerning. "Yes."

"Good. Then you have nothing to worry about," I say, hoping that's the end of that discussion and the previous one as well.

"We got off track. Tell me what's going on at school," he says more seriously this time.

"Seriously, it was nothing. It was just a little prank. It was nothing compared to what happened at my old school." I try to ease his worries.

"Promise me you will be careful and will let me know if anything else happens," he demands.

"Of course." But only if Ben knows of it because he will tell him no matter what.

"Alright, I just wanted to check on you. I love you."

"Love you too. Bye."

I hang up the phone and then realize that I'm still in the car with Declan and Barry. My eyes meet Declan's in the rearview mirror.

"What happened at school, Everly?" he asks.

"It was nothing. Just a little prank," I repeat for the twentieth time today. I don't want to make a big deal out of this, nor think about it.

"Tell me," he says sternly.

Ugh. Why did this have to happen? I was really enjoying the past month. I should be thankful that I got a month this year that was actually good. Sometimes I wonder if I did something in a past life to deserve what is happening to me now. Then again, I just wonder if everyone's life is like this. Everyone said junior year of high school was horrible and that was when it all started. It just doesn't seem to be ending there for me.

I sigh. "Adam had someone leave a note for me on my locker."

I pull out the note and read it to him. "Then when I opened my locker, red paint spilled all over me. See, just a dumb prank."

I see Declan clench the steering wheel, and Barry shifts in his seat. I really don't want them to do anything about this because it's going to make it worse.

"Look, Adam has a lot of friends. Can we just drop it? I can handle these dumb pranks, but if something bigger happens, I'll tell you, okay? I don't want this to get worse."

I can tell Declan is thinking about it, and he glances over at Barry. Declan finally nods. "Alright."

I feel my phone vibrate to see a new message in the boys' group. That's what I named our group messages with Jake, Ben, Bash, and James.

James

Everly and I are officially dating.

Well, I did not expect that, but it makes me smile.

Ben

I'm shocked.

Jake

Noo!! Everly you dare betray our love?

Bash

It's about time.

Why do none of you seem surprised?

Ben

We found you in his bed at the beginning of the summer remember?

Nothing happened.

Jake

So you're saying you haven't slept with him?

Well I didn't say that.

The group message keeps going on, but I ignore it as I text James separately.

That means a lot to me that you told them. Thank you.

James

I'm glad I did. But you could've left out the part about sleeping together.

I wanted Jake to know how serious I am about you.

James

So you admit he likes you?

No but if it's a concern to you then it is to me.

James

I love you Everly

I love you too James

# Chapter Four

I'm currently in the car with Declan heading to James' apartment. We don't need a second security guard since I'll be with James mostly at his place. We're thirty minutes away from reaching our destination and my nerves are getting the better of me. Maybe I shouldn't have done this.

I texted James at midnight this morning wishing him a happy birthday, but I haven't said another word to him since. The school day went fine, and nothing has happened since Monday. I'm not convinced that it's over, but I'll take the bit of peace that I can get at school.

When we pull up to his apartment, I hesitate to get out.

"Is everything okay?" Declan asks.

I look over at him. "Yeah, I'm just nervous. I didn't tell him I was coming."

"Well, I'll be out here all night if you need anything," he says.

I always feel bad when my security team has to sleep out in their car. At least, I hope they get some sleep. I'll be leaving early in the morning to not ruin the plans James has with his friends. I just really miss sleeping in his arms.

James said that he usually gets home around five from classes on Friday. He got stuck with one of the later classes this year, which stinks especially on Fridays. I only have fifteen minutes to get my act together before he shows up, so I shove the nerves down, climb out of the car, and sprint up the stairs to his apartment. I pull out the key he gave me and let myself in.

It's a large apartment, bigger than the average house. Thankfully, the noises of the city are drowned out. The insulation and soundproofing are pretty good here. Instead of looking around his apartment like I want to, I quickly head to the bathroom to make sure I still look okay. I fix up my hair and thankfully my makeup is still perfect. I take off my shirt and pants, neatly folding them on the bathroom sink. I look at myself in the mirror and can't help but smile. I think James is going to like this.

I couldn't figure out a good birthday gift for him, so I thought maybe I would be enough. I have on the lacy red bra and thong that I bought from the lingerie store last weekend. I go to the living room and plop myself on his couch. I move around for a few minutes, trying to find the best position that I think would be sexy for when he walks in the door. He will have to round the corner before he sees me.

I hear the key in the door and quickly get into the position I decided on. I have my elbow on the arm of the couch with my head in my hand. I'm laying across the couch with my left leg bent up. I try to straighten my shoulders and body to push out my breasts a little, but not to look like I'm trying too hard. I hear his footsteps enter and see him round the corner.

He immediately spots me, and his face lights up as he throws his keys on the counter.

"Well, this is a surprise," he says while placing his messenger bag on the stool and walking toward me.

I look up at him and say, "Hopefully a good surprise."

"Mmm..." he says while sitting on the couch in front of me and pulling me into a kiss.

I roll to my back, and he straddles me on the couch. I'm thankful his couch is so comfortable and a lot deeper than a normal one.

He parts our kiss and looks me up and down. His fingers trace the lacy bra around my breast and then he trails his fingers down my stomach doing the same thing around my thong.

"I think this is the best birthday yet," he says looking at me like he can't hold back any longer.

He leans forward and kisses me again while cupping my breasts through the bra. I want to tease him a little more with this, but I'm so turned on by the way he's just looking at me. I unbutton his shirt and take it off him within seconds. I trail my hands up and down his chest enjoying every inch of him and his beautiful abs. It should really be a crime to have abs this sexy.

It takes less than five minutes for us to lie completely naked on the couch. I spent a hundred and fifty dollars on this lingerie set for it to last five minutes. With the way James looked at me, it was worth every penny.

James trails his kisses down my neck, over my breasts, stomach, and to my thighs. He's kissing me everywhere except where I want him to. He knows it's torture. Finally, he takes one long stroke with his tongue exactly where I need it.

"Mmm... You have no idea how much I've missed tasting you," he says as he begins eating me out like he's starving for me.

It doesn't take long for me to climb to the edge, but right before I climax, he pulls away. I let out a groan.

"I want to us to come together. Hang on, let me grab a condom."

He's about to get up when I pull him back down on me. "Don't you dare leave me like this."

He laughs. "Baby, I need to be inside you."

I pull him in for a kiss and wrap my legs around his waist so he can't let go. He's just a centimeter away from entering me.

"I'm on the pill," I say, and he doesn't need any more convincing before he thrusts inside me.

He tries to go slow, but we both need more. He thrusts fast and hard, which makes us both come quicker than we would've liked. I can feel the warmth of him as he releases inside me. I've always used a condom before and this new feeling without one is amazing.

He rolls off me and kisses me on the temple. He pulls on his boxers and goes into the kitchen for something. While he does that, I figure I'll go get cleaned up in the bathroom real quick. I stole one of his t-shirts earlier from his closet and had it waiting for me. I throw it on but keep my bra and underwear off. His shirt covers me enough that you can't see anything unless I bend over.

When I come out of the bathroom, James is sitting back on the couch with some water for me. I take a sip and sit down next to him, leaning my head on his shoulder. He has the tv on, but neither of us are watching it.

"I've missed you," James says stroking my hair.

I smile. "Me too."

"How long are you staying for?" he asks.

I sit up and look at him, hoping to get a read on that question. Does he look like he wants me to stay, or does he look like he wants me to leave? I'm thinking it looks like he wants me to stay.

"Well... I was hoping you didn't have any plans tonight. I was thinking we could eat some dinner, and I could spend the night. I'll leave tomorrow morning because I know you have plans with your friends," I say, really hoping that he's okay with that.

He kisses me on the lips and says, "That sounds perfect, except leaving in the morning. Can you stay all weekend? You can come with me tomorrow. I'd like to introduce you to my friends."

I know my entire face lights up when he says that. "Really?"

He laughs. "Yes, really. You don't think I'm trying to hide you, do you?"

I shrug. "The thought crossed my mind. I thought you might be embarrassed to be dating someone still in high school."

He grabs my face and looks directly into my eyes. "I could never be embarrassed by you. They are all going to be jealous that you're mine."

I feel my cheeks heat as I blush at what he said. He knows exactly what to say to me to make me feel good.

I text Declan the change of plans and he's going to have Barry drive up as well since I'll be here all weekend. James orders some Chinese so we don't have to leave his apartment and can stay in all night.

When he comes back from ordering, he looks me up and down. "I love seeing you in my shirt. It looks much better on you than me."

I grin. "It's comfy and you're not getting it back."

After dinner, James puts on a movie, but we are not paying attention at all. We start making out and it quickly turns to more when he moves his hand up my shirt to realize I have nothing on underneath it.

He groans. "Everly... What are you trying to do to me?"

I giggle, but that quickly turns into a moan as he licks between my legs again. It feels so good.

He pulls back for a second to say, "God, you taste so good. I'll never get enough of you."

I can feel my cheeks heat with his words. His talking dirty to me is new. It's somewhat embarrassing, but I would be lying if I said I don't love it. He enters two fingers inside of me as he continues to lick and brings me through another climax. He crawls on top of me and starts kissing me again.

When we part, I push him off so I can get down on my knees in front of him to return the favor, but he stops me. "Let me just enjoy you for a little bit. We have all night."

He pulls me into another make-out session, and the whole world slips away for the rest of the night while we enjoy each other's company and make love more times than we have in the past.

# CHAPTER FIVE

James and I stay in bed until lunchtime, reluctantly getting up because our stomachs demand it. I go to the kitchen to make a couple of sandwiches to eat while he takes a shower. When I hear the water turn off, I race back into the bedroom to sit on the edge of the bed. I'm still only in a t-shirt, and I'm very sore from last night's activities.

James comes out with a towel wrapped around his waist, and his hair is dripping wet. Holy crap, he is hot. This is exactly why I ran back into his room before he stepped out of the bathroom. I didn't want to miss this.

He smirks at me as he notices I'm staring at him. "I thought you were getting lunch ready."

I smile. "I was, but I heard the shower turn off and I didn't want to miss the show."

He stalks toward me and stands directly in front of me. "And what show is that?"

I reach out, placing my hand on his chest. "This. Your perfect abs on display and your hair dripping wet. I'm so turned on right now."

He pushes me onto my back and starts kissing me. I moan. I want him so badly again even though my body protests after how many times I had him last night.

James pulls back. "I think we need a break, but I'll have you again in my bed tonight."

I groan in protest. "You're torturing me."

He laughs. "Not as much as you're torturing me. Go get ready and I'll finish making lunch."

Without arguing, I head into the bathroom and turn the shower on. I take a quick shower and get dressed for the day, putting my hair up in a messy bun because I don't feel like drying it right now. I need to eat first.

By the time I make it out to the kitchen, James is fully dressed, and our sandwiches are ready.

"I was hoping you would still be in a towel when I got out here," I say to him.

He smirks again. I love that smirk. "I think you're worse than me."

"I am not," I say, fake pouting.

He kisses me again and leads me to the stool at the island, pushing the sandwich in front of me. "I don't want to be a bad influence. You need to eat."

I do what I'm told and eat every bite. I'm starving.

"The sandwich was amazing. We make a great team," I say because it does really taste good. Maybe it's just because we skipped breakfast and worked up quite the appetite.

James laughs. "It was really good, but I think it was even better because of the company."

James leans over and starts kissing my neck. I laugh and swat him away.

"What happened to needing a break and waiting until tonight?" I tease.

This time, he groans in protest. "I forgot I said that. Can I take it back?"

I stand up to put some distance between us. "Nope. Now let's go."

I walk toward the door to put my shoes on, but he wraps his arms around me from behind, lifts me up in the air and plops me on the couch.

"We can take a few minutes to enjoy each other," he says while kissing under my ear and down the side of my face to my neck.

I giggle. "So, this is why you wanted me to stay. You're just using me for my body."

James stops kissing me and puts his forehead to mine before pulling away to look me in the eyes. "While I do love your body, Everly, I love everything about you. When I'm not with you, you're all I think about and the only person I want to be spending time with. You've invaded every thought that I have."

I was just joking about the using me for my body comment, but dear God James has just made my heart swell. I thought that

I was being a needy teenager because I can't stop thinking about him either when I'm not with him. I can't get enough of him when I am with him and never believed true love existed, but I'm pretty sure I've found that it does.

James walks me around campus to show me where he goes during the day. I enjoy seeing the places he likes to sit to study and hang out with his friends. It's nice to be able to picture where he is when I'm talking to him. He leads me to the frat house where we'll be celebrating his birthday. I'm surprised that he's not part of a fraternity with how popular he is, but he has a lot of buddies in them that he hangs out with.

I didn't expect to be coming to a party with him, so I didn't bring anything nice to wear. I'm just wearing my short jean shorts and a tank top. At least it has a graphic of flowers on it, so it's not plain. I did dry my hair and tried to make it look decent. It's straight since I didn't have my curling iron with me. I spent more time on my makeup than normal to make up for my appearance.

As if James can tell what I'm thinking, he says, "You look fantastic tonight, Everly."

I smile up at him. "Thanks. So do you. I really love you in those button-down shirts with jeans."

He smiles back and I can tell he's making note of what I just said. Good. Because I find him really hard to resist when he looks like that. I find it even harder when his hair looks a little messy, as if I just ran my hands through it.

He introduces me to some of his friends, who already seem to be drunk. Actually, it seems like they are still partying from the night before. Is that what happens on the weekends at college in a frat house? Regardless, his friends are kind, and no one seems to be bothered by the high schooler in attendance. It's crowded, and the music is loud, but it isn't exactly what I expected. I thought there would be more people making out in corners, but I suppose they have rooms they can go in. I'm curious about what I would find if I went upstairs.

James leads me to the counter with the beers. He grabs each of us one, and we find a spot on a couch to sit and relax for a bit. I enjoy his company while people watching. James has his arm around my waist and his thumb is rubbing the top of my thigh, higher than he should be. He knows what he's doing.

We both finish our beer before Bash shows up. I love the fact that they are going to the same college and are still best friends. We all plan to attend here next year which is comforting to me. It's going to be a lot of fun hanging out with them all year before James and Bash graduate. I can't even imagine the things we are going to do and the trouble we are going to get into. If our parents thought we were bad as kids under their roof, then imagine us when we are adults with no rules. Not that we have very strict parents to begin with.

"Happy Birthday, James," Bash says, giving him one of the guy hugs with a pat on the back.

He comes up to me and gives me a hug, whispering in my ear, "They're out front."

I nod, release him, and watch him walk off toward the front door. James doesn't know it, but I texted Jake and Ben about tonight. Bash agreed James would love to have them here, too. Getting the five of us together without adult supervision is never the best idea, but it always makes for great memories.

I lean into James and give him a kiss on the lips. "I need some fresh air for a moment. Come with me?"

I wasn't really asking, as I didn't give him a chance to answer. I grab his hand and pull him toward the front door. Once we open the door, he immediately spots our friends and his face lights up.

"Hey!" he yells over toward Jake and Ben.

Jake smiles wide and Ben yells out, "Happy Birthday, man."

After catching up for a moment outside, James leans into me. "Did you plan this?"

I smile but don't respond. I don't need to. I'm just so glad that he is happy to have them here and isn't embarrassed by his high school girlfriend and friends intruding on his college life. I was afraid that once he went back to college, he would regret being with me. I was wrong.

As the night went on, the drunker I got. The drunker we all got. I decide to take a breather and sit on the couch while watching James and his friends play beer pong. I'm not sure that they all need to be drinking more, but who am I to tell them to stop? I enjoy watching James like this. He's so carefree and laughs with his friends. I feel like he has to be so serious most of the time because he has a lot of pressure on his shoulders to take over his father's business. I know he wants to take over, but I think he feels like he doesn't have any room to make mistakes. I can't imagine that feeling. Regardless, I'm glad that he feels comfortable letting go occasionally around us.

A random guy comes to sit next to me on the couch. He's good looking, but not my type. Well, maybe he would've been if I wasn't with James. I definitely would've been flattered by the way he's looking at me, but I can tell he's a player. He probably gets laid every weekend by a different girl. His dark hair is spiked up, and he has big hazel eyes. Surprisingly, he doesn't look all that drunk.

"I haven't seen you here before," he says, leaning in closer so I can hear him over the music.

I laugh. "That is the worst pickup line ever, and everyone knows it."

He gives me a smile and I can see why girls would throw themselves at him. "It was just an observation, not a pickup line. Do you go to school here?"

I shake my head. "Nope. I'm a high schooler."

I figured that would get him to go away, but surprisingly, it doesn't. Noted. He's one of those that doesn't care how old or who you are as long as he can get you in bed.

"Ah, senior right? You've chosen the best way to tour a college. Experiencing the night life at a frat party will tell you everything you need to know." Shockingly, he seems like he isn't being serious about that.

Before we can continue our conversation, James comes over and swoops me up so he can sit and places me on his lap. He places a kiss on my lips and looks over at the guy that's sitting too close to us for comfort.

"Hey Brad. I see you met my girlfriend," he says possessively.

Brad's grin widens as he looks between us, and he puts his hands in the air like he's surrendering. "I get it. Happy Birthday James." He stands up and looks back at me. "It was nice meeting you. Hope to see you here next year."

I nod but don't say anything back. I smile at James, but he doesn't exactly look happy.

"What's wrong?" I ask.

He shakes his head. "You're too beautiful for a place like this. Too many guys are going to be hitting on you, and I don't want to get in a fight tonight. Let's get out of here."

I laugh. "James, you have nothing to worry about. I want you to have fun tonight with your friends."

Jake and Ben come over toward where we're sitting, and Ben pipes up into the conversation. "He's right Everly. Let's head back to James' apartment. I have something fun for us to do, anyway."

I shrug and follow their lead. If they all want to get out of here, who am I to oppose? It's been a couple of hours, anyway.

I'm already on the verge of being drunk, and I'm not sure I want to go down that route again right now.

It didn't take me long to figure out why everyone was okay with going back to James' apartment. Ben brought some joints for us to enjoy, and I'm kind of excited about the idea. I've never seen James high before, or any of them, for that matter. I'm fairly certain this good night is about to turn into an epic night.

As we enjoy the drugs and alcohol that are continuing to flow between us, none of us can stop laughing. I'm not even sure what we've been talking about for the past half hour, but it's hilarious, obviously.

"Who is ready for something fun?" Bash asks the group. He's already the drunkest of all of us, so this should be good.

We all raise our hands like we are back in the classroom.

"Old Dude Nicholas needs a makeover. Shall we dress him up?" he asks, barely keeping a straight face.

Who is Old Dude Nicholas? Regardless, I'm down. "I'm in!"

They all look at me and laugh. "Do you even know what I'm talking about?" Bash asks.

"Nope, but who cares? It'll be fun," I say, shrugging my shoulders.

James explains they call the giant statue in the middle of campus Old Dude Nicholas. I vaguely remember seeing it when he was taking me on a tour of the campus earlier. That statue is like at least twelve feet tall if not taller. I'm pretty sure it's taller. I'm too drunk and high to be able to tell how tall something is. Regardless, this is going to be fun.

# Chapter Six

It's now past midnight and everyone is either still partying or sleeping in their dorms. There's no one anywhere near Old Dude Nicholas, and it's dark except for a couple of lamps lighting the path around us.

Bash pulls some items out of his backpack, and I have no idea where he got it all from. I don't even remember him going back to his place to get the backpack. Regardless, I watch as he pulls the items out. A giant roll of pink tulle, duct tape, a floral dress, and a woman's tea party hat.

I laugh as he looks so serious, placing them all around the statue. "Where did you get all these things and why do you have them?"

He looks at me like I asked him the dumbest question on earth. "Why wouldn't I have them?"

I shrug and drop it. I'm too wasted to care. The boys go back and forth about the plan. Apparently, we're going to be using the tulle to make a skirt for him and the dress is going to be his shirt. That's a good idea. Then, obviously, we're going to be putting the hat on top of his head. Not sure how we're getting all the way up there, though.

"You coming, Everly?" James asks from on top of the base of the statue.

I look over and Bash has Jake on his shoulders on the other side of the statue from James. When did they all get up there and what did I miss? I shrug my shoulders and hop up on the base next to James.

James kneels down and says, "Get on."

Oh! I'm supposed to be on his shoulders like Jake is on Bash's. I get it. Don't know why, but sure.

I laugh as I hop on James' shoulders, and he stands up. From the other side, Jake reaches around the backside of the statue and hands me the roll of tulle. Oh!! We're making the skirt. Good idea on how to do it. How did I miss this conversation?

Jake and I pass the tulle around the statue for what feels like twenty minutes. The fact we've only done a few passes makes it seem like it's probably a lot less time. We drop the roll a few times and stumble quite a lot, but we all survive. So far.

The roll ends on my side, so James hands me the duct tape. I have trouble getting the duct tape off the roll to start, but eventually get it. I don't know exactly how this is supposed to work, but I start it at the top of the skirt and bring the tape all the way down to the bottom of it. I do a couple of passes, and I think it's going to stay. Before I can debate putting more on, James kneels, and I crawl off him.

He turns toward me smiling and whispers in my ear, "I can't wait to get back to the apartment and have you on me again."

I smirk, but he plants a kiss on my lips. Hard, sloppy, and wet. Yeah, we are both wasted.

"Get a room!" Jake yells out, even though he's standing right beside us.

I pull away from James and look at the statue. It looks great, like he really has a skirt on. I'm proud of the work we did.

"Alright, you ready Everly?" Bash asks me while handing me the hat.

"Huh?" I ask as I take it.

Ben laughs. "We're going to help you get on Old Dude Nicholas' shoulders so you can duct tape the hat to his head."

Wow what? Did I agree to this? That looks pretty high up, but sure. "Okay. What about the dress?"

They all look at me, confused. I look back at the statue to see the dress taped to the front of him like it's a shirt. When did they do that?! And that makes a lot more sense. I guess that wouldn't fit over the statue.

"So, you want me to get up on his shoulders so I can put the hat on? How is this going to work?" I ask, looking between the four of them.

Jake responds, "You're going to stand up on James' shoulders and then climb to the statue's shoulders and put it on. It'll work. You'll see."

"Won't I fall? I don't know..." I say, a little concerned, but not really caring at the same time.

"Don't you trust us?" Ben asks with a mischievous grin that I certainly don't trust.

"No," I say too seriously as we all laugh and fall to the ground. I haven't laughed this much in a while.

After we all settle, I find myself standing on James' shoulders. Bash is on one side, holding one of my legs, as Ben is on the other, holding the other leg. Jake is below us with his arms out like he's ready to catch me if I fall. He certainly is not going to catch me if I fall.

I can reach the shoulders at this point, so I hold on with dear life and jump up off James' shoulders. I hear him go crashing down, but I don't have the luxury of looking because I'm trying to pull myself up on this slippery statue. Why is it so slippery?

I finally get my grip and sit on his shoulders with my thighs gripping his head like I'm trying to squeeze the life out of him. I place the hat on top of his head, but it's like half the size, and I realize that I don't have the duct tape with me.

"Guys! You forgot to give me the duct tape!" I yell down to them like they are a hundred feet under me.

"Shhh! Don't be so loud Everly, we can hear you," Jake says, hushing me and everyone looks around to see if anyone heard.

They each try throwing the tape up to me and keep missing, not even coming close. It hits me on my forehead one time because my reaction time is way too slow. After trying what seemed like five hundred times, Ben finally gets up on Bash's shoulders and hands me the tape. I wrap the tape around the hat and the face of the statue a bunch of times. I have no idea what this is going to look like, but whatever it'll stay on.

Once I finish, I throw the tape to the ground and hear Ben yell, "Ow!" Oops, I must have hit him on the head with it.

I don't remember the plan to get down, but it's really not that high up. I move my legs to hang behind the statue and hold on to its neck. My hands slip and I drop down to the base of the statue, feeling the pain in my legs as I hit it. I stumble backward and fall off the base when I land backward on a hard body.

"Shit! Everly, what the hell?!" Bash groans below me as I realize I landed directly on him.

"Oh! Sorry!" I say, pushing off him to stand up. I didn't realize that I pushed directly on his package, and he let out another cry of pain and curls to his side as I stand up.

"Crap! Sorry Bash!" I feel horrible for causing him pain, but thankfully, it didn't seem to last too long.

"Remind me never to do anything like this with you again," Bash says, standing up slowly, trying to catch his balance.

I look around the statue to find that we are the only ones left. "Where did they go?" I ask Bash and he shakes his head like he doesn't know.

We see flashlights coming our way and hear voices yell out, "Stay right there!"

Oh crap! Is that campus security? Police? Bash and I turn to each other wide eyed and run in the opposite direction as they run behind us. We are both out of breath as we round a few buildings and finally throw ourselves into a bush. We crouch down, trying to stay quiet and ignoring the branches sticking us. We listen for any footsteps while our hearts continue to race, but we never hear anyone come our way.

Once we're sure they are gone, we make our way out of the bush. There's a nearby bench I go to sit on to get all the bush pieces off me.

I look over at Bash and laugh. "You look like a giant walking bush! Bush Man! Ohhh, it's so close to Bash. I'm forever calling you Bush Man!"

He looks at me with a concerned face, but then dies of laughter. We both sit on the bench, picking pieces of the bush out of each other's hair and clothes. There's a twig that somehow made its way up my shorts, sticking out.

"Did they really ditch us?" Bash asks before pulling out his phone and texting the boys.

There's no immediate response, so we walk back toward James' apartment, and I start to shiver.

"Bash, I'm freezing!" It's a cool September night, and I'm only in a tank top and shorts.

I see some fire pits in one area that James said they like to hang out at. I questioned why the campus allowed these because I feel like they would be a safety hazard, but I'm glad they do.

"Do you have a lighter?" I ask Bash and he immediately pulls one out of his pocket.

Why does he have a lighter on him? I didn't place him for a smoker, but whatever, I'm glad he does.

We head to the fire pit to light it. We figure we can hang out for a bit here until the guys respond with where they are. My stomach growls. I'm starving.

Bash keeps trying to light it, but it isn't lighting. I go to grab it from him to try, but apparently my coordination is a lot more off than I thought it was. Somehow, I end up lighting up his sleeve and it starts to burn.

"Holy Crap!" Bash yells, hitting his sleeve against the side of the fire pit.

I panic and take the bottom of my shirt to try patting it out, but instead of the fire burning out, my shirt catches on fire.

"Oh, my God!" I yell, running around trying to hold my shirt out, so it doesn't touch my skin.

Bash's body slams into me, pushing me over toward a giant fountain I didn't even realize was there, and we both fall in. I just miss hitting my head on the bottom. Pushing myself up above the surface, I cough up the water I inhaled on the way in. I must have gasped as he pushed me into the water.

I look over at Bash sitting in the fountain next to me, soaking wet. We both stare at each other and laugh. Hard. I splash him and then tackle him into the water, so he knows what it feels like.

He continues to laugh with me still on top of him, trying to get him back. "Everly, I tried to save your life. You were on fire!"

I continue to laugh, knowing that's the case, but want to get him back. "I thought you were just trying to get me back for basically punching you in the dick."

Bash is trying to push me off when we hear James yell, "What the fuck is going on?"

I look over at James, who is holding a takeout bag in his hand and has a scowl on his face. I should feel guilty being in this compromising position with Bash, but I don't. Bash and I stare at each other, our faces mere inches apart, and burst out laughing again.

James pulls me off Bash and out of the fountain. I shiver as goosebumps line my whole body. I was cold before and now I'm freezing. My teeth begin to chatter.

"Jesus, Everly. Here..." James says, putting the bag on the ground and unbuttoning his shirt.

I smirk. "James... I don't think now is the time..."

He wraps his shirt around me and buttons it up. Oh! He's giving me his shirt to keep me warm. How sweet and not at all what I thought he was doing. Now James is shirtless, and I'm confused because I could've sworn he had an undershirt under it. I can't help but rub my hands over his chest.

James leans over and whispers in my ear, "Not now, princess."

Princess? Has he called me that before? I kind of like it.

I step back and Jake throws a pebble at James' chest. "What the fuck?!" James yells.

I look at Jake, wondering the same thing.

Jake laughs, "Come on, man! Pop your pecks! Let's make these rocks fly. Ready?"

We all just exchange looks, but James steps back and stands with his back straight and shoulders back. "Ready!" he yells.

Jake throws little rock pebbles at James' chest, some hitting and some missing completely. James tries to "pop his pecks" whatever that means, but the pebbles mostly just roll down his stomach after hitting him.

"Work it, James!" Ben yells out with a catcall.

Bash whistles and I fall to the ground, dying of laughter. I have to pee so bad and if I stand, I'm pretty sure I'm going to pee myself. Then again, I am soaked. So, will anyone know? I look around to see if there is anywhere to go, but James' place is too far away, and the buildings are clearly not open, whatever time it is.

I see some bushes by the building and as much as I don't want to go back into a bush, I'm going to pee my pants. Beer goes right through me, and I'm pretty sure it's been hours since I last went.

"Don't look, I'm going pee," I say, running over toward the bushes. Of course, I look back at them and they are all staring at me. "I said don't look!" I yell as they turn in the opposite direction.

I pull my wet shorts and panties down and squat, releasing the burning sensation in my bladder. After what feels like a twenty-minute pee, I decide wiping with a bush leaf doesn't sound pleasant, so I skip the wiping all together. My shorts are hard to pull back up as they are wet from the water in the fountain. I'm also pretty sure I accidentally peed a little on them too, but whatever.

Apparently, everyone else has to pee too, so they all go to the bushes and pee together as I look away. Those poor bushes.

We make it back to James' place in one piece and scarf down the burgers and fries they got when they ditched us. Apparently, there's a 24/7 diner right next to the campus they went to. They could've told us that before leaving us to run from the police. We drink some more beer with our dinner or midnight snack, whatever, and laugh the night away.

# CHAPTER SEVEN

The nausea in my stomach and pounding in my head wakes me up. I try not to move as I open my eyes to take note of my surroundings. When I pry them open, I find myself curled up beside a body and my head lying directly on someone's junk, thankfully with boxers on. My heart begins to race, as I'm certain this is not James. I don't move my head as I force my eyes to wander down to the face of the person who owns these boxers. My breath hitches as I see Bash dead asleep. I quickly roll to my other side. I close my eyes as pain shoots through my body and head. I feel myself hit another body as I pray it's James. I open my eyes to find a penis directly in my line of sight, and this one is not in boxers. I sit up quickly and notice Jake lying right next to me.

Oh my God, what had I done last night? Did I have a three-some, and it wasn't even with James? Where is James? I stand up, feeling dizzy and like I'm going to throw up. I sit on the couch until my stomach settles and take in my surroundings.

There are takeout boxes and beer scattered everywhere. The place is a mess. Ben and James are nowhere to be found.

As I stand to walk toward James' bedroom, I notice that I'm only in the sexy bra and panties that I wore the first day to James' apartment. Not only did I get half naked, but for some reason I changed into these? What did I do?

When I reach James' bedroom, I can't help but smile at the sight before me. James and Ben are in his bed comfortably where James is spooning Ben. I let out a loud laugh, which wakes them up. James looks disgusted with himself as he pushes off Ben and Ben falls onto the floor. I continue laughing because I mean, they're brothers. Whatever.

James rubs his head and looks at the clock on his end table.

"What happened?" he asks, looking at me like I have the answers.

I can't help but stare at him, since he's only in his boxers. Then I notice Ben is too and staring at me. He looks like he blushes and walks past me out of the room. I smile as I watch him go.

"I have no clue. I woke up between Bash and Jake on the floor in the living room. I was hoping you could tell me what happened," I say as I cringe.

James just stares at me with an emotionless expression and shakes his head. Yeah, he has no idea either and is not about to start throwing out accusations.

I take some clothes out of my bag and head into James' bathroom. I really need a shower and to get dressed. When I open the door, it smells awful. There are clothes thrown all in a pile on the floor and what looks like vomit all over the toilet, floor, and the clothes. Like everyone's clothes. The sight and smell make me need to vomit, but thankfully I'm able to hover over the toilet and do it in there. I quickly turn the shower on and try to hold my breath as long as possible while in the bathroom so as to not smell it and throw up again. I feel like I have vomit all over me, so I need this shower. It's the fastest shower in the history of showers ever.

I come out only in a towel and get dressed in James' room. I make sure to put the fan on in the bathroom and keep the door closed. I feel like I should be the one to clean that up, but at the same time, I do not want to be the one to clean that up. That's something we're going to have to deal with later, which is clearly what we all thought last night.

By the time I come back out to the living room, all the boys are dressed and sitting quietly on the couch. Except Jake, who is laying on his back on the floor looking like he's going to die. At least he had the strength to put his clothes on and not lie there naked. They all turn to me as they hear me enter, and James gets up to hand me a glass of water, aspirin, and crackers. I drink, take, and eat it all, trying to keep it down as the nausea continues.

We are all quiet and looking like death. I'm not sure if it is because we all feel miserable or we are trying to figure out what happened last night. I rack my brain to remember the events. They aren't clear, but I do remember the party, the statue, hiding in bushes and eating burgers last night. I feel like there are quite a few gaps, especially how the three of us ended up on the floor naked or half naked.

I shift in my seat and cross my arms over my stomach. I wince as my left arm hits my stomach right under my breasts. There's a stabbing, burning pain. I lift my shirt to look, to find a huge nasty looking mark almost the size of the palm of my hand. How did I miss this until now? I guess I've just been concentrating on not throwing up.

"What happened?!" James comes running over to me, holding up my shirt and inspecting it. "It looks like a burn."

He runs off toward his bathroom. Does he know what's currently inside that bathroom? If not, he's going to be surprised once he steps foot in there. I hear retching from the bathroom and cringe. Yep, he's just as surprised as I was.

Shortly after he finished vomiting, he comes out with a giant bottle of aloe. He applies it to the burn, I'm assuming, and it hurts like hell. Tears form in my eyes from the sting.

To get my attention off the pain, I ask, "Did you enjoy the nice surprise in the bathroom too? I did the same thing when I went in there."

He doesn't look up at me, but he laughs. "That's disgusting. I already texted Alice this morning to come clean, but I'm going to have to pay her a lot more to deal with that. She'll be here in about thirty minutes."

I cringe again, but not because of the pain. "That's so gross. We can't let her clean up that mess."

He looks me in the eye. "That's what I pay her for. It's fine. This isn't the worst she's seen."

I want to ask if he means that it's been worse for him before or if, just in general, she's seen worse. The nausea continues to bubble in my stomach, and I decide now is not the time to know details about that information he just shared.

"How bad can it be?" Bash gets up and opens the bathroom door. He immediately slams it closed and asks, "What the fuck happened last night?"

James finishes applying the aloe to my stomach, and I notice a similar mark on Bash's wrist as he walks by me. I grab his arm above the mark, and he stops.

I turn his arm over and say, "It looks like you got burned too. Here," I hand the aloe to him. "Do you remember how that happened?"

He shakes his head and sits down, applying the aloe to the burn on his wrist. He winces a few times, but it needs to be done.

"Oh! When we found you two after getting the food, we found you molesting Bash inside the fountain," Jake says as he finally sits up, looking somewhat human again.

Bash and I snap our heads toward each other, staring into each other's eyes, willing the memory to come back to us. Apparently, it works because we both smile and start laughing at the same time. I wince as laughing makes the burn hurt more, but I can't stop. I can't believe that happened.

James looks confused and maybe a little concerned, like he thinks something was going on between me and Bash last night.

"Okay, I was not molesting Bash last night. Apparently, we don't know how to light a fire or put one out. I caught Bash's shirt sleeve on fire and then I tried to put it out with the bottom of my shirt. Needless to say, we both were on fire, and he pushed us into the fountain to put it out," I say, continuing to laugh at the end.

We all laugh and occasionally get quiet as I think we're all fighting the nausea and headaches. We finally put all the pieces together except for how we all ended up where we fell asleep last night.

Ben explains the lack of clothes situation, though. "Everly, you threw up all over me last night, which in return made me throw up on Jake. Then apparently everyone was throwing up and everyone's clothes were covered. I'm assuming that's the mess currently in the bathroom?"

No one responds to what Ben just explained, as we all look green at remembering the incident. It will forever be known as the incident we won't be talking about again. A knock on the door breaks our silence as James gets up to let an older woman inside. She carries cleaning supplies. This must be Alice.

I get up and thank her for her help but cringe again at the thought of what she'll be dealing with. "Alice, can I help with the bathroom before you go in? It's bad."

She smiles at me and says, "You must be Everly. It's nice to finally meet you, but no, I got it."

"Um. It's really bad and gross. I don't think it's fair…" she cuts me off.

"Really Everly, it's okay. Whatever it is, I've seen worse. Trust me." She smiles and walks off toward the bathroom. To my surprise, she doesn't make a sound as she walks in there and starts cleaning.

I think about my clothes and figure I really don't want them back. Plus, my shirt is probably burnt and not salvageable, anyway. I tell James to have her toss them and everyone else agrees to toss theirs too. As much fun as we had last night, we do not need those clothes as a reminder of how the night ended.

I hate saying goodbye to James, but I need to get back to get ready for school tomorrow. I want to write down in my journal everything that I can remember about yesterday. After the year I had with Adam, I found myself writing down all the good memories as they happened. Sadly, there aren't many entries in my journal last year because of that. Most of the pages in the journal are from last summer.

I have Declan drive me home because I can't sit in the back seat of the car driving back with Ben and Jake. I'm still nauseous and while I don't often get car sick, I have a feeling I would today if in the back. About ten minutes into the drive, it apparently didn't matter that I was sitting in the front seat. Declan pulls over as I throw up on the side of the road. He waits for me in the car, and I groan as I sit back down and buckle my seatbelt.

I hear him laugh. "I had a feeling you were pretty wasted last night."

I look over at him and give him the stink eye. "How did you know?"

"Everly... You don't think I just let you go to a frat party and walk around campus with your clearly drunk friends alone, do you? I was following you, and James gives me access to his cameras in his apartment," he says, like it's all common sense.

"Wait... what? He has cameras in the apartment?"

I stop for a moment, thinking about that. Oh my God... Did Declan see us having sex? I blush and look away from him. Suddenly I'm feeling nauseous again.

As if he knows what I'm thinking, he says, "I don't watch them all the time. I just check in to make sure everything's okay."

I don't believe him, but if James gave him access to the cameras, then clearly, he trusts Declan.

A thought occurred to me about the cameras. "Does it record or is it a live feed?"

He glances at me for a moment before saying, "It records."

I have mixed feelings about this, but I can use it to my advantage when it comes to last night. "Can I see it? Just a part from last night that I can't remember..."

He interrupts me, "No. I'm sorry, but I promised James I wouldn't let anyone, including you, have access to the cameras."

I don't respond to that, as it makes me feel uncomfortable. James doesn't want me to be able to see what he's doing. Why? I mean, I wouldn't sit there and watch him, but it made me feel uneasy, like there's something to hide.

Again, as if he knows what I'm thinking, he states, "It's just a privacy thing, Everly. But are you wondering how you woke up between two boys that aren't your boyfriend this morning?"

I blush again, thinking about how he must have seen what happened last night, and I was in my sexy bra and panties. Geez, how can he sit here and pretend like all of this is normal? This is so awkward. I can't hold in the nausea again. He pulls over and I barely make it, leaning outside the car door, emptying the rest of the contents in my stomach.

I lean back in the car and get comfortable, as if nothing happened. "Yes. That's exactly what I was wondering."

He smirks. "Nothing happened. After you all had a vomiting party, everyone took off their clothes. James and his brother passed out immediately after in his bed. It looked like you debated joining them but went out to the living room with the other two. You guys just laughed and eventually fell asleep."

I smile, thankful that's all that happened and to have the memory filled in. I don't remember any of that, but it makes sense.

Declan looks serious and like he's contemplating saying something else, but he doesn't.

"Just spit it out Declan. What do you want to say?" I ask in a demanding tone.

He doesn't look at me as he says, "I just worry about you. You were having fun last night, but you've drank a lot the past few months. You mixed it with drugs this time, and I just want you to be careful, okay? If you ever feel like you've had too much, you know to call me."

I nod and am not sure if he's able to see since he's driving. I'm not mad at what he said. It makes me happy that he is concerned for me. It seems like he actually cares about me versus just keeping me safe for the money that my father gives him. He feels like... a friend.

"Declan," I say.

"Hm?" He glances at me, then back to the road.

"Thank you," is all I say and need to say.

# Chapter Eight

It's Friday night, and it's the homecoming game. It's intense, for me at least. There are so many students in the stands screaming and throwing things around. My anxiety is getting the best of me, so I leave my group of friends to fend for themselves in the stands. I keep getting hit by random objects every few minutes and arms or legs are hitting me in the back or on my head. I just can't take it anymore.

I make my way to the bathrooms to get some peace. I feel bad I left Ashley alone, but the boys will keep her company. Lauren wasn't allowed to come to the game tonight because she had a date with her fiancé. Ugh, fiancé. I hate saying that. After I compose myself in the bathroom, I come out and lean against the brick wall, getting fresh air far away from the stadium. I can still hear all the ruckus though, as if I'm in the middle of the stadium. Why do people like these things?

A boy I've never seen before walks past me and bumps into me. What the heck? I'm leaning against the wall, so unless he's drunk, that was definitely on purpose.

"Oh, sorry, I didn't see you there," he says while standing way too close to me.

I don't respond. I go to move away, and he steps in front of me, blocking me. My heart rate picks up at his proximity and the way he's looking at me. Yeah, that wasn't an accident, and whatever he is planning isn't good.

"Excuse me, but my friends are waiting for me," I say, hoping he will take the hint and move out of my way without any issues. Of course that doesn't happen.

He puts his arm on the wall and his body is basically against mine, blocking me in. My heart continues to beat out of my chest in fear, but I don't let it show. I glare at him like this is nothing but an annoyance.

"Have you been enjoying this year so far? I've heard you're too scared to use your locker anymore," he says with a smirk.

So, this must be one of Adam's friends and one that has put things in my locker. I no longer use my locker, but I have found notes in and outside of it the past few weeks. There haven't been any more pranks, just mean notes. All of them were about the same, basically calling me a slut and other unoriginal things.

He moves closer where I feel his body press against mine and leans to whisper in my ear, "I've heard how much you like to suck cock. How about we go elsewhere, and you can show me?"

I feel bile rise in my throat at what he just said. How can there be so many disgusting guys out there, like Adam? How do none of them have any consequences happen to them? Oh, that's right, money. I honestly hate money. Does this stuff happen in other schools that aren't based on money?

I snap out of my thoughts as I feel his breath on my neck. Shortly after, he places a kiss on my collarbone, and I really think I'm going to throw up at this point.

"Stop," I say as a warning.

He doesn't stop.

"I said, stop!" I raise my voice this time, hoping he'll get the hint.

He still doesn't stop.

I close my eyes to collect myself and push the fear away. Declan has been training me for months. This is exactly the reason I wanted to train with him. I'm sick of these bastards trying to take advantage of me.

I put my hands on his hips to steady myself and give myself leverage to pull my knee up as hard as I can to his junk. He's stunned and groans as he stumbles backward, holding himself. He looks me in the eye, and he looks so angry, but I don't stick around.

I push past him, but he grabs my wrist and pulls me back, making me fall hard onto the ground. I wince at the pain in my arm, but it leaves quickly as I hear him call me "bitch." He places his knee in the middle of my stomach to pin me down as he catches his breath from me kneeing him.

My left arm is free, and while it's not my strongest, it's all I have. I punch him as hard as I can in his nose, which makes a cracking noise, and blood immediately starts dripping. A few drops are on my hand and then my shirt and face. Okay, there are definitely more than a few drops and I'm pretty sure I just broke his nose.

I take that moment to roll out from under him and start running again. This time he let me go, but I don't look back. As I round the corner of the building, I run directly into Declan's chest.

"Are you okay?" Declan asks, looking at me up and down.

I nod but don't say anything.

"Come on, let's go get you cleaned up." He leads me toward the school, but I stop him.

"No, I'm ready to go home. Can you take me home?" I ask, hoping he won't argue, and he doesn't.

When we get in the car, we are silent for a few moments. I'm surprised he hasn't asked me what happened. When I look over at his face, he's smiling.

"What?" I ask him, confused.

He shakes his head but keeps the smile on his face. "I'm just proud of you."

"Why?" I ask, still confused.

"I saw you take care of yourself back there. You did good, Kid."

The adrenaline of what just happened is still wearing off, but I can't help but smile. That means a lot to me for him to say that.

"Wait, does that mean you were there the whole time and watched what happened without helping?" I study him.

He nods. "I was ready to jump in if needed, but I wanted to give you an opportunity to help yourself. You did."

I smile again. "You know, I'm pretty sure my dad would fire you if he knew that you didn't step in immediately to help me."

He glances at me, then back at the road. "Actually, he's the one that suggested it. It was hard for me to sit back and watch, but when we talked about your training, he said he wants to make sure you can take care of yourself and if a situation like this happened, to not jump in immediately. He loves you Everly, and he wants to make sure you are protected, but that you can protect yourself if ever needed."

Everything he just said makes my heart grow. The fact that my dad is the one suggesting that to ensure I can care for myself, tells me how much he loves me. Then the fact that Declan said it was hard for him to watch and not jump in shows me how much he cares for me too.

The rest of the ride home I text Ben, Jake, and Ashley that I left. I don't want to tell them what happened, but they keep pushing me, so I finally cave and tell them. Within a few minutes of texting them, I get messages from James and Lauren as well. Apparently, my life is not private by any means.

"Before I forget again, I've been meaning to give you this," Declan says while pulling a box out of the middle console.

"What is it?" I ask as I open it to find a beautiful watch.

"It's a watch, but it's in case you find yourself in trouble and unable to get to your phone. Do you see the button on the side? If you push it three times, it'll alert me that you're in trouble and

I'll come," he says as I locate the little button on the side of the watch.

I click it three times and Declan's phone makes a horrible screeching sound like an alarm. He hits a button on his phone to make it stop.

"Okay cool, thanks Declan," I say as I put it on my wrist. After what happened today, I'm thankful for it. If I wasn't able to defend myself and Declan wasn't around, there is no way I would be able to reach for my phone to call him.

Ashley shows up first to get ready for homecoming and Lauren says she is running an hour behind. Ashley takes a quick shower in my bathroom because she says her hair is a disaster and we won't be able to work with it in its current state. When she comes out of the bathroom, I tell her I'm going to go downstairs to get some drinks and snacks.

As I head back to my room with way too many snacks in my hands, Ben catches up to me on the stairs.

"Want some help?" he asks, while taking the water bottles out of my hands before I drop them.

"Thanks, I might have gone overboard on the snacks." I shrug my shoulders and regret it as I drop a couple on the floor.

Ben immediately picks them up and continues following me to my room.

I bang on the door with my shoulder and yell, "Ashley! I'm coming in and Ben's with me in case you're not decent!"

She doesn't respond, so I maneuver a few packages under my arm so I can open the door. Once we are in, I don't see Ashley anywhere in the room. I peek into the bathroom to find she isn't there either.

"I don't know where she went," I say, confused about where she could've gone.

Maybe she went downstairs to help me with the snacks, and I somehow missed her. Ben shrugs his shoulders, and we leave the room together, but I leave the door open.

As we are walking down the stairs, Ben says, "So, I need your help..."

I look toward him and ask, "With what?"

He doesn't answer immediately, so I take the opportunity to keep looking for wherever Ashley went. I don't see her in the kitchen, in the foyer, or in the hallway to my room. Where could she have gone?

"Well... I accidentally let a squirrel in my room and need to get it out before my mom sees, or she's going to freak out. Jake can't come over right now, so I was hoping you could help me," he says, looking serious.

I laugh because he's joking, right? When he doesn't join me in laughing, I realize he's not joking.

"Wait, what? How on earth did you accidentally let a squirrel into your room and why?" I ask, wanting to know the story because I'm sure it's good.

"I'm not going to answer that. This is a help and don't ask questions situation." His eyes are pleading.

Ugh, pulling the help and don't ask, I hate when the boys pull that. But I agreed long ago to it, so I have to continue with it. One day I may need to pull that too. We walk back to his room, and he has a box outside his door. I'm not sure I like where this is going. Is there really a squirrel in his room?

"Alright, so I was thinking I'd open the door and try to scare the squirrel over to you and you could throw the box over it," he says, like it's a good plan.

It's a horrible plan, but I'm supposed to just help, so I'll do just that.

"Ready?" he asks with his hand on the doorknob.

"Ready," I reply, holding the big box in front of me.

He opens the door and we both slide in, closing the door quickly behind us. I look around the room and don't see or hear anything.

Ben is sneaking around, looking under his bed, in his bathroom, closet, everywhere and he can't find it.

"Do you think it somehow got out?" he asks.

"I don't know. Did you leave the door open at all?"

Right when I ask that question, I see movement out of the corner of my eye by his window. I look over to see something on the top of his curtains and then that something is flying at my face.

I let out a loud scream and lift the box up to cover myself from being attacked by the killer squirrel and it somehow lands in the box. I throw the box instinctively on the floor and Ben runs to close it. The squirrel is running around inside, making a bunch of scratching noises.

"What do we do now?!" I ask with my heart racing.

"Open the window!" he yells.

I open the window, and Ben brings the box over to it. Before I can tell him to wait, he throws the squirrel out the window, which lands on a nearby tree. I let out the breath I was holding, because I was about to say the poor squirrel might die throwing it out of a second-story window. He closes the window and we both stare at each other for a minute before we laugh hysterically.

"Well... That was fun. Anything else?" I ask, while already halfway out the door.

If there is anything else, I'm not sure I want to be a part of it. That was enough excitement for the day. He shakes his head, no.

Ben walks with me back to my room, where Ashley still isn't anywhere to be found. He thanks me again and goes on his way as I close my door to take a breather before I start searching for Ashley again. Capturing and throwing a squirrel out of Ben's room is just a typical task, sure. So back to reality, if Ashley went outside, then I'm going to need a sweater. I open my closet door and am startled when I find Ashley standing inside my closet in the dark.

"What are you doing?" My heart rate picks up from being startled.

It's super creepy finding someone standing in your dark closet. Especially after being attacked by a squirrel.

"Is he gone?" she whispers.

Is she talking about Ben? If so, and if he wasn't gone, then why was she whispering? He'd know I'm talking to someone in here.

"Yes. Have you been in here the whole time?" I can't help but laugh, thinking about her hiding out in here.

She looks embarrassed but starts laughing with me. "Yes, I can't believe I just hid in your closet from him."

"Why were you hiding?" I ask, but I'm pretty sure I know the answer. It would be the only reason that I would hide in my best friend's closet.

"I didn't want him to see me. I don't have any makeup on..." she trails off at the end.

My eyes widen. "Do you like Ben?"

"What?! Psh.. No..."

If that wasn't an admittance to liking him, then I don't know what is. I just shake my head and step back so she can leave my closet.

Once Lauren arrives, we help each other get ready by doing our hair and makeup together. I tell Lauren about finding Ashley in my closet and we can't help but make fun of her, though

I feel a little bad that she will be going to the dance with us and watching Ben with his date tonight. She said it's really nothing, but I'm not sure if I believe her. Then again, I thought she liked Declan. I wonder if she's over him now.

Once we finish getting ready, I stare at myself in the mirror and can't help but smile. I look amazing. The dress I chose goes to my ankles and is fitted, showing off every curve of my body. There is a slit on one side going up to the middle of my thigh, and it has a high neckline. It's dark blue and sparkly, like the night sky. Even though the only skin showing is my leg where the slit is, it looks pretty sexy. Lauren curled my hair into loose waves and Ashley did my makeup. The bright red lipstick looks amazing on me.

I stare at Ashley and Lauren in their dresses as well. Lauren's is a modest pink dress, but Ashley's green dress shows a lot more skin and some cleavage, but it's not slutty.

Ashley grabs my phone and takes a picture of me. She takes an extra minute before placing it back on the desk. I assume she was cropping it or using a filter to make the lighting look better.

After finishing Lauren's hair, I hear my phone buzz to find a text from James.

James

> Jesus Everly. You look hot. Tell me you're skipping homecoming and coming here.

I feel myself blush at what James says and while I want to be mad at Ashley for sending it to James, I can't bring myself to be. I probably would've sent it later anyway to show him what he's missing out on. I'm not exactly sure why he couldn't come home this weekend, but I didn't really feel like asking either.

"You're so lucky to have someone like James who looks at you and finds you so attractive..." Lauren says with a longing in her voice.

Ashley and I both exchange looks. "Lauren, you look hot. Does Lorenzo never compliment how you look?" I ask, even though I already know the answer.

She shakes her head. "No, not really. He always just looks at me and quickly looks away. It's like he just sees me as a child or something."

Ashley scoffs. "Well, you are basically a child to him. He should be happy he gets someone as hot as you for his wife."

Lauren blushes but doesn't say anything.

"Do you ever text him?" I ask.

She nods. "Yeah, not often, but mainly when we're making plans for our dates. I'm pretty sure he's not into this arranged marriage any more than I am."

Well, that is even sadder than I thought. I can't believe her parents are forcing her into this marriage. As much as I'm not a fan of Lorenzo, it makes me feel a little bad for him as well, knowing that he's also being forced into it.

"Well, let's send him a picture of you as well and see what he says," I say, taking her phone from on top of my desk.

She gasps. "No! That'd be... unprofessional? I don't know. It wouldn't be right."

Ashley and I both laugh. I ask, "Really? Unprofessional? I know this is like an arranged business marriage thing but come on. You two are going to be married. He should see what he's marrying."

She sighs, knowing that we aren't going to give up. "Okay, fine."

She gives a small smile to the camera. She looks gorgeous, but her smile doesn't reach her eyes. Her eyes look so... sad. When's the last time she genuinely looked happy?

I send the photo to Lorenzo from her phone, and his message comes back almost immediately.

Lorenzo

Lauren, you look beautiful. Be careful tonight.

"See! He said you look beautiful. Maybe he won't be the worst husband," Ashley says. She's always trying to make Lauren feel better about the arranged marriage because what else can we do?

Lauren looks mad at what Ashley just said. Clearly, it was the wrong thing to say. "Then you marry him, Ashley. He's not a good man, and he's so closed off. He doesn't want me anymore than I want him. You can have him and live happily ever after throwing away all your dreams to become his wife and a mother to his kids."

She stomps off into the bathroom, slamming the door closed. Ashley and I look at each other. We don't say anything. There is nothing to say. Lauren has every right to be angry at the situation. She's losing everything she's always wanted and dreamed about to do what her parents tell her to do. To marry a much older guy that she barely knows and won't even get any freedom as an adult. She goes from her parents' rules to his rules. It's not fair, and it honestly pisses me off every time I think about it. I just wish there was something we could do for Lauren.

# Chapter Nine

We drive up in style, in a limo, to the dance like everyone else in the school. I don't think I saw a single student driving themselves, which isn't that unexpected considering how rich you have to be to attend this school. Declan and Barry followed behind us, as usual. Jake and Ben both have their own dates to the dance, so they went with them in another limo.

The whole school was transformed for this one night. I don't think it had a particular theme this year, or at least I don't know of what it is if they did. I'd say the theme is how much money can you spend on one night because the décor is ridiculous. There are chandeliers on the ceiling, which clearly are real, but I have no idea how they have them all set up. There are a few tables scattered around the edges of the auditorium completely decked out with what look like pure gold vases filled with roses. A red carpet leads into the auditorium like we are famous, with flashing lights of the cameras taking pictures of each student and their dates.

Ashley, Lauren, and I walk up to get our pictures taken. We pose regally for the first one, but then quickly shift into our silly, giggly poses. I think we got one good picture out of that before we got into a huge fit of laughter, and to think we hadn't had anything to drink. We planned to spend the night together after the dance, but it was a stretch getting Lauren's parents to allow her to come here in the first place. Ashley and I didn't feel right having a sleepover without her, so we're just going to have the most fun we can while here and forget everything else.

I've never noticed how many slow songs played during these types of dances before. Whenever there was a fast-paced song, we went out to the dance floor and danced like crazy. Arms flailing, jumping up and down, and spinning in circles, running into each other type of crazy. We're having fun and we couldn't care less what anyone around us thinks. After three songs in a row, it turned to another stupid, slow song. The song itself is completely fine, but I think I'm a little salty from the fact that James isn't here to dance with me. I'm doing my best to stay positive as I always do, but the ache in my chest from missing him is strong tonight, especially as I look around the dance floor at so many cute couples.

"You're missing James," Lauren says as a statement, not a question.

"Yeah, I am. The long distance is hard. I wish we still lived in the same house, so I can go to his room to see him whenever I want," I say, sighing.

Sometimes I get a little depressed thinking about the fact that I wasted the whole summer. If only I had sat down with James at the beginning of the summer and told him how I felt, then maybe we could've gotten together sooner. Then we could've at least had almost two months to hang out and we could've snuck into each other's rooms every night.

Those what-ifs tend to bring me down, so I shove them away and try to think about all the fun I had this summer with the boys. While I sometimes wish I would've done things differently, I know everything worked out the way it was supposed to.

"Everly!" Jake says excitedly as he puts his arm around my shoulder.

I look over and smile. "Hey, Jake. Where is your date?"

He shrugs. "She's somewhere over there with her friends. I think she got sick of hanging out with me. Wanna dance?"

I look toward the dance floor where all the couples are dancing closely together. My eyes scan the rest of the room, and I see Declan leaning against the wall with his eyes on me. I don't see Barry anywhere, so I'm assuming that he's outside monitoring things. Is it a betrayal to James to dance with Jake? I don't want James to be upset, but it would be nice to dance with someone.

"It's just a dance Everly. I promise I won't try to kiss you," he says with a wink.

I laugh and look toward my friends, who are basically pushing me to go dance with him. Are they trying to tell me something? Like they think I should be with Jake? No, they are just being good friends, saying it's okay to go. I think. I'll need to have that conversation with them later to find out the truth because I feel like they've been team Jake.

When we get on the dance floor, the song ends and another slow one comes on. Seriously? How many slow songs are we going to play? Not everyone has a date...

Jake pulls me close as we dance. I'm not a great dancer and not sure exactly what to do with my arms. I place them on his shoulders as he puts his on my waist. Is this right? Or should it be the opposite way? Ugh, now I'm just not going to enjoy myself because I think I did this wrong and now I can't change it, but he would've changed it if that was the case, right?

Jake looks back and forth between my eyes. "What are you thinking about, Everly?"

I let out a nervous laugh. "Honestly? I'm thinking about how I really don't know how to slow dance and wondering if I'm doing this wrong."

He smirks and pulls me in closer, basically like a hug. "Well, there is way too much space between us. Just take a look around at everyone else."

I do what he said and watch the couples around us dancing. Might I add, way too close. Like, I didn't know you could get that close and why are the chaperones allowing this? Isn't there supposed to be a rule to keep a ruler's length of space between you at all times? I'm inappropriately close to Jake, but dear God, I'm not that close and what is the couple beside us doing? I want to say they are kissing, but the guy is basically eating her face.

How is that even fun, hot, or whatever it is they want that to be?

I look at Jake, and he's reading my mind. "Yeah, I'm not sure what's going on there, but forget what I just said. Let's just concentrate on each other."

I smile back up at Jake because that's a great idea. We sway back and forth to the music, which feels like we're in junior high, but this is comfortable for us.

"So, your girlfriend isn't going to be upset that you're dancing with me?" I ask.

He frowns. "No, she's not my girlfriend."

"Ah, so she's just someone you brought to the dance so you could have some fun with after, right?" I don't mean for that to sound so judgy, but it definitely does.

Thankfully, he laughs. "You know me too well, Everly."

I cringe and put my head on his chest. I love Jake, as I've come to realize, like a brother. I want him to be happy, but I hate that he's like this. I want him to have a girlfriend and know what love is. Sleeping around with a bunch of girls isn't going to make him happy like he thinks it will, but it's his life, so I can't say anything.

"How are you and James doing?" he asks.

"We're doing good," I say, keeping it simple.

"I'm sorry he wasn't able to make it tonight," he says, looking at me for a reaction.

What is this about? Was James right and Jake does still like me? I feel horrible if that's the case, so I'm not even going to think about it. He has all these beautiful girls that want to be with him. There's no way that he still wants me. Right?

"I don't really want to talk about James right now," I say, giving him a small smile.

"I get it," he says and pulls me even closer.

I lean my head on his chest, and we finish out the song dancing until the next song comes on which is finally a fun, upbeat song.

I pull away. "Thanks for the dance. I should probably go find Ashley and Lauren."

"They look like they are having fun talking to my friends over there. Let's dance some more."

I look around at all the couples dancing, and it feels like we are in a nightclub and not at a high school homecoming dance. Girls are grinding up against their boyfriends and their boyfriends have their hands all over the girls' bodies. Why are the chaperones allowing this? Oh, that's right, I'm sure they were all bribed with money.

I give him a wary look and he pleads, "Come on, just one more dance."

"I really don't know how to dance to this type of music," I say, still trying to get out of it.

"Yeah, you do. I saw you dancing with your friends," he says with a gleam in his eye.

I laugh. "Yeah, I probably looked like a baby deer that was just born and trying to learn how to walk."

"You looked amazing, Everly," he says seriously.

I steal another glance at the couple next to us where she is still grinding against him. Yeah, no. I'm not doing that with Jake.

Jake laughs again and grabs my hands. "Come on Everly, we're dancing."

He tugs on my arms and waves them around floppily. I laugh hard, having trouble keeping myself upright. He jumps up and down as I follow his lead, still holding onto his hands.

"See! Just let loose and have fun!"

I continue laughing as we continue to dance like crazy people. Occasionally, Jake lets go of a hand and makes me do a spin and whistles at me. He dips me a few times and we just... have fun. I glance over toward Declan, who is still standing in the same spot and smiling at me. I know I'm going to hear about this later and how crazy I look, but I don't really care at this moment.

Just when the song ends, Jake makes me do one more spin, lets go of my arm, and pushes me toward the crowd. I stumble forward, right into a strong body, catching me and setting me up right. I feel so embarrassed and so mad at Jake.

"I'm... I'm so sorry!" I say as I straighten myself up.

When I look up, I see a familiar face smiling down at me. James.

"What are you doing here?" I ask, shocked to see him.

He told me he wouldn't be able to make it to the homecoming dance, so I didn't expect him to be here. I tried not to show how disappointed I was, but I'm pretty sure that he knew, anyway. It's just like James to show up and surprise me. God, I love him. I can't help but admire him in his fitted gray suit.

I think he looks amazing in his casual clothes, but this is even better.

"I'm sorry I'm late, but I wanted to come for as much of the dance as I could." He smiles at me and pulls me into him to dance slowly together.

The song is not a slow song, which is surprising considering more than half the songs have been, but we dance like it is, anyway. I lay my head on his chest, and I know that I have a huge grin on my face. When my eyes find Ashley and Lauren dancing, they both give me a thumbs up and goofy grins. I suppose that's their way of saying I'm off the hook for the friends' homecoming.

After a few more dances with James and him not letting me go the whole time, Homecoming is winding down.

"Are you ready to go?" James whispers in my ear.

I lean back to look at him and nod.

He grins. "I got a hotel room for the night." I look up at him, shocked, and he laughs as he continues, "Don't look so shocked. I want to spend the night with you without my family around."

I give him a wicked grin. "Oh yeah? What are you planning that you don't want your family around for?"

He leans in close again to my ear. "I plan to have you screaming my name all night long."

I clench my thighs together at the thought of what he plans to do to me tonight. If tonight is anything like last weekend, then I know I'm going to be in for a long, pleasurable night.

"What about your mom? She's expecting me home," I ask.

He shakes his head. "Not anymore. I told her you would spend the night with me."

My eyes grow wide. "But... She knows we are together, right?"

"Of course she does. She knows everything."

"So, she's okay with that?" I ask, surprised.

He shrugs his shoulders. "I mean, you're almost 18 and I'm in college, so what's the point in stopping us? She wants the truth more than anything."

I suppose that's true, and it's just like Declan. He doesn't care what I do as long as I tell him, and it's safe. I'm not sure if my father would agree to this, but I'm thankful Mrs. Crawford does. I wonder if Ben will also get a hotel room tonight with his date.

"Stop overthinking and let's go," he says, leading me toward the door.

I pull on him to stop for a moment. "I need to tell Declan where we're going."

"I already told him where we're staying and that you'll be leaving with me. He's already following." He nods in Declan's direction, who sure enough, is already following us.

I don't hesitate any longer as he leads me to his car and opens the door for me. When I get in, he leans over and buckles my seat belt. He's never done that before. When he clicks the seat belt in, he gives me a quick kiss before standing up straight and walking to the driver's side. He's been a lot more affectionate now that everyone knows about us, and I like it.

The moment we open the door to the hotel room, he pushes me against the wall and kisses me. He grabs my face, and I grab his forearms as he continues to kiss me hard, and his tongue tangles with mine. Both of our breaths are ragged, and we can't get enough of each other.

He's not wasting any time as he slips my panties off from under my dress.

He pulls away from me for a quick moment to see what I'm wearing. "Did you wear these thinking you would do this tonight with someone?"

I smirk because it is unusual for me to wear a lacy thong unless I planned to be seen in it. However, it was the only underwear I currently had clean that didn't show an outline with the dress I'm wearing, but I didn't need to go into detail and kill the mood.

"I can always hope, can't I?" I smirk as he pulls me a few steps, pushing me onto the bed.

He hovers over me with both arms on either side of my head. "I hope you were only thinking of getting lucky with me."

My response comes out breathy as he leans closer to my face. "Of course. You're the only one I want, James..."

He covers my mouth with his and runs his hand through my hair. He now leans on his forearm versus just his hand to hold himself steady above me. His body is on top of mine, but his weight is mostly on his arm.

His mouth leaves mine as he trails kisses down my neck and stops quickly when he realizes the dress is in the way of accessing the rest of my neck and body. He helps me stand up and get out of the dress. He takes my bra off quickly, following my dress.

He steps back and groans. "You looked beautiful in that dress tonight, but I prefer you like this."

I feel myself blush as he admires my body. I'm still pretty self-conscious, but I'm trying my best to appear confident and not hide myself.

I look at him and find the situation to be completely unfair. "I also love your attire from tonight, but I prefer some layers to be taken off."

He takes off his suit jacket as I start unbuttoning his shirt. He throws both to the floor and I work on his pants next. Once those are off, his erection springs free through his boxers. He's so ready, which is good because so am I.

This time I take the lead by putting my hands on his chest, turning us around, and pushing him down on the bed. I crawl on top of him, hovering over him just as he did moments ago.

"Oh, you want to be in charge tonight?" he growls.

I lean down and cover his mouth with mine to silence him. While our mouths are busy, I position myself over his erection, teasing him by keeping his tip just at my entrance.

He groans and pulls away from the kiss. "Baby, you're torturing me. Please let me be inside you."

I can't help but smile. "Well, since you asked so nicely."

I tease him a little longer before lowering myself completely onto him. He moans and grabs my hips to help set the rhythm. I feel self-conscious as my breasts bounce with each thrust, but

I can't bring myself to care because it feels so good. I continue to ride him as he pulls me down to kiss me again. As we move faster together, we both find our release at the same time.

Once we come down from our high, I slip off him and roll to his side, laying my head on his chest. He kisses the top of my head and sighs.

"I wanted to take my time with you when we got here, but I have to say that I really enjoyed you taking charge," he says.

I let out a sigh and look up at him. "Well, we do have all night."

He pushes me onto my back and rolls on top of me again. "Is that so? What do you have in mind?"

I lean forward and kiss him for a moment before breaking it off. "Oh, I was just thinking we should order room service."

He laughs and rolls off me, sitting on the edge of the bed. "Not a bad idea. You'll need your energy for what I have in store for you tonight."

I laugh as I sit up as well, grabbing the clothes he must have laid out for me before we got here. I also notice that my overnight bag is in the corner of the room. James thought of everything. The more time I spend with him, the more I fall in love with him. My heart is so full, and I cannot imagine my life without him.

# CHAPTER TEN

The weekend went by too fast, just as it always does. It'll be another two weeks before I see James again, and I'm really struggling with that. I don't know when it happened, but I'm completely dependent on and attached to him. I text him on average every thirty minutes during the day. I get antsy when he doesn't respond immediately, like now. It's lunchtime, and he hasn't responded since this morning.

Lauren bumps her shoulder into mine, pulling me from my thoughts. "What's wrong?"

I take a bite of my sandwich and shrug. "Nothing, I'm just waiting for a text back from James."

Ashley laughs. "You are seriously addicted to him, Everly."

"No, I'm not," I respond way too quickly.

Everyone at the table laughs, including Ben and Jake, who are sitting with us today. I don't particularly find it funny.

"I've seen how often you and James text or call. I'd say you're obsessed with him," Ben teases.

"Well, I just don't have anyone better to talk to or spend my time with," I say while sticking my tongue out at him.

Everyone continues to laugh but eventually moves onto different conversations. I have trouble paying attention because I can't stop thinking about James and what he's doing. He doesn't have a class at this time, so I'm not sure why he's not responding. What if something happened to him?

"Earth to Everly!!" Jake waves his hand in front of my face.

"What?" I ask.

"Are you still thinking about James?" He actually looks concerned.

"No." Yes, but I'm not going to admit it.

"Well, are you going to answer our question?" he asks.

"Sorry, what was it?"

"Are you going to the fair?" Lauren asks.

Oh, I completely forgot that the fair was in town this week. Unfortunately, it will be gone before James is able to come back to town. I really have no intention of going without him. My father took me to the fair when I was little, but I feel like if I go now I would just want to go with my boyfriend.

"I don't think so. What about you?" I look back and ask Lauren.

She shrugs her shoulders and looks away for a moment. "Lorenzo asked if I wanted to go with him, but I don't really know that I want to. I feel like I would just be so stressed out going with him. He's not the fair going type. Or date type. Or any type..." Lauren's words start drifting off.

I hate this for Lauren. I know she's not interested in Lorenzo, but I wish she would try a little harder. If he asked her to go, then I feel like she should go. What's the worst that could happen? If it's an awful time, she can just feign being sick and go home or something. This is on her though. I shouldn't be judging.

Ben and Jake are both going to the fair this weekend with the dates they went to homecoming with. I'm honestly surprised Jake is going with her again since they didn't seem like they were really interested in each other. Maybe I misread that between them.

I continue to check my phone throughout the day almost every five minutes. James still hasn't texted, and it's the end of the school day. Maybe they were right, and I do have a problem. Is it normal to feel like this? I want to be with James every second of the day, or at least talk to him. Maybe this isn't normal.

The moment I get home, I go up to my room to call James. I didn't want to do it in front of anyone because I don't need them to call me out again. When I open my door, I find the best surprise. I can't help the smile that spreads across my face when I find James lying on my bed against the headboard, reading a book. He uncrosses his legs to get up, but before he can, I jump on top of him and kiss him.

James laughs. "Well, hello to you too, baby."

I pull back but don't roll off him. "I'm so glad to see you here, but why haven't you been answering my texts? And what are you doing here?"

He kisses me again and scoots out from under me so we can both sit comfortably.

"I didn't trust myself to not ruin the surprise, so I forced myself not to text you. And I'm here because I'm taking you to the fair tonight."

I squeal, like a fangirl squeal. "Really?!"

He laughs again. "Yes, really. I take it you're excited?"

"Excited is an understatement!"

We make out on the bed for a few minutes, then he pulls away once again. I don't want him to pull away and by the way his body is responding to me, it seems he doesn't want to either.

"Let's go get dinner and head to the fair. I have another surprise for you too," he says with a grin on his face.

"Oh yeah? What more can you possibly offer me?"

"Will you play hooky from school tomorrow to find out?"

My eyes widen. "You... James Crawford is asking me to play hooky from school? What have you done with my boyfriend?"

James smirks. "One of my classes is canceled tomorrow, and I figured I'd skip the other. I want to take you out. We don't get a chance to go on many dates, so I thought this would be the perfect opportunity."

I'm still finding it hard to believe that he's skipping a class and asking me to skip school. Maybe he's just as addicted to me as I am to him. Clearly, we are both a bad influence on each other. I'd do anything for him and I'm pretty sure he'd do anything for me. When did we get to this point? I remember having a crush on him and never thinking he could feel the same way about me. Now we are both equally obsessed with each other.

"James, you could ask me to skip the country with you and I'd follow without question," I say seriously.

"Good to know, but I'm just asking you to go to the fair with me tonight and spend the day together tomorrow," he says with a smirk.

I roll my eyes. "Fine, if that's all... Then I suppose I could do that."

He rolls on top of me and tickles me. I laugh and squirm underneath him. I love serious James, but silly James is another of my favorite versions of him.

"Do I really have to get on that?" I ask James as we get closer to the front of the line.

"Yes. It's what every couple goes on at the fair. It's the most romantic thing to do."

"But... It looks like it's going to fall over. What if it falls over?" I cringe while listening to the Ferris Wheel make all sorts of creaking sounds.

"What happened to skipping the country with me and not asking questions?" he asks, trying to hold back his laughter.

"Well, I'm not going on a death trap by skipping the country. We'd be very much alive on the other side of the world. Would you like to do that? I'd much rather leave now and head to Ireland or wherever you want to go." I try to tug on his arm to get out of line.

This time, he doesn't hold back his laughter. "Everly, we will be fine, I promise. Do you trust me?"

My nerves relax a little at his words. "Of course I trust you."

"Then let's get on this thing and enjoy ourselves. I promise it'll be romantic."

I sigh but nod. I don't know how something can be romantic when my heart is beating out of my chest, and I feel nauseous. It's almost like I'm going zip lining again. James should know by now that my luck is horrible. It's my luck that some important bolt on this ride would come loose while we're at the very top and then come tumbling down to our deaths. Though, I suppose it wouldn't be so bad to die with James beside me.

We finally get on the ride and I'm sitting on the same side as James, so close to him I'm basically on his lap. When we finally start moving, we jolt forward, and I grip onto his arm for dear life. I hear him chuckle, but he doesn't call me out on it.

We finally make it to the top and the Ferris Wheel stops.

I don't notice I have my eyes closed until James says, "Everly, open your eyes and look."

I do as he says and look out in the distance. We are really high up, but at this moment I'm not feeling as scared as I was before. Everything is so beautiful at night. The lights in the distance from the city are shining and above us you can see the stars. There's not a cloud in the sky. The moon looks like it's almost a full moon and so bright. This really is perfect and romantic.

"It's beautiful," I whisper.

I feel James' gaze on me as he says, "It is, but not as beautiful as my view."

I can feel the heat rising in my cheeks as I look toward him. I've never had someone look at me the way he's looking at me. He makes me feel beautiful and loved. My heart squeezes at the thought.

He pulls me into a gentle kiss. The Ferris Wheel moves forward again and stops a couple times before we part. We are halfway back down to the bottom, and I don't want this to end yet. Even though I didn't want to get on to begin with.

James pulls something out of his pocket and holds it in his hand. I can't see what it is as it fits inside his hand and is completely covered. James takes his other hand and puts it on my cheek to hold my face and look directly into my eyes.

"Everly, I want you to know that I've never felt this way for someone before. We've known each other for basically our whole lives, and I can't imagine you not being in my life moving forward. I've fallen completely in love with you, and while we are still young, I know that I want to spend the rest of my life with you. We're not ready to get engaged, but I want to make this promise to you and give you this promise ring to signify it. I promise to love you forever and one day, I'll be proposing for real. Will you accept this promise ring?" James holds out his palm, showing me the ring.

I can't see the ring well in the dark, but I know it is perfect. Everything he just said was perfect. My heart is so full at this moment, and I'm so giddy with his promise ring proposal. I never saw this coming.

"Yes, of course," I say as he slips the ring on my right-hand ring finger.

I put both of my hands on each side of his face and kiss him hard. I pull away and look him in the eyes. "I love you so much, James. I promise to love you forever, too. No matter what life throws our way, I'll always love you."

We kiss the rest of the way down until it's our turn to get off the Ferris Wheel. James steps out first and holds his hand out for me. I take it and step off. We don't let go of each other's hands until we have to.

We do a couple more rides, but I'm not a huge fan of fair rides. James plays some fair games to try to win me a stuffed animal. When he plays the balloon dart game, he actually does a great job. He wants to get me the large panda stuffed animal, so he keeps playing until he wins it. At the end of the game, the guy says that he owes $80, which is ridiculous. We could've bought that bear at the store for $20, but James doesn't care. He just wanted to win it for me, and I love that. I'll forever treasure the bear.

On the ride home, I have the bear in the front seat with me and I can't stop staring at my ring. I was able to get a good look at it in the lights earlier and it is gold with a beautiful emerald, my birthstone, in the center. It's simple, but perfect. I still can't believe he gave me a promise ring.

When we get back to the house, we both quickly change, and he wants me to meet him in his room. On the way to his room, I'm looking down at my ring and literally run into Ben in the hallway.

Ben puts his arms out to steady me. "Sorry Ben, I wasn't paying attention."

Ben chuckles. "Something else on your mind?"

I smile because, of course, he knows it's his brother. His brother is always on my mind. I don't have to say it.

"I can't wait to hear all about the fair tomorrow at lunch," he says while stepping out of my way.

"Actually, I'm skipping school tomorrow," I say nonchalantly.

Ben raises an eyebrow in question.

"James asked me to skip so we can spend the day together," I say while shrugging my shoulders.

Ben lets out a long laugh and then studies me. "Wait, you're not joking? James is skipping classes tomorrow and asked you to skip school?"

"Yeah, I know. I was just as surprised as you are."

"Huh. Well... I'd say you're a bad influence on him, but he needs to lighten up a little and have fun. Good for him. I'm glad he has you Everly," Ben says while patting my shoulder and walking off.

"Good night, Ben."

"Good night," he calls over his shoulder with a little wave.

I quickly walk into James' room to find him already lying in bed. He looks exhausted, and honestly, I feel the same way. I crawl into bed and cuddle with him.

Neither of us say a word as we just enjoy each other's company. I drift off to sleep quickly with his arms around me.

# Chapter Eleven

I wake up the next morning confused about where I am. I'm not in my room and it's pitch black. Is it still dark outside? I go to grab my phone to realize I'm trapped underneath an arm. Oh, that's right, I slept with James last night. I cuddle up closer to his body and enjoy being in his arms. I wish I could wake up like this every morning with him.

I feel my phone vibrate with a text and a quick panic shoots through me. I completely forgot to tell Declan I'm skipping school today. Hopefully it's not too late, and he's worried about where I am since I'm not in my room and didn't meet him to bring me to school.

I push James' arm off me and roll a couple of times to the end table where my phone is. I pick it up to realize it's already nine in the morning! I can't believe we slept in that late, and I also can't believe those blackout curtains work so well.

"Come, lay back down," James says groggily, holding his arm out for me.

"I have to text Declan that I'm not going to school today." I scramble, trying to pull up my texts from him. I'm surprised he hasn't texted me yet.

"I already told him and my mom. Now come lay back down."

He thought that much ahead that he already told them? I can't believe how thoughtful he is with everything. How can I deny his request now? I take my phone with me as I snuggle back in under his arm.

I pull my phone back out to see who texted me. It was Ashley in my group chat with Lauren.

Ashley

> Are you okay Everly?

Lauren

> It's not like her not to respond to messages...

Ashley

> Should I text Declan to make sure she's okay?

Lauren

> Give her until 9 to respond.

Ashley

> It's past 9 now I texted Declan and he said she's skipping school today to spend time with James and that she's probably still sleeping.

Lauren

It was literally a few seconds past 9 when you sent that but okay. Glad she's okay.

Sorry guys I'm fine. James took me to the fair last night and asked me to skip school today to spend the day with him.

Ashley

How was it?!

It was amazing. He gave me a promise ring!

*Picture of promise ring*

Ashley

That is gorgeous!!! I cannot even! *Swoons*

Lauren

Wow! So pretty. James really loves you.

He does. Sorry I forgot to text you last night. Have a good day at school and I'll give you all the details later!

I hear James groan. "Everly, who are you texting?"

I smile. "Lauren and Ashley. They were worried about me since I didn't show up at school and then I wanted to brag about the promise ring you gave me. They both said it was beautiful."

I can't see James' face, but I know he's smiling. I love bragging about James to my friends. I wish they both had a love like I do and sometimes I feel bad for bragging, but he deserves all the praise.

James scoots closer to me and starts kissing up my neck. When he gets to my ear, he nibbles on it and says, "I love that you talk so highly of me to your friends."

I giggle. "How could I not? You're the best thing that ever happened to me, James."

I turn over and kiss him. "I love you," I add.

James kisses me back before saying, "I love you too, Everly. You're the best thing that happened to me."

We lay in bed for a few more minutes before he rolls off and opens the curtains. I fling my arm over my eyes and want to hiss at the sunlight shining in through his window now. I feel like a vampire.

James rubs his eyes. "Okay, that was brighter than I thought it would be."

We both laugh and I get up as well. "So, what are your plans for us today?"

He pulls me in close. I love that he always wants to touch me.

"Well, I was thinking we could start off by getting breakfast. Then I thought we could go for a walk in Central Park since it's nice outside. Do you remember that castle there?" he asks.

I gasp. "Are you seriously questioning if I remember that castle? Of course, I remember the castle! My dear prince, however do you think I could have forgotten?!"

James laughs. "Good. There's an outfit on your bed. Go get dressed."

He kisses me on the forehead and shoos me out of his room. When I open my door, I see a beautiful dress sitting on my bed. It's not a normal dress, it's a dress like in a fairytale fit for a princess.

After getting myself zipped up in it, I look at myself in the mirror. The dress goes all the way to the floor and has ruffles and lace along the sides and front of the dress. It has long sleeves which are perfect for a chilly day. There's a beautiful lace design from the shoulders to the chest and down each arm. The back has a small hole just above where my bra strap is. It's a beautiful taupe color. I go to my closet and pull out some gray lace-up boots that I thought would match this perfectly. They go up to my knees, so it will help keep me warm.

I finish my look by doing my makeup more than I normally would and adding some loose curls to my hair. I have no idea what James has planned for us, but I'm excited. I'm assuming we will go to the castle. I'm not going to lie, I'm loving the idea of dressing up while being there. It is quite the walk, but I think these boots will be comfortable enough and the fact I get to walk around looking like a princess excites me even more.

After I finish getting ready, I go back to James' room. He should be finished getting ready by now since I took so long.

When I walk into his room, he's still in the bathroom, so I sit on the bed and take a selfie of myself. I send it to the girls' group, which I named for the group chat with Lauren and Ashley.

My phone chimes with a text almost immediately after sending it.

Jake

> You look hot! Why are you not at school and where are you going looking like that?

Oh my God! Did I accidentally send it to Jake?! I quickly fumble through my phone to see I not only sent it to Jake, but I sent it to the boys' group! My heart stops for a moment as I panic. I can't believe I sent it to the wrong group. I rarely mis-send texts.

> I meant to send that to Lauren and Ashley sorry. James and I are playing hooky today.

Bash

> Well you look amazing Everly and did you say James is playing hooky today?

After feeling better about sending the text to the wrong group, I finally get the courage to send it to Lauren and Ashley. I triple check to make sure I'm sending it to the right thread.

James comes out shortly after my mishap, and my jaw literally drops when I see him. James is dressed up like a prince. He has on dark brown pants with black boots that also go up to his knees. His top is leather with a belt and what looks like a cloak on his shoulders. The padding on his shoulders is a lighter brown that is fuzzy. I can't stop staring. James has a smirk on his face as he stalks over toward me. He knows exactly what he is doing to me. I don't want to go anywhere now. I just want to stay here, undress him, and jump in bed with him. Then again, I don't want to undress him because he looks so good in that. My own prince. He is every girl's dream.

"What do you think?" He leans down and whispers in my ear.

I feel goosebumps rising on my neck and arm.

"James... You look hot. Please tell me your plans for today include time for us in your bed," I say, all breathy.

He smirks. "Oh, I fully intend to get you in bed at the end of the day, but first I want to spend the day out with you and make your dreams come true. When you were younger and we went to the castle, you mentioned wanting to dress up like a princess to find your prince there. I want to be that prince you were looking for."

Can this man be any more perfect? That had to be like seven or more years ago, and he remembered what I said.

Before we leave, I take a selfie of us together and send it to the boys' group. This time I mean to send it to them. I know they will probably make fun of James for this, but I don't care. They need to know how amazing James is and how cute a couple we are.

James has Declan drive us to breakfast and then to Central Park. Declan parks close to where the castle is, so we don't have to walk too far. It would only take about ten minutes. Declan doesn't say a word to me the entire drive or walk up to the castle, but I keep seeing him take glances at me and smiling. Sometimes it looks like he's holding back a laugh, like he finds this to be entertaining.

I feel like I should be embarrassed because who goes around dressed like a prince and princess randomly? I'm not embarrassed though because James is not the type to do something like this and he's doing it for me. He should be embarrassed, but he hasn't made it seem like he is at all or like he doesn't want to do it. In fact, he's acting like this is the best thing ever. Either he really wanted to do this for me, and it makes him happy, or he secretly is enjoying it himself.

When we stand in front of the castle, I have to say it is a lot smaller than I remember it being. I knew it wasn't big, but it felt much bigger when I was little.

"What are you thinking?" James asks.

"I'm thinking about how it looks a lot smaller than I remember, but it's still amazing."

He laughs. "Yeah, now that we're older, it does seem smaller. Let's go."

James links our arms and brings me up in the castle where there are some men playing music on their cellos. It's the perfect music to dance to and apparently James feels the same way because he pulls me in and starts dancing. The first song we dance to is slow and I enjoy every second of it. I truly feel like I'm in a fairytale dancing with my prince.

The second song is faster with a fun beat. James and I are dancing around each other, skipping, and have our arms linked, letting go and coming back together again as we dance. I can feel everyone's eyes on us and feel silly, but I don't care. We dance around each other and spin around, having the time of our lives. I don't want this moment to end.

When the song ends, James leads me to the top of the castle. We walk up the narrow staircase and I trip on the second to last step. I was doing so good the entire way until the very end. How typical of me. James steadies me and helps me up the last two steps. Once we get to the top, we look around and enjoy the beautiful views of Central Park and the city. James pulls me close to him and kisses me. I melt into him and feel the wind whipping around my hair. Once we pull apart, I lean the side of my head into his chest as he holds me close with his arm around my waist. We stand there longer than we probably should have, but I think we both know that soon our day will be coming to an end, and we'll have to go back to reality. I am rather enjoying this fairytale, and the best part is that I'm with James.

Reluctantly, we head down the stairs, but don't head back the way we came. James leads me further into Central Park by the lake. He leads us over to a blanket that is set out on the lawn with a picnic basket. Did he really have a picnic set up for us?

He opens the basket and brings out the food. My favorite sandwiches, chips, and chocolate chip cookies. I keep saying I don't know how I could fall more in love with this man, but I do. He keeps giving me more and more reasons to love him.

We mostly sit quietly, eating our food and watching the people around us. We talk occasionally, but just enjoy each other's company. I've never felt comfortable in silence and always felt a need to fill it, but I don't with James.

After finishing our picnic, we go back to the car and Declan drives us home. I know James is going to have to leave soon because he still has to drive back to college. I don't want this day to end.

When we get back to his room, I can't take it anymore. I pull him toward the bed as I fall on it, and he lands on top of me. We're already making out, and I want him to tear off my clothes already.

James groans. "Everly, I love you in this dress and don't want to take it off, but I want to end this day making love to you."

This man knows how to make me swoon. He wants to end it by making love to me. He always knows the perfect thing to say. I agree with him though; I don't want his clothes off because he looks so hot in them.

"Then let's make love, but leave everything on. I can't get enough of you in this outfit. I hope you're going to keep it and wear it again," I say while tugging on his shirt to bring him closer to me.

"I'll do anything for you."

James lifts my dress above my hips and pulls off my underwear over my boots. He then unbuckles his pants and pulls them down just enough to let his erection spring free. He leans over and kisses me as he enters me slowly. One of his arms is on the side of my head and the other holding my waist. He continues to kiss down my neck and back to my lips as he thrusts in me over and over again. It's slow, and it somehow feels so different from what we've done in the past. I know we've made love before, but this time feels like so much more. After we both climax and come back down, he lies beside me and holds me. I can't help the emotions that are overtaking me, and a few tears slip from my eyes. I try to wipe them away before he sees them, but of course, he never misses anything.

"What's wrong?" James asks, looking at me with concern.

I shake my head. "Nothing is wrong. I just... I'm emotional. That was amazing, and it just felt different. It felt like... I don't know how to explain it."

He leans over and kisses my forehead. "It felt like making love. I love you so much, Everly. I know we were pretending to be in a fairytale today, but we are our own fairytale. This is never ending love. We have a love that will never fade, I know it. I can't imagine my life without you in it."

Well, I was getting my emotions in check, but then he had to go and say that. I hold back a sob and look away for a few moments to compose myself.

James grabs his phone and says, "Check your email. I just sent you something."

I pull out my phone and go to my email. I open his to find a bunch of pictures attached. When I open the pictures to look at them, I see they are from today. There are pictures of us dancing, laughing, at the top of the castle, and at our picnic. I didn't even realize anyone was taking pictures of us. I was so consumed with James that I had no idea.

"Did you have someone take pictures?" I ask, trying to rein in my emotions.

"I did. I thought you'd want to remember today. When you feel lonely or when you're mad at me for whatever I do, I want you to have these pictures and this ring to remember that our love is forever."

What is happening? How am I going to be able to let him leave for college now? I need him so badly that my heart hurts thinking about him leaving.

"I love you so much, James. I'll never forget today."

# Chapter Twelve

School has become an annoying part of my day. I'm ready to graduate and move on with my life. Meaning, I'm ready to get to college and spend every minute with James that I possibly can. Staying invisible this year has been harder than I thought it would be, but I've succeeded for the most part. I occasionally get glared at by girls and they snicker as I walk by, but I just keep walking. I don't care what they think about me or if they have a problem with me. I'm staying to myself and my little group of friends.

"Alright, we're going to team up. McKayla and Scott, you're the captains, so go ahead and pick your teams." And there goes that. The coach decided it's dodgeball day.

McKayla and Scott go back and forth, picking someone to join their team. Jake and Ben are both in my PE class and, of course, they both get picked first by Scott. McKayla picks her best friend Samantha first, which is dumb because she stinks at dodgeball, but whatever. I'll let myself get hit so I can sit out immediately and not endure this stupid game.

To no one's surprise, I'm picked last. Ben and Jake give me a look of pity, and I just shrug my shoulders at them. Unfortunately, I'm not on their team. I'm on the team with mostly girls.

As I walk up to my team, I notice McKayla roll her eyes and hear her whisper to Samantha, "Of course we get stuck with her."

My heart skips a beat, and I feel anger rise immediately. Wow, where did that come from? Usually I let these things slide, but for some reason, I have the urge to tell her off.

"Sorry, I didn't hear you. What did you say?" I ask with attitude.

She scoffs and says, "I don't know why we always get stuck with you."

"Why?" I ask. I don't really care for her answer, but I'll play along for a moment.

"You're horrible at all the games we play in PE," she snarls.

I shrug my shoulders. "Yeah, okay."

Samantha chimes in by coughing out, "and" cough, "a slut," cough.

I had just turned away from them, but my head whips back quickly at what she just said. "Excuse me?"

"You heard her. Slut," McKayla says.

I'm really beginning to hate anyone with the name Kayla in it. My heart is now racing along with my mind. I think about fifty different things I could say and do in this situation right now. The one that sounds the best is to punch her in her smug face, but I know that isn't the right thing to do. I should walk away right now, but of course I don't.

"I'm pretty sure you're the slut," I state back casually.

She gasps. "Well, I'm not the one that slept with all the boys you're living with. You've been here, what? A couple months and you have slept with both Jake and Ben? I heard you slept with their brothers too."

I can feel the anger and adrenaline now rushing through my veins. Who the hell told her that? Is Adam spreading this rumor? Are these girls part of his friends' circle and here to rile me up on his behalf?

"You should really check your facts before making accusations about people," I state, trying to stay diplomatic and calm. I'm anything but right now.

"Hmm... You're right. It's not fair to Ben. He's sweet. I doubt he would sleep with a slut like you," Samantha butts in again.

I ignore the comment and try to find the will to just walk away. I don't know what it is about these two, but they make me want to stay and fight with them. Pure rage is burning inside me, and I feel like any second I'm going to snap.

"Oh, you're right Sam. Ben is too good for her and there's no way he would take Jake's seconds. We all know he's a man whore who probably has..."

And that's what it takes me to snap. The moment she started talking badly about Jake, my arm and fist had a mind of their own. I wind back my arm and smash my fist into McKayla's face. She makes a pained sound as she steps back, holding her nose.

"You bitch!" she cries out with the words muffled.

Another one of her friends runs up to her to see if she's alright. While I'm still fuming with rage and watching McKayla, I don't even notice Samantha come up beside me and yank back my hair, hard.

My head flies back and the pain in my scalp makes my heart race faster and another shot of adrenaline hits. I grab her arms to pry my hair out of her hands, but am unsuccessful, so I headbutt her and when she lets go, I knee her in the stomach as she falls to the floor. The sound of the coach's whistle going off is barely audible in my already ringing ears.

I go to get a kick in on Samantha, but I feel arms wrap around me from behind and then find Jake standing in front of me with hands on my shoulders.

"Hey, Everly. Let's walk away," he says while completely in my face, blocking my view from everything happening around us.

"Principal's office! Now!" the coach yells at me.

Jake exchanges a few words with the coach as I notice Ben is the one holding me from behind. When Jake finishes, Ben lets go and Jake walks me toward the gym doors. I hear her tell the other girls to go to the nurse. Everything around me sounds muffled, but I can feel Jake's arms around me as he leads me through the doors and down the hall. When we make it out of earshot of the gym, he turns me around and places my back against the lockers.

"Hey, what happened?" Jake looks at me with such concern in his eyes.

"Nothing," I say in a monotone voice, avoiding his eyes.

He laughs, but it's not a real laugh. "Shit, don't tell me nothing. Tell me what happened. You don't just snap like that."

I shake my head and think for a moment. I want to spare him from what they said about him, but I know he won't believe me if I said I punched her because she called me a slut. He knows I don't care about that enough to get physical with someone. Crap, why did I turn this physical? That was stupid. I know I have more self-control than that.

I sigh. "They were calling me a slut and then started saying mean things about you and I just lost it."

Jake stares at me without saying anything. He doesn't ask me what they said, and he doesn't tell me I shouldn't have done it. He doesn't say anything. He just pulls me into a hug and holds me there for a moment. Eventually, we have to make our way to the principal's office.

When I make it to the office, I'm immediately pulled in with the principal and assistant principal. Jake is sent back to the gym. I wish he could've been here for support, but I guess it's probably best he isn't. I tell the principal exactly what happened and what was said.

"Everly, you're a senior. You know fighting doesn't solve problems, words do, or you walk away," Principal Sanchez says.

I nod and don't say anything. There isn't anything to say. He's right. At this point, it's best not to argue and just accept whatever punishment they decide to give me.

I'm asked to wait out in the main area of the office while they call my father. I sit in the chair with my leg shaking up and down. I feel nauseous thinking about what he's going to say. I'm not afraid of my father or that he's going to ground me or anything. I am afraid of him telling me he's disappointed in me. There's been very few times he has told me that in my life, and I'm hoping this isn't going to be one of them.

After what feels like five hours, but in reality, it's five minutes, the principal calls me back into his office.

"I spoke to your father, and we agreed that since you have no prior issues, not even a detention, that we will let you off with just a one-day suspension. You'll go home now and take tomorrow off. I want you to take the time this weekend to think over your actions and come back Monday refreshed and apologizing," he says.

Ugh, apologizing. I'll have to get up the courage to do that over the weekend. Right now, I don't feel sorry for hitting either of them. They started it and said some nasty things. I've never done anything to those girls before, so why they felt the need to be that way toward me is what bothers me.

Someone knocks on the door and once it opens, Declan comes walking in. "Ready, Kid?"

I look back toward the principal, and he nods. I get up and walk out with Declan right behind me. I get in the car and sit in the backseat. Neither Declan nor Barry say a word to me. I know my father called Declan to tell him what happened. I wonder what he's thinking.

My father hasn't reached out to me yet, which I still expect him to tell me he's disappointed in me. God, I hate when he's disappointed. The fact Declan isn't speaking makes me wonder if he's disappointed as well. A lump forms in my throat as the adrenaline and rage wear off. No, I'm not going to cry.

I hate that I'm losing control of myself. As much as those girls deserved it, I should have never touched them. I know that, but I was just so angry. That lump in my throat gets tighter and damn it, tears start dripping down my cheeks. Ugh, come on. I will not cry, in the car, in front of Declan and Barry.

I'm not going to cry. Think about something else. I start thinking about James and the fun time we had the other night at the fair and the next day at the castle. That makes me lose it. Damn it, that was supposed to help. The tears are coming fast now, and I do my best not to make a sound. I stare out the window and I hold my breath. Stop freaking crying. What is wrong with you?

I'm getting angry again and damn it, that makes me cry harder. A sob escapes, and I gasp loudly as I let the air seep back into tight lungs. I take a quick glance in the rear-view mirror and Declan's worried gaze meets mine. Ugh.

I pull my legs up and bury my face in my knees, hugging them tightly. I usually wait until I'm alone to let myself feel my emotions, but clearly that's not happening. I angrily cry into my knees as silently as possible, which isn't silent at all. When we're getting close to home, I regain control of myself and swipe at my tears like I'm trying to hide them. Clearly, both Declan and Barry know I've been crying. At this point, I just need to own it.

When we finally make it home, I stay in the car for a minute longer as Barry takes a quick glance back at me and then heads into the house. Declan waits outside the car. When I get out, I try not to look at him as I bolt for the front door. Declan catches my arm, and I stop in my tracks. I don't look back at him and don't move. He comes closer and unexpectedly wraps me in a tight hug.

Crap, I just got my emotions in check and him doing this makes me want to cry all over again. I don't break the hug, and he stands there with his arms wrapped around me for as long as I need. After a minute or two, I pull away and finally look at his face. I can't read his emotions.

"Meet downstairs in ten?" he asks.

I nod and head back inside to get on some workout clothes to spar with Declan. When I make it downstairs, he's waiting for me. We warm up, and we still haven't said a word to each other, but I know it's coming.

After five minutes, he finally speaks, "So, tell me what happened."

I shake my head. "It was dumb. I got angry at what they were saying and couldn't control myself. I punched her. Then her friend attacked me, so I attacked back."

Declan stares at me like he wants me to continue.

I sigh. "I know I shouldn't have done it, Declan. I lost control. It won't happen again."

"You're right, it can't happen again. We have all lost control before, but now you have to learn from it. It's okay, Kid," he says while letting me throw some punches at him while he blocks.

I throw a few more punches at him before he continues, "So tell me what they said to get you so upset."

I shake my head. It isn't necessary for him to know, and I honestly just want to forget about it.

"Everly. Tell me," he demands.

I sigh again. "She called me a slut and then started talking bad about Jake. It was stupid and I shouldn't have let it get to me, but it did once she started talking about him."

He nods. "Feeling the need to defend others is a good quality. You just need to make sure you do it in the right way."

"I know," is all I say.

We continue sparring until I'm sweating and ready for a break. My anger and sadness have left me completely. This always helps.

"You're not mad at me?" I ask him as I take a drink of water.

He looks me over for a moment before saying, "No."

"Disappointed?" I ask.

"No," he states.

I look back and forth between his eyes. "Really?"

"Really. Like I said, we've all lost control before. I can see you understand your mistake and you'll learn from it. You're good, Kid," he says.

I give him a small smile and head out the door.

"Everly," he says, stopping me.

"Yeah?" I ask.

"You need to call your dad now."

Crap, I knew it. My father probably told him to make sure I called when I was ready. I sigh as I head back to my room, shower, and change. Once I finish stalling as long as I can, I pick up the phone and click on my father's name, dreading the conversation to come.

# Chapter Thirteen

I returned to school after my suspension, and everything was back to normal. Thankfully, my father dealt with the two girls' parents and came to an agreement that they wouldn't press charges against me. I'm not sure what my father said to convince them, but I'm thankful he did.

I dreaded that phone call with my father, but he surprisingly wasn't disappointed. He, of course, told me that's not how we deal with our issues, but then he proceeded to act like he was kind of proud of me. The school wrote off my one-day suspension like it never happened. I know that was also my father's doing. Either way, everything seems to be back to normal and those girls haven't even spoken to me since that day. I also was never forced to apologize to them.

I'm currently hanging out at Ashley's house, where her brother, Dillon, is throwing a Halloween party. Their parents are out of town, so he came home for the weekend to use their house. It's a nice house with plenty of room for hundreds of teenagers and young adults to get drunk and have a good time.

Unfortunately, James and Bash couldn't make it home for this party. They had committed at the beginning of the year to help with some frat party at college. He invited me to come but said he probably wouldn't be able to spend much time with me since he'll be helping out. I decided to stay home and come here to hang out with my friends. I'm a bit disappointed. It would've been fun to have a boyfriend to coordinate costumes with.

"Everly... I'm really disappointed in you," Ashley says while looking me up and down.

"Why?" I question her, even though I already know the answer.

Ashley is in a sexy Harley Quinn costume. This character is a popular choice this year for Halloween and there are many variations to it. Mine being on one end of the spectrum and hers being on the other. While she barely has on any clothes, my body is covered. I'm wearing skinny jeans with a jacket in her colors. Both of us have our hair pulled up like hers and each pigtail dyed pink and blue.

"You have a hot body. Why not show it off a little?" she asks.

I shrug my shoulders. "I have a boyfriend who isn't here, so I don't feel the need to look hot. I'm just here for fun."

She rolls her eyes. We didn't plan to go as the same character. In fact, we didn't plan our costumes at all. If we were smart, we would have planned something fun for Lauren, Ashley, and me to wear. With that being said, Ashley and I showed up as the same character. We're not sure what Lauren is yet, since she is running late.

We head to the kitchen and find the famous bowl of alcohol spiked with punch. We both fill our red solo cups and take a swig.

I cough. "Ashley, I swear this is getting worse. Is there any punch in this alcohol this year?"

She laughs. "If there is, I can't taste it. I don't think we should drink more than one this time."

I agree with that. The last party I attended here didn't end very well, and I was so drunk. I'm going to stick with the one cup this time. Plus, I have Declan watching my every move and I can feel the judgement coming off him already. Alright, he never judges me out loud, but I just know that he is on the inside.

When Ashley and I finish our drinks, we head out to the dance floor. She sent Lauren a text to see where she was, but she hadn't responded yet. I'm starting to think that she wasn't able to sneak out of her parents' house. They weren't supposed to be home this weekend, but maybe something changed.

Ashley and I have danced to four songs, and we are both sweating and feeling the effects of the alcohol. Seriously, who makes that punch? I'm starting to believe they just completely forgot to put the punch in it.

I feel hands wrap around my waist from behind. "Hey baby, can I join in?"

I laugh as I swing around and swat at Jake, who is all decked out as the Joker. "Where's your hookup for tonight?"

He smirks. "I'm looking at her."

"In your dreams, Jake," I say while dancing with him, anyway.

"Oh, you don't want to know what happens in my dreams."

I feel more hands on me, pulling me away from Jake before I can respond.

"Stop hitting on my brother's drunk girlfriend," Ben jokes while nudging Jake with his shoulder.

"Hey, I'm not drunk!" I can't help but laugh because he's right. I think I am drunk.

Ben and I dance through the song together while Jake is dancing with Ashley. Those two look perfect together with their costumes. They both went all out to look exactly like their characters. They look amazing.

"So, did James ask you to keep an eye on me tonight?" I ask jokingly.

"Maybe," Ben says.

I gasp. "Wait, seriously? Did he really?"

Ben shrugs his shoulders, which gives me my answer. I'm not surprised that he sent his brother to keep an eye out on me. It kind of makes me want to do something crazy just so Ben has something to report back to him.

"So why aren't you dressed up?" I ask looking him over because he's in normal clothes.

Ben shrugs. "I wasn't in the mood this year."

"Well, that's no fun. You can't come to a Halloween party without dressing up. Promise me next time we go to one, you'll dress up," I say.

He smiles. "Sure."

I excuse myself to head to Ashley's room to use the bathroom. The one downstairs always has a long line, so she lets me use hers. When I make my way up the stairs and to her room, my hand stops on the doorknob before turning it as I hear voices inside.

"We need to talk about this," I hear Lauren's voice say through the door.

"We shouldn't talk about this here. We'll find time to talk later," a male voice that I don't recognize says.

"We never have time," she argues.

I hear footsteps get closer to the door, so I step back quickly, trying to pretend like I wasn't close enough to hear anything. The guy walks out with Lauren right behind him. She notices me immediately and freezes, but he continues to walk past me and down the stairs. I don't recognize him, but he also has on a mask.

"Who was that?" I ask her as she walks closer to me.

She shakes her head. "No one important."

I want to press her further, but she looks upset. She clearly doesn't want to tell me who that was, so I know she won't tell me what they were arguing about.

"We didn't think you would make it. You didn't respond to our texts."

"Sorry, I had bad service. My parents also left late, so I was running behind," she responds.

I decide to change the topic. I look over her outfit and say, "Ashley is going to get a kick out of your costume."

She smiles and looks me over. "We probably should've coordinated. I didn't think you would dress as Harley Quinn too. You make a better one."

I laugh. "Well, I actually think Ashley makes the best one."

"No way! Ashley too?" Lauren laughs and starts walking toward the stairs.

"I'm hitting the bathroom, and I'll come find you. Just a warning, they left out the punch when making the alcohol spiked with punch," I offer the advice to her.

After the bathroom, I find Ashley and Lauren in the living room. Lauren is talking to Ben while Ashley is talking to Declan. I make my way toward Ashley, and I notice her flirting with him. Ugh, I thought she was over him when she started to have a crush on Ben. Or I'm pretty sure she just has a crush on everyone. Either way, I figure I need to save Declan from this awkwardness.

When I get closer, I hear Declan's laughter and watch Ashley put her hand on his arm. He doesn't move back. That's... surprising. What is going on here? I continue to watch for a little longer and Declan doesn't seem to mind, so I guess he doesn't need saving. I head toward Ben and Lauren.

"It's just a stupid story to keep kids out. It's not real," Lauren says.

I jump in on the middle of their conversation so I'm not sure what they are talking about. "What story?"

Ben looks at me seriously as he says, "The abandoned house at the end of the street. It's haunted and they say if you are in the house at midnight the week of Halloween, you won't come out."

I look at my phone to see there's twenty minutes until midnight. That should be plenty of time to get down there if we want to go. Do we? I'm not superstitious and I don't believe in haunted houses. It's abandoned, so it has to be creepy and most likely dangerous, like the floor may fall in or something. Lauren's right, they probably say that to keep kids out.

"Let's do it," I say, but don't know why.

"Really?" Ben asks, looking excited.

"I'm assuming you haven't been?" I ask.

He shakes his head. "No one would ever do it with me. Jake refuses because he believes in all that ghost stuff."

I shrug my shoulders. "Yeah, I'm down for it. Lauren, are you in?"

"No thanks, I'll stay here," she replies while taking a sip of her drink and looking off toward the corner of the room.

I follow her gaze to find her staring at the same guy she was talking with earlier. He's completely dressed up in his costume, so there's no way to know who it is. Does he go to our school? Does she like him? My heart clenches at the thought. I hope not because that would be awful considering she's getting married in less than two months.

"Ben, this was a terrible idea," I say as I tug on his leg to get his foot unstuck from the floorboards.

"It's really stuck. I don't understand how it's so stuck! Shine the light on it," he says quickly.

We made it to the alleged haunted house five minutes ago. It is right down the street from Ashley's house, but its long driveway places it in the middle of the woods. It's a huge house, and it didn't look too run down. We walked inside and it did feel spooky, but I'm sure that was just our imaginations. We walked through the foyer and went straight upstairs because he wanted to check out the upstairs first. That's how he ended up with his foot stuck in the floor.

I shine the light on his foot and there's barely a little hole that it fit through. We pull his pants up to see if we can get a better look, but it doesn't help.

"Is your shoe stuck on something? Can you slip your foot out of your shoe?" I ask, thinking that's the only explanation on why it's stuck.

"I'll try," Ben says while wiggling his foot to try to get it out of his shoe.

A door slams in the distance and we both freeze. I shine the light in the direction we heard the noise, but nothing is there. We both listen intently to see if we hear anything else, but there's nothing. Not even a footstep.

"It was probably the wind," Ben says with his voice shaking.

"Yeah, you're right." He's wrong. There's no way the wind just shut a door inside this house, but let's just say that to make him feel better.

We bring our concentration back toward his foot and try to get it out of his shoe. Moments later, we hear footsteps. I shine the light again in the general direction I thought it was coming from, but I think it may be downstairs.

"Someone else must be here doing the same thing as us," I say while walking toward the stairs.

"Hello?" I call down the stairs.

There's no answer.

"Is someone else here?" I yell again.

Silence.

My heart rate picks up, and my chest tightens. Okay, it's fine. It's probably just some animal or something and maybe Ben was right. It could have been the wind. I turn back toward Ben who is trying hard to get his foot out, and I can tell he's panicking. I want to help him, but I don't know what I can do.

I walk back toward him when we hear a door creak open and slam again.

"Ben! It's time to leave," I whisper shout.

"I'd love to Everly, but I'm a little stuck here," he says while sticking his hands in the hole, doing his best to loosen his foot.

I stomp at the wood around his foot thinking that maybe we can make the hole bigger to make this easier. My adrenaline is starting to kick in when I think I hear more footsteps.

The footsteps get louder. Okay, I definitely hear footsteps. The stairs make a creaking sound, and we hear a thud, then another, and another, as it sounds like someone is slowly coming up the stairs.

"Oh my God, Ben, someone's coming," I whisper.

The steps get faster, and I shine my light over toward the stairs to see a figure coming up it. I literally jump at the sight as my heart is beating out of my chest and I feel sick.

The figure races the rest of the way up the steps and all I see is a glowing white head as it races toward us. I panic and jump on Ben as we both fall backward and start rolling on the floor, screaming. I try to right myself, but I'm so freaking scared I don't even know what to do that I'm basically burying myself under Ben for his protection.

Just when I think I'm about to have a heart attack, cry, or whatever, I hear laughter. Familiar laughter.

"Jake?!" I yell and cry out.

"What are you guys doing?" He continues to laugh as he turns on a lantern that lights up the whole hallway upstairs.

Ben stands up and helps me up. My right arm hurts as I think he crushed it in the landing, or maybe when I was trying to place myself underneath him like he was a shield.

"What are you doing?!" Ben asks angrily.

"Lauren told me where you guys were, and I thought I'd come too. You both sounded scared, so I thought I would pretend I was a ghost," he says with a grin on his face.

Okay, he looks really creepy all dressed up like Joker and in this weird lighting in a haunted house. I mean, abandoned house. Obviously, there's no such thing as haunted houses.

I look back toward Ben to realize that his foot is now unstuck. "Well, at least that got your foot out."

Ben laughs, and it sounds like he's still coming down from being scared. "I guess so."

"Well, I've had enough excitement, and it's past midnight. I'm ready to go. What about you?" I ask, looking toward Ben.

"Yep, let's go," Ben says, leading us back toward the stairs.

We make our way down to the front door and Jake twists the knob to open it. It doesn't budge, and he tries unlocking it and locking it over and over.

"Let me try," Ben says, pushing him out of the way.

Ben does the same thing and then shakes the door like he's just trying to pry it open. It's not working.

"Want me to try?" I ask, but Ben shakes his head and continues to try.

After a few more moments, we all hear a loud thud behind us. We twist fast, facing the direction of the noise and once again, there's nothing there.

"Hello?" Jake yells out in a high-pitched voice.

There's no response.

"Jake, did anyone else come with you?" I ask, hoping the answer is yes.

"No," he says, and my hope deflates.

"Alright, come on Ben, let's get out of here. This isn't funny anymore," I say as my heart races again.

This is exactly like horror movies. The stupid teenagers go into a haunted house thinking it's all fun and games until they are murdered. I'm not afraid of ghosts, but I can picture some crazy murderer being in the house right now just waiting for stupid kids to enter thinking it's fun. Well, it's not fun, and this was the stupidest idea I've ever had.

Ben continues to try the door when another loud crash happens behind us followed by what sounds like something running across the floor.

"Oh my God, we need to get out of here right now. NOW!" I yell and start panicking.

I run toward the front window and try opening it, but it won't budge. Ben is now body slamming the front door with Jake like they are just going to break it down. I'm fumbling with the locks on the top of the window, trying to figure out the combination to unlock them. Why are these stupid latches so difficult to figure out?

Another thud and the sound of something rolling toward us makes me jump and contemplate breaking the glass in the window. Thankfully, I figured out the correct position for the latches and lift the window up that is screenless.

"The window!" I yell to the boys as I throw a leg through the window.

A loud screeching sound occurs and more thuds coming toward us which propels me quicker out the window. Scratch that, Ben literally propels me out the window as he follows, and Jake is pushing him out. Ben falls onto the porch next to me and Jake falls right on top of Ben. We all scramble to our feet and start racing down the driveway when we hear laughter coming from the trees beside us.

My heart is still racing, but we all stop in our tracks to look at the source of the laughter. Lauren and Ashley come out of the trees and Declan walks out of the front door, laughing. I laugh hysterically because if I don't, I'll cry. I'm fairly certain I was seconds away from peeing my pants.

Jake and Ben both let out a heavy breath and then laugh with us. I look back toward Declan, who makes his way over to us.

"Did you guys all plan this?!" I glare at the three of them.

Declan smirks. "It was Lauren's idea."

We all look toward Lauren, who just continues to laugh harder. I don't think I've ever heard her laugh this hard before.

"Seriously? Declan, you almost gave me a heart attack. I thought I was going to die!" I yell at him while pushing his shoulder.

Declan shrugs. "I figured it would teach you a lesson on leaving without telling me."

I shake my head. I didn't really think about it since I was with Ben, but I should have told him. Declan just usually keeps a close eye on me and follows. Okay, lesson learned.

# Chapter Fourteen

I've been looking forward to Thanksgiving break with James. We were only able to see each other two more times between the fair and this break. We have been texting constantly and talking every night on the phone. When he's not with me, I feel like I'm missing part of my heart, which I'm pretty sure he will forever own.

Ashley's family is hosting a Friendsgiving at a fancy hotel in a ballroom the weekend before Thanksgiving. She said they have been hosting one every year since before she was born and it's always a memorable affair. Her family agreed to invite all the boys, me, and Lauren. Her brother, Dillon, made mention this is the most friends Ashley has ever invited. He seemed like he was happy for his little sister to be making friends. Now if only we could get her a boyfriend.

"Everly, are you ready? You're taking forever," Ashley says, peeking into the bathroom to see what more I could possibly be doing.

James is coming as my date, so I'm trying to look my best, especially since I haven't seen him in a while. Lauren helps put loose curls in my hair and pins up my bangs with a beautiful silver barrette with a butterfly on it. My dress is a gold and sparkly fitted floor-length gown. I thought it may be too fancy, but looking at Ashley, I can tell it's not. Her short dress barely reaches her knees, and it's a fitted black and sparkly dress with a slit up the right thigh. Lauren's maroon dress is more of a cocktail dress.

"You look gorgeous. James is going to love it," Lauren says with a sad smile on her face.

The closer we get to Lauren's wedding, the sadder she seems. She keeps a smile on her face, but it never reaches her eyes. I know her and she's pretending to be happy when she's clearly not. I wish there was something more I could do for her and that she could find true love. Or that Lorenzo would step up and treat her better. I don't know what all goes on in their relationship, but with what Lauren describes, he doesn't seem too interested in her. Lauren said they did end up going to the fair together, but it was awkward. She hasn't felt like sharing any details.

We leave the hotel room and go down to the ballroom, where guests are arriving. James, Ben, and Jake should all be here shortly. Just enough time for me to explore, as I love to do.

The ballroom is huge and completely decked out. There are at least thirty tables with ten chairs at each and a huge dance floor. The décor is a sophisticated fall theme. There are a few random statues in the corners and plants surrounding them. I go up to one to get a closer look.

This one is of a man holding a gun. I'm not sure of the significance, but it looks so real. Like if I touch it, then the skin will be warm, and he will move like a normal person. The temptation is too hard to resist, so I touch it. I place my hand on the cold statue's hand and feel how smooth it is. Suddenly, without any force, his finger falls off. I stand completely still, continuing to hold out my hand to the statue with the evidence broken off into my hand.

Did that really just happen?! I hardly touched it, why me? I take a quick glance around to see if anyone noticed me breaking the statue. It doesn't look like it. What do I do with it now? I try to stick it back on, but without any glue, it's never going to stay. I could lean the finger on the gun, but then that would just be too obvious to have a detached finger sitting there. I don't have any pockets to put it into, so that's out of the question. I notice the large plant sitting close by, so I quickly toss it in the plant and rub my hands down the sides of my dress, pretending like I didn't just break the statue and stash the evidence in a plant.

Before I have a chance to turn around, I feel hands on my hips and warm breath next to my ear. "Did you just throw a finger in the plant?"

My breath catches and I spin to face James, who has an amused look on his face.

I can't help but giggle. "I have no idea what you're talking about."

He cocks an eyebrow. "Oh really? Should I just take a look in here then?" he asks while getting closer to the plant.

I grab his arm. "Oh no, there's no need for that."

He pulls me in closer and kisses me. I melt into him as I always do as everything around us fades away.

Someone clears their throat from behind us. I quickly pull away from James to find my father and Mr. Crawford standing a few feet away. I feel myself blushing as I put some distance between James and me.

"Dad! What are you doing here?" I ask trying to pretend James and I weren't just making out in a very public setting. What was I thinking?

He eyes James for a moment before saying, "We are back in town for the week and the Hills invited us to their party."

I walk up to him and give him a giant hug. He squeezes me back. "I'm so glad you're home. Why didn't you tell me you were coming?"

We part and he says, "Well, I wanted it to be a surprise, which I see it was for you as much as it was for me."

I feel myself blushing again and step further away as James stretches his arm out to shake my father's hand. "It's good to see you again, Mr. Monroe."

My father shakes his hand and nods. This is so awkward, even though I have been open with my father about my relationship with James. Knowing that we are dating is completely different from seeing us make out. I'm just glad that we kept it PG because it's been hard to do that lately.

As more guests arrive, we find our seats at the table. Ashley sits to my left and James sits to my right. Lauren, Jake, Ben, Bash, my father, Mr. Crawford, and Mrs. Crawford also sit at our table. I can't help but just sit there and listen to all the conversations going on around me. This is my whole family right here. My father, my best friends, basically my second parents and siblings, along with my boyfriend, all at one table. How could life get any better than this?

I feel James place his hand on my thigh as he leans in to whisper in my ear. "Everything okay? You're quiet."

A smile stretches across my face. "Yes. I was just thinking that everyone I love is currently sitting at this table. I couldn't ask for a better night, and I wish it wouldn't end."

Before the food is served, Mr. Hill makes a nice speech thanking us all for attending and for our friendship. While I haven't seen him around much, the way Ashley describes him and how he spoke today tells me that he is a good man.

Our food starts arriving in front of us on those fancy silver plates with lids. While I've been to many fancy dinners, this is only the second time I've seen this presentation for a meal. I feel like a princess in a castle right now, and I'm loving every second of it.

Once everyone at the table gets their plates, I follow their lead to lift the top. When I lift mine, I find a disturbing sight and smell that makes me slam the top back down and want to vomit. I immediately stand, forcing my chair to fly back and fall to the floor. James, my father, and Mr. Crawford all stand up as well.

I'm holding my breath, and my hand is over my mouth to keep myself from vomiting.

My eyes are wide as my father asks, "What's wrong?"

Before I can say anything, James lifts the lid to see for himself. He places it back quickly, grabs it, and hands it to my father, who is now by my side.

James wraps his arms around me and whispers in my ear, "It's okay, we've got this handled."

I'm still in shock as James leads me out of the ballroom toward the lobby. I suppose they want me out of there to avoid a scene with the rest of the guests. Now that I'm sitting here with James' arms still wrapped around me, I realize that the whole room was silently staring at me. I can't believe I reacted that way.

James and I are sitting on a bench in the lobby as Barry stands in front of me talking on his earpiece walkie with some other guards, which I assume are the Hill's guards. As the door to the ballroom opens, I see all of my friends come toward me and hear my father shout inside the ballroom. I can't make out what he was saying, but he is not happy.

"No one come any closer," Barry says as he steps directly in front of me and holds a hand out to my friends.

Why was he telling them not to come closer? Did he think one of them did this?

I stand up, put my hand on his shoulder, and say, "Barry, it's okay. None of them were involved in this."

He doesn't look at me as he says, "It's just a precaution until we figure out who did it."

I nod and sit back down with James. My friends are ushered back into the ballroom, and no one is allowed to leave the building. I have a feeling we won't be finding the person who did it in there because they are probably gone or were never here to begin with. I'm positive Adam is behind this, even if he had someone plant that disgusting plate in front of me.

I try not to think about what I saw and smelled, but it's impossible. I relive the memory of seeing about ten dead frogs on the plate. I think there was a note, but I didn't dare keep the plate open long enough to read it. I'm sure they are though, and I have a feeling it didn't say anything good if everyone is reacting like this. If it was a little prank, it might have been investigated but laughed off. Knowing Adam, there was a threat involved.

My father finally comes out and whispers something to Barry before coming toward me. "Sweetie, Barry is going to take you and James back home. I want you to stay in your room until I get home, okay? We made sure the house is secure, so you will be safe there."

I take a deep breath and ask, "Are you sure that's necessary? It was just a dumb prank, right? I hate to ruin everyone's night."

He puts his hand on my shoulder before saying, "It's not your fault, you didn't ruin anyone's night. You understand? But I want to make sure you are safe, so please do as I say."

I nod. "Where's Declan? I don't want to go home without him."

"He's helping investigate who did this. Barry will take you home."

I look at Barry and then back at my father. "I don't mean any offense to Barry, but I want Declan."

My father searches my eyes for a moment and whatever he finds makes him sigh. "Alright, Declan and Barry will switch places if that makes you feel more comfortable."

I nod. I do trust Barry and he's been nothing but good to me, but I just feel better with Declan. I spend most of my time with him and we have a mutual trust with each other. I also know that he will tell me what is going on and what the note said. Barry is more tight-lipped about things.

Once we get home, I go straight to my room like I promised my father. James isn't going to leave my side, and I ask Declan to come to my room as well. As we sit there, Declan looks at me like he's worried.

"Spill it," I say, knowing that he knows exactly what I mean.

Declan leans against the wall by the door with his arms folded. "The note was a threat to you, your friends, and your family. There were ten frogs for the ten people at that table. We are assuming the threat indicates they plan to kill everyone."

My heart skips a few beats, and I have to tell myself to breathe. "So, do you think it was a real threat, or it was just a prank? It's Adam, right?"

Declan nods. "We don't know anything for sure, but we're investigating it. My assumption is that it is Adam, and it's most likely not a real threat. Just a threat to scare you."

I sigh and sit down on the edge of my bed with James. James has been quiet this whole time, but when I look over at him, he looks furious. I know he wants to take this into his own hands with Adam, but he can't. I won't let him.

"Thanks Declan. Let me know if you find anything else out?" I ask but know that I don't need to.

Declan nods and leaves the room. I look over at James. "I know what you're thinking, and I don't want you to do anything. Let them handle it, okay?"

James doesn't say anything, and he clenches his jaw.

"James! Promise me that you won't do anything. I couldn't live with myself if anything happened to you," I say, while holding both sides of his face in my hands.

"Okay," is all he says.

That's not a promise, but it's good enough for now. I'll just have to keep him even closer to me all week to ensure he doesn't do something stupid and calms down about the situation. Hopefully, it will be dealt with before that point, anyway.

# Chapter Fifteen

The threat from the other day is still being investigated, but it seems they are at a standstill. They were able to find who put the plate in front of me, but the server was just doing his job and had no idea what was inside. He has been with the company for many years, so he is trustworthy, and he has no connection with Adam. The cameras just so happened to not be working in the kitchen that night, so they couldn't see who put the plate together. Unfortunately, with no proof that it was Adam's doing, they can't do anything about it right now.

I haven't left the house much in the past few days, but when I do, Declan follows me closely. Thanksgiving break was supposed to be fun with my friends, but it's honestly just been depressing. I'm trying to stay positive as I have most of my life, but it's getting hard. It seems the more friends that I have, the more threats are being made against them. I worry because I don't know what Adam is capable of anymore, and I've clearly pissed him off.

James rolls over on his side to face me as he wakes up. I've been awake for a while as I've been having trouble sleeping.

"Good morning," James says while pressed up against me and pushing my hair behind my ear.

I give him a small smile. "Good morning."

"I like waking up to you every morning. I've been spoiled these past few days," he says, watching me closely.

"Me too. I'm going to miss you when you go back to college."

I've been sneaking into James' bedroom every night after everyone's in bed. Not much has happened except last night, and the only reason it did was because I initiated it. James has been so sweet with everything that has been going on and has just been there to comfort me, as he always does. We've been spending time together watching movies and cuddling. We've spent some time with the other boys, but we've mostly been keeping to ourselves when I'm not with my father.

James starts kissing me, and I groan in his mouth. I push him away and not because I want to. I glance over at the clock and sigh. I have ten minutes before I need to be downstairs training with Declan. Yes, it may be Thanksgiving, but I still need to train, and I want to. With the threats that keep coming in, I want to not only be able to protect myself, but to protect my friends too.

"Stay in bed a little longer. You can be late one day," James says, while tugging me back toward him and kissing my neck.

"James... I want to, but I can't be late. Declan will destroy me in training if I am," I say, while still allowing him to kiss me.

He pushes my shirt up and kisses his way down to my stomach. I arch my back toward him and then my stupid brain keeps reminding me that I now only have seven minutes until I need to be downstairs. I groan again as I pull him up to kiss me on the lips before pulling away again.

"Alright, I get it. Come see me after training?" he asks right before biting my earlobe.

"It'll be my first stop after my shower."

Before I can change my mind, I jump out of bed and race out of his room to mine. I get dressed in my workout clothes in record time and make it to the training room without a second to spare.

Declan looks at his watch and smirks. "Cutting it close today. It seems James has been a bad influence on you this week."

I can feel myself blush as I say, "I've been on time every day."

"That you have," he replies.

We warm up together in silence, which isn't unusual, but I can feel some tension in the room. Something isn't right.

"What's going on Declan?" I ask while holding a squat, stretching my legs.

He pauses for a moment, like he is trying to figure out how to tell me whatever it is that he wants to say. "Have you talked to Ashley lately?"

I shake my head. "No, I mean, I did yesterday morning. She's been sick since the party, so she hasn't been saying much, but she said she was feeling better. Why?"

He nods and my heart starts racing on why he is asking that. "Well, she isn't sick. She was poisoned. I'm going to be honest with you because I always am. She was poisoned that night in her drink, and we aren't sure if she was the target or if you were. You were sitting next to her, but everyone was threatened that night in the note."

I stop stretching and sit on the floor as I suddenly feel nauseous. Would Adam really try to poison me? Or would he really poison my friends? What is even happening right now? Is this real life? I thought this type of stuff only happened in movies. Then again, what if this isn't Adam? My father did say that it is dangerous. I don't know the extent of his business or job, and I don't care to. Is he working with some shady people that might want to kill us?

Declan puts his hand on my shoulder to pull me out of my thoughts. "Hey, it's okay Everly. We have so many extra precautions to keep you and your friends safe, okay?"

I nod but don't feel any better about that. We already had extra security at the party and yet someone still got to us. I need to know if this is Adam or someone else. I feel sick thinking about even talking to him, but I'm going to have to. But, before that, I need to take training even more seriously. I feel confident that I could hurt someone enough to be able to escape, but I want to be sure that I can fight and protect those I love as well.

"Declan, I want to learn how to use a weapon. I know I can't walk around with a gun, but I can with a knife. Will you teach me?" I step closer to him, staring into his eyes, determinedly.

He studies me for a moment before answering. "Alright, I'll have to get some training knives and a real one for you to carry around, but we can start practicing without. Are you sure that's really what you want?"

Without hesitation I answer, "Yes."

He steps back and sighs. "Everly, with what I've been teaching you, it would hurt your opponent and allow you the opportunity to escape. If I teach you how to use a weapon, you could kill someone. I want you to think seriously before we really practice with knives, and you carry one with you."

I understand what he's saying, but I need to do this. "I know. Declan, I'll be honest. I don't know how I would feel if I killed someone, but I do know how I would feel if someone killed a person I love and I didn't do anything about it. I wouldn't be able to live with myself if that's the case, especially if the reason was because of me."

Declan nods and starts teaching me about knives and safety. He teaches me exactly where I need to stab someone to slow them down and where I need to stab to do more damage. I'll admit, this isn't the most pleasant training session, and I really do not want to have to ever kill someone, but my circumstances have changed.

Once training is finished, I go upstairs to take a quick shower to clear my head. I know I shouldn't do what I'm about to do, but I have to. I pick up my phone and stare at it for a moment, trying to keep the nausea at bay. What's the worst that'll happen? It's just a phone call with one question.

Before I chicken out, I dial the number which is engrained in my head.

He answers on the first ring. "Everly, what a pleasant surprise to hear from you. How are you doing?"

My throat gets tight when I try to respond. I clear it and say, "Adam, I just need to know... was it you?"

I hear him laugh on the other end of the line. "You will need to be more specific, Everly."

I feel the tears burn behind my eyes, but I push them back. "Did you send me that dish at the party the other night with the note?"

He's silent for a moment before responding, "Ah, that... Yes, did you like it?"

Is he serious right now? Did I like it? He really is mental. How did I ever get mixed up with someone like him?

I ignore his question and ask another. "Did you mean to poison Ashley, or were you trying to poison me?"

He continues to laugh, yes laugh. How is any of this funny? "Of course I wasn't trying to poison you. Why would I do that? I told you that your friends would be in trouble if you told anyone, and you did. I mean, I'm not against poisoning you, but what fun would it be to accidentally kill you before you see your friends suffering?"

Kill me?! Did he actually mean to kill Ashley?! I need to call her after this to make sure she's okay. Could she have died? Did he give her enough poison to do that?

"What do you want, Adam?" I whisper into the phone only because I can hardly bring myself to talk anymore.

Adam sighs. "I want you to understand the consequences to your actions, Everly. Not only did you make a fool out of me by breaking up with me, but you told everyone when I told you not to. You got me in a lot of trouble with my father and I don't appreciate that. So, you and your little friends will pay for what you've done. It sounds like Ashley got lucky, but I'll tell you what, I won't target her again so soon. Maybe your other friend, what's her name... Lauren, right? She seems like an easy target. Or maybe I'll go after your boyfriend. There's so many to choose from."

I'm not sure how much longer I can hold back vomiting, but I need to fix this. This is all my fault. "What can I do to make this stop?"

He makes a tsking sound before saying, "It's too late now Everly. I'm sorry, but you need to learn what happens when you mess with the wrong people. Now, I do appreciate the call, but I must go. I hope you have a Happy Thanksgiving."

I don't say anything back, and he hangs up the phone first. I still feel sick, but it quickly turns to anger. I throw my phone on the bed and can't control the anger that came out of nowhere. I pick up the pillows on my bed and throw them against the wall with a scream. It doesn't help, as I can feel my anger rise even more. I swipe all the papers and junk off my desk onto the floor and pound the desk a couple of times with my fist, continuing to let out unnatural screams. I need to punch something. Hard.

I try to calm myself enough to go back down to the workout room so I can punch a punching bag fifty times.

I stalk toward my door and yank it open to find Ben standing on the other side, wide eyed.

"Everly, are you okay?" he asks, putting his hand on my shoulder.

The anger slowly fades as I stare into his eyes. My heart sinks thinking about Adam possibly hurting him. My friend, basically brother. What would I do if Adam hurt him?

I finally let the tears fall, and Ben immediately pulls me into a hug. I bury my face in his shoulder and continue to cry out my frustration, anger, sadness, fear, everything. I don't know how long I stand there crying, but it's long enough that when I lift my head from Ben's shoulder, my father, Declan, and James are all standing there watching me.

There's no use hiding that I contacted Adam. I know they are going to be mad at me for doing it, but at this point, there's nothing to lose. The concern is written on everyone's face, so I walk further into the hallway to tell them what happened. I don't feel like going to sit down in an office. I just want to get this off my chest now.

I lean against the wall with my arms hugging myself as I clear my throat. "I called Adam..."

My father steps forward like he is going to interrupt me, and I shake my head. "Before you interrupt me, let me just finish. I called Adam because I needed to know for sure it was him and it was. He didn't deny it. He is angry with me for telling on him and getting him in trouble, so he wants revenge. He intentionally poisoned Ashley and said he will continue going after my friends. There's nothing I can do to stop him at this point."

I feel so defeated saying that, but it's the truth. I hate feeling so out of control in this situation because there's nothing that he wants from me anymore other than for me and my friends to suffer. At least last year I was able to have sex with him when he wanted, to keep him from hurting my father, but now there is just nothing.

Declan and my father exchange a few words before my father stands in front of me. He pulls me into a hug and squeezes me.

"Everly, I don't want you contacting him again, okay? If you feel you need to, then let us know and we will do it together. I'm not going to let anything happen to you," my father says before letting me go from the hug.

"That's just it, I'm not afraid for myself. I'm afraid for my friends and you. I don't know what I would do if anything happened to any of you," I say as my voice trails into a whisper.

Each of them is saying something along the lines of not worrying about anyone else, but how can I not? Declan and my father walk off to figure out how to proceed with the situation. Ben leaves James and me alone, which we go back into my bedroom. He helps me clean up the mess I made before laying with me in bed. I feel comfortable lying in silence with James as I fall asleep for a quick nap.

I sit at the large dining room table, looking around at the feast being set before us. The Hales joined us for the Thanksgiving lunch that Mrs. Crawford planned. While the adults sit at one side of the table, the boys and I sit at the other. I rarely get to see Mr. and Mrs. Hale, but they are nice enough and always treat me well. They act much stuffier than the Crawfords, though. If I were to stay at their house every summer, I don't think I would have the same relationship with Mrs. Hale as I do with Mrs. Crawford.

After my nap with James earlier, I feel much better. There is nothing I can do at this moment about Adam, so I decided that I'm not going to let him ruin this holiday for me. He would love to know that I'm miserable right now, so I'm not going to let him win. I have my whole family here, and I'm going to enjoy them as much as I can. Especially with what I have planned.

Jake kicks me under the table and raises his eyebrows. I smile and try to contain my laughter, thinking about what we are going to do. Jake and I have been texting back and forth the past week, trying to come up with a prank during our Thanksgiving lunch. We haven't told Bash, James, or Ben what we have planned, which I feel will make this a lot more fun.

I take a sip of water, trying to hide my smile because I know everyone will be able to see the mischief on my face. I love pranks, but I sometimes struggle to keep my emotions in check while doing them. Jake has complete control of the situation now. I look across the table at Jake and he mouths, "Ready?" to me.

I nod and clear my throat once again, trying not to laugh.

I feel James' hand on my thigh. "Everything okay?"

I smile at him and just nod. I don't think I can get any words out at the moment.

Just as I go to take a bite of my turkey, a loud farting sound comes from the adult side of the table. Everyone pauses eating and talking for just a split second, before continuing like nothing happened. Somehow, I contain myself and ignore it as well. In this situation, ignoring a fart is the polite thing to do.

Bash and Ben look around at each of us with a smile and make eyes like they couldn't believe that just happened, but again, it's polite not to bring attention to it. A minute later, a louder and longer fart sounds from the same spot as the last one. This time, everyone stops and looks around the room, trying to figure out the culprit. My father and Mr. Hale are looking at each other since it sounded like it most likely came from one of them.

Once again, nothing is said as everyone continues with their meals. Even though it's rude, I place my elbow on the table to hide my face from the boys as I'm smiling and having trouble containing my laughter. Bash lets out a quick laugh with a cough to cover it up. After shoving my mouth full of mashed potatoes, I make the mistake of looking at Jake.

He has the biggest grin on his face and a gleam in his eyes. I don't think I have seen him smile so wide before and I suck in a laugh, but the mashed potatoes go down my throat, choking me. I have a coughing fit for a moment and try to drink some water regretting putting so much mashed potatoes in my mouth. James is patting me on the back like that would help my coughing fit. Why do people think that helps?

After that embarrassing moment of everyone staring at me and checking to make sure I was okay, the conversations continue. I look at Jake once again and can tell he is dying on the inside as he's squirming in his seat. He mouths, "again?" to me and I put up my finger for him to wait a second.

The servers are clearing the table and bringing out our dessert. I figure this is the best time to go for the third fart. I'm thinking a third fart will be difficult to ignore. Once everyone receives their dessert, I go to kick Jake to let him know to push the button, but I guess I accidentally kick Ben instead.

"Ow!" Ben says, leaning down, rubbing his shin looking across the table at James.

James looks at Ben confused, and I whisper, "Sorry!"

Before I can try kicking Jake again, James whispers in my ear, "What is going on?"

"You'll see," is all I reply with before kicking Jake harder than I need to.

I'm pretty sure that'll leave a bruise on both Jake and Ben. Jake and I stare at each other with the biggest grins on our faces. I know the other boys now know that something is going on.

Jake makes his fingers halfway visible for me to see him counting down from three. On one, he pushes the button, and it's the loudest fart yet, but what makes it the best is how wet it sounds. For some reason, it sounded like it came directly from Mrs. Crawford.

This time, Jake and I can't hold back. We both burst out laughing as Bash, James, and Ben join us.

"Children! Let's not be rude!" Mrs. Hale shouts down at us, but it makes us laugh even more.

I hear Mrs. Hale whispering something to Mrs. Crawford, but I can only hear Mrs. Crawford continually denying that it was her. No one will own up to that horrible sounding fart, and I feel so bad for Mrs. Crawford because everyone is clearly blaming her.

While they are all talking, I lean forward to whisper to Jake. "Alright, let them know what it was. I don't want her being blamed."

"Aw, are you sure?" Jake asks.

I nod and continue laughing. Jake pushes the button three more times in a row, which makes different farting sounds, and everyone catches on.

"Jake!!" Mrs. Hale yells at him.

Jake puts his hands up like he's innocent and asks, "Why are you blaming me?"

"Son, we all know it was you. Hand it over," Mr. Crawford says, holding out his hand for the button.

Just when I think he is going to hand it over, I feel something land on my lap. Jake threw the button on my lap to blame me! Am I supposed to take the blame?

Jake stands up with his arms up in the air. "See, I don't have anything."

Jake pulls his phone out of his pocket and pats the rest to show there is nothing in them. Everyone then looks at Ben.

"Don't look at me!" Ben stands and does the same thing as Jake. They look back and forth at James and Bash, who both shake their heads. I can't help but start laughing. At this point, why not? I lift my hand with the button in it and push it, revealing that I have control of the fart machine. Every single person at the table is now laughing.

My father grabs the little fart machine that's taped under the table and brings it up. He holds his hand out for me to give the button to him, and I do. He shakes his head, but still has a smile on his face. I think this is the best Thanksgiving that my father and I have ever had.

# Chapter Sixteen

I sit in the passenger seat of the car in awkward silence while eating my ice cream. The ice cream itself is amazing. Plain chocolate in a large bowl, just as I like it. The company sitting in the driver's seat is the problem. I don't know why I thought this was a good idea, but clearly, I was mistaken.

Barry sits silently in the driver's seat, looking straight ahead out the windshield. I didn't need to get ice cream on this cold November day, but I wanted some alone time with Barry. He wasn't interested in bringing me dress shopping for Lauren's bachelorette party alone. Declan took the day off, and he has been tight-lipped about what he's doing today. Why I thought I could get that information out of Barry is beyond me. New determination enters me as I've already finished half my ice cream and only gotten a few grunts and yes or no answers out of him. I tried to start small, but it's time to move onto bigger questions.

I place my left arm on the console and lean closer to Barry, inspecting him. As the time passes that he doesn't look my way, I continue to stare at him and lean closer. While doing so, I study his appearance. He's always wearing medium colored wash jeans and a polo shirt. Today, he's wearing a navy polo shirt. He typically wears darker colors, which I suppose blends in better. He's bulkier than Declan, though they are about the same height. Barry looks like he's in his late thirties, or maybe it's the scruff on his face that makes him look older. He keeps his dark brown hair short and always looks perfect without a hair out of place.

After leaning in so far that I'm basically on his lap, Barry finally turns to face me, and I stare into his dark brown eyes.

"Can I help you?" he asks in his gruff voice.

I smile and sit back in my seat. I don't know why, but I really want to mess with him today.

"I was just smelling you and admiring your scent. Do you wear cologne?" I ask with a serious face.

"No," he states back in his typical serious manner.

Barry looks straight ahead again and occasionally looks out each of our windows and in the rearview mirror. Is all this as uncomfortable to him as it is to me? Why is he always so serious? I sit back in my seat and sigh, taking a couple more bites of my ice cream before it completely melts.

I lean against the door and look back over at him. "What is Declan doing today?"

He doesn't look my way as he answers, "It's his day off."

No duh. "I know that, but what is he doing?"

This time, he takes a quick glance at me before looking straight ahead again. "You'll have to ask him that."

I roll my eyes, even though I know he doesn't see it. I know I don't spend that much time with Barry alone, but I really would like to get to know him a little better. He's been with me for a few years. I feel like by now we should be well acquainted, and I should be able to break down his hard exterior a little bit.

"What do you do on your day off?" I ask.

"I don't take days off," he says.

Yeah, that's what I figured he would say. Declan doesn't usually take days off either, so that's why I'm curious where he is. Is he out on a date? I can't really imagine that being the case because I don't know where he'd meet someone. He's always around me. If he's not, then he's usually sleeping. There are times that Mr. Crawford's guards take their place, especially with the night shifts, but I've never noticed Declan leaving his room or the house during those times.

"Why not?" I ask.

Barry sighs like I'm annoying him. "This isn't a typical 9-5 job. We're paid to not have days off."

I cringe at his words. "Does my father not allow days off or vacations?"

This time, he looks at me and doesn't look away as he speaks, "Your father is a good man. He would allow for time off if we asked, but I have a feeling we were chosen for our jobs, knowing that we wouldn't ask."

I finish with my ice cream and hold up my bowl, letting him know that I'm going to throw it away. The moment I'm out of the car, Barry is beside me. The trashcan is literally ten steps away from the car. I could've rolled down the window, threw the bowl out, and most likely made it in the trashcan. It's that close, but I know Barry takes his job seriously and would never risk it.

When we get back in the car, he starts driving home. I'm fairly certain he's annoyed that I asked him to drive me for ice cream when we have plenty in the kitchen at the Crawford's house. I thought he might get the hint that I wanted to spend some quality time with him, but I guess not. Or he knows that and just isn't the type of person to spend quality time with someone.

We're halfway home and driving in silence again. I look at my phone to see a message from Ashley that was sent over an hour ago. How did I miss this?

Ashley

**I'm going on a date wish me luck!**

**What?! Who are you going out with?**

I await her answer, but she doesn't respond. She hasn't told me she was seriously interested in anyone or that anyone asked her on a date. My mind tries to come up with who she's gone out with, and it can't be Ben because he's still at home, and I'm pretty sure he's dating that one girl he took to homecoming. My heart skips a beat for a moment as my mind drifts to Declan. Could he... No, he wouldn't go out with Ashley.... Right?! Now I'm panicking and need to know. I text Ashley a couple more times, but she's not responding. She's clearly still on the date.

"Are you sure you can't tell me where Declan is?" I ask Barry.

He just shakes his head in response.

I let out a low growl in irritation. "Is he on a date?"

Barry looks at me and does a quick study of my face before looking back to the road. We pull into the driveway, and he puts the car in park. Neither of us get out of the car.

"Are you worried he's on a date?" Barry asks, and I swear he's amused.

"Huh? Why would I be worried? I just want to know if he's on a date." I say a little too quickly. I am worried. I'm worried he's on a date with Ashley because that's just not going to end well. He wouldn't be dating Ashley, would he?

"Why do you want to know so bad?"

I study him for a moment to see if I can figure out the answer to my question. I am positive that he's not going to answer my question.

"I just want to know what he's doing. He never takes a day off and that seems like a reasonable guess," I state.

"What if I said he was on a date?" he asks, still completely serious.

"Is he?!" I ask a little too quickly and loudly.

The side of Barry's mouth twitches up for a quick second and I know he is indeed amused. "Are you jealous?"

Oh, Oh!! That's why he looks amused. He thinks that I'm wondering because I'm jealous and I like him. I mean, we do spend a lot of time together, but he knows that I'm with James, right? Though I'm not with James right this second... James said he had work to do with his father today, so that's why I figured this was the perfect opportunity for Barry and I to have some bonding time.

Now the question is, where do I go with my response? Barry is engaging me with questions and possibly some answers, and that's because he thinks I like Declan. Should I continue this, so he keeps talking? Why not?

"So what if I am?" I ask.

I'm not going to say that I am, but it doesn't hurt to ask a question back. That seems to be what people do when they don't want to answer a question, right?

Barry shakes his head. "I think you should concentrate on James, Everly."

Okay, that didn't last long. I can't help but smile and start laughing.

"Sorry, I don't like Declan. At least, not in that way. This is the most you've talked to me, so I thought I'd try to go along with it."

Barry studies me more. He's studied me a lot during this car ride, like he's never been around me before.

"Do you want me to talk more?" he asks.

"Yeah. I mean, I'd like it to be less awkward and to get to know you better," I say.

Barry nods. "Okay, I'll try to talk more."

I smile at him before opening the car door to head inside. "Thanks Barry."

# Chapter Seventeen

The weeks after Thanksgiving break went by quickly and without any issues regarding Adam. I thought for sure I would hear from him again, but everything had been eerily quiet. Ashley was fine once the poison got out of her system, but she and her family are wary now. I have been mostly left alone at school, minus a couple of ugly notes still being posted on my locker by his friends.

Ashley and I are taking Lauren out for her bachelorette party. Her wedding is a couple of days into Christmas break, so we figured to do it the weekend before. We're heading to the club that the boys and I went to over the summer and doing a sleepover at my house afterward. James got them both fake IDs so we would have no problem getting in. Of course, Lauren's parents think we are just going to see a movie and then have a normal girls' night in.

Barry and Declan accompany us inside the club and thankfully we have no issues getting in. Ever since my one-on-one time with Barry, he's been more talkative. By more talkative, I mean he says one or two sentences to me each time I see him. I find our time alone together to have been a success, even though I never found out what Declan did on his day off. I tried everything to get it out of him by even making bets with him during training, which I lost every time, and he won't budge. I think he finds it entertaining to torture me.

Ashley had finally gotten back to me that night about who she went on a date with and, thankfully, it wasn't Declan. It was a boy in her class named Shawn. He's not very popular and seems to be kind of a nerd. I've only seen him on a few occasions, but he seems nice enough. They decided to give being boyfriend and girlfriend a go.

Lauren, Ashley, and I sit at the bar and order a round of shots.

As we wait, I ask Ashley, "So how are you and Shawn doing?"

She makes a cringey face and says, "I guess we're okay. He took me to play Dungeons and Dragons with his friends the other night."

By the way she said it, it doesn't sound like that was her favorite thing in the world to do.

"So, you didn't have a good time?" Lauren asks, while downing her shot and shaking her head from the burn.

Ashley shrugs her shoulders. "I thought it might be fun, but that's definitely not my thing. We're also not going to talk about the kiss we shared."

Oh no, we're certainly going to talk about that. "What happened?"

Ashley downs her second shot and says, "I just said we're not going to talk about it!"

Lauren and I both laugh. "Well, you can't bring it up and not share the details, so spill it," Lauren demands.

Ashley groans. "Fine... It was the worst kiss I've ever had. It was sloppy and so inexperienced. I was hoping it would get better with time, but it's just getting worse."

"That sounds awful. So did you break up with him?" I ask.

"No... not yet. I didn't want to hurt his feelings," she replies.

Yeah, Ashley's not very good with that type of stuff. If we weren't here for Lauren's bachelorette party, I would force her to call him and break it off. We're here to have fun though with Lauren and try to make this crappy situation with Lorenzo better.

After another round of shots, we take to the dance floor. We dance like we did during Homecoming, but this time it seems like we're dancing a lot better, I think. Or maybe that's the shots talking. We were going to take it slow, but clearly, we decided to go ahead and get drunk fast so we could enjoy ourselves more. It seems to work because I'm not as self-conscious as I was at Homecoming. We must look pretty decent because a couple of guys come up to us to join in. One has his hands all over Ashley and the other is right behind Lauren, trying to dance with her.

Just a couple of seconds after they both join in with us, Asher appears out of nowhere. I smile at him but notice his expression as his eyes are locked on the guy behind Ashley. He almost looks like he wants to murder him. I wonder if he knows him and doesn't like him.

Asher clears his throat, changes his expression, and says, "Ladies, come join me at my table."

He pushes himself between the guys that came up and puts his hands on Lauren and Ashley's lower back as he nods to me to follow. Lauren and Ashley both pause for a moment, until I give them a nod and a reassuring look. Once we reach the table, Lauren and I sit on one side as Ashley sits on the other. Asher says he'll be right back and leaves us at the table. Thankfully, it's the furthest away and a lot quieter over here, so we don't have to scream at each other to be heard.

"Who is that?" Ashley asks.

"That's Asher. He works here. He's really nice and helped me out last time I was here," I say, reassuring them.

"Why did he bring us over here?" Lauren asks.

I shrug. "Not sure, but he didn't seem too happy with the guy behind Ashley. Maybe he knows him and wanted to get us away because he's no good."

Asher comes back with three waters and hands them to us. We all take a drink of them immediately, and I can't help but notice him watching Ashley intently. Is he concerned for her?

"Ladies, if you need anything, feel free to ask for it. Hang out here as long as you want and order some food. Everything's on me tonight," Asher says.

He stands up straight and meets my gaze. He nods his head toward the back, indicating for me to follow, and I do. I tell the girls I'll be right back and to order something good for us to eat along with some margaritas or something.

Once we make it to the hallway, he stops where we can still see the table where my friends sit. I look over at Asher to find him wearing an oddly colorful suit, but he makes it work well. I'm not half as drunk as I was the first time I met him, and I still can't help but notice how gorgeous he is. He seriously should be a model with his perfection. I try to take a peek at his ears, but they are completely covered by his hair. I remember the first time I noticed how pointy they were. I wonder if they really are or if my drunk mind made that up.

"It's good to see you, Everly," he says, taking his gaze off the table and finally on me.

I nod. "You too. Thank you for offering us whatever we want tonight, but we'll pay. We're doing a bachelorette party for our friend."

Asher's eyebrows scrunch together as he looks at me. "Which friend is getting married?"

"Lauren. She's the one that was sitting next to me," I say.

I swear Asher looks relieved after I say that. "She seems a little young to be getting married."

"Yeah, she just turned 18. It's an arranged marriage, and she's not looking forward to it," I respond.

"Well then, make sure she has a good time tonight. And yes, everything's on me. Let me know if you need anything. But I just wanted to pull you back here and ask how you were doing."

I'm honestly shocked at how he genuinely seems to care about me. I really didn't think he would remember me.

"I'm actually doing pretty well. You'll be glad to know I did talk to James. We're dating now," I say with a smile.

"Good, you deserve to be happy," he says and then glances back at the table.

"You're doing alright?" I ask.

He looks back at me and replies, "I'm doing great. I won't keep you, Everly. Seriously, if you need anything, let me know."

I thank him again and walk back toward the table. I bump right into Declan's chest because I didn't realize he was standing right around the corner watching me. Maybe I've had too much to drink already.

"Sorry..." I state and back up a step as he grabs my shoulders to steady me.

"Next training, we're going to talk more about keeping an eye on your surroundings," he says.

I roll my eyes at him, and his frown indicates he doesn't find that amusing. I sigh.

"What's the point of that when I have you and Mr. Serious over there?" I point toward where Barry stands.

"Clearly you're drunk, so we'll talk about this later."

Declan moves to the side to let me pass, but for some reason, that makes me kind of mad. I don't often get angry at Declan, but it seems like he's in a mood tonight. I grab Declan's arm and pull him further into the hallway toward the offices where I met Asher the first time.

"What's going on Declan?" I ask and he just stares at me, confused.

"You're in a mood. What put you in that mood?" I ask again.

"I'm not in a mood," he says while folding his arms over his chest.

I laugh because, yes, he's in a mood. Or maybe I'm in a mood. I don't know. I continue to stare at him in silence because I'm not leaving until he speaks. Eventually, he gives in.

Declan sighs. "It's just been a long week and I'm tired. Come on, let's get back to your friend's bachelorette party."

I really look at him and he does look exhausted. I feel bad for dragging him out here like this. I know that he's my guard, but I also know he takes it upon himself to make sure Ashley and Lauren are also taken care of, especially when we are in a place like this drinking.

"Thank you, Declan, for always taking care of me," I say, and we walk back.

I pause halfway there with a random thought in my head, and because I'm drunk, I ask, "Why do I have guards and no one else does?"

He pauses with me and replies, "What do you mean? You know your father is rich and in a dangerous business. That's enough reason to have a security team."

"I know, but why don't Ashley and Lauren?" I ask.

Declan shrugs his shoulders. "Ashley's family isn't nearly as wealthy as your father, and I'm pretty sure Lauren's family doesn't have much right now, but her fiancé has her taken care of."

"Wait, what does that mean?" I ask out loud versus in my head like I thought I did.

"Lauren has someone assigned to watch out for her by her fiancé. She's followed when she's out to keep her safe."

Well, that is news to me, and I'm pretty sure Lauren doesn't know that. Should I share this bit of information with her? How haven't I noticed before?

"Is he here now, watching her?" I ask.

"Yes," Declan answers.

"Where?" I look around the room, trying to find someone that looks like they might be watching her. I don't see anyone.

"You don't need to know," he says.

That's probably for the best. I don't want to know because I'll probably just watch him all night, and then I'll want to tell Lauren. She has enough on her plate as it is. I don't want to tell her that her fiancé has been spying on her and watching her every move if she doesn't already know.

"What about the boys? Why don't James and all of them have someone?" I ask.

Declan looks at me, confused. "They do. The Crawfords and Hales have their own security teams at home and they all have someone, too. James has someone living in the apartment next to him on campus. They don't need to be followed as closely or all the time like you because they can take care of themselves."

Well, isn't all this information interesting? How have I seriously not known any of this before? James has someone living in the apartment next to him? I kind of feel dumb not knowing any of this. Maybe Declan is right. I need to be more observant. I will definitely be revisiting all this during our next training session.

After feeling stupid about not knowing all of what Declan said, I took a quick moment to brush it off before heading back toward the table. Ashley, Lauren, and I spend the next couple of hours eating lots of fried foods, drinking margaritas, and dancing. Oddly enough, no other guys try to dance with us, which I'm okay with. It makes it awkward since I'm with James and not interested in anyone else. Also, since Ashley is still technically with Shawn, who she has said, she'll break up with him first thing in the morning. Then, of course, Lauren is engaged to Lorenzo.

Once we made it back home, we turned on the tv in my room for a movie, but none of us made it past the first ten minutes. Lauren passed out first, followed by Ashley. I send a quick text to James letting him know we made it home safely, and we had a great time before letting myself fall asleep.

# CHAPTER EIGHTEEN

I'm finding it hard to believe that Lauren is getting married in a few days. I hate that it's not a time to celebrate. It's more like we're getting ready for a funeral. Christmas break begins today, and I'm going to be spending the next couple of days before the wedding at Lauren's house. Ashley is going to join us tomorrow night, on Christmas Eve because yes, they are getting married on Christmas Day. I hate to be missing out on time with James, especially since I haven't seen him since Thanksgiving break, but Lauren needs me.

"So, what do you want to do tonight?" I ask her as we get home from school and throw our bags in her bedroom.

She shrugs her shoulders and plops herself on her bed. She looks like she's giving up and I can't have that.

"Come on Lauren, we only have a few days left. Unless you decide to take me up on the offer to get you out of here. I know we can hide you," I say, really hoping she'd take me up on the offer.

"I promise they will find me Everly," she says like she knows that for certain. She may be right.

I sigh. "Fine, then we need to make these last few days before your marriage fun. What do you want to do? We can do anything you want."

She sits up in the bed and looks at me seriously. "You mean anything that I want in the house? I'm not allowed to leave until after the wedding. Which I'll be leaving with Lorenzo and into his bed." She shivers at the thought.

I do too. I'm so angry at her parents for forcing her to do this. "I'm going to go get us some snacks."

Cookie dough always makes her feel better. Me too. I go downstairs to the kitchen and open the fridge. I find an un-opened roll of cookie dough that she hides in the back. I take it out and don't even bother cutting some of it. We will be eating the whole thing tonight.

Just as I'm about to leave, her mom comes into the kitchen. I hide the cookie dough behind me.

I nod. "Mrs. Faucett."

She nods back. "Everly." She looks at my arms behind my back but doesn't say anything about it. "How is Lauren doing?"

I glare at her. Seriously? "Do you want me to be honest?"

She nods.

"Then she's doing horribly. She doesn't want to get married, and she's scared. He's not nice to her," I say, trying to keep my voice calm.

She sighs. "She's young. She will grow to love him. She has a good life carved out ahead of her with him and she will see that in the future."

She sounds so rehearsed. Does she really believe that or is she just trying to convince herself?

"Please forgive my rudeness, but I have to say this at least once. What you are doing to her is wrong," I say in an accusatory manner.

She furrows her eyebrows at me. "You don't understand Everly. I appreciate you being a good friend to her, but right now she just needs a friend beside her, so I won't keep you."

Well, clearly, she doesn't want to hear what I have to say and now she is dismissing me. I walk past her without another glance. At least she doesn't say anything about what I have behind my back. Maybe she does feel bad a little bit, but not enough.

We spend the rest of the night eating cookie dough in bed and binge-watching anime. We've been obsessed with *Marmalade Boy*, and it really makes for a depressing night... more depressing. It's almost midnight, and it looks like Lauren fell asleep, so I take my phone out to text James. He's usually still awake at this time.

I miss you.

James

I miss you too.

I wish I could be home when you get home tomorrow.

James

I won't be home until late anyway. I'll see you at the wedding. Concentrate on Lauren.

Thank you for being understanding.

James

You're a good friend

I love you

James

I love you too

I put my phone down to find Lauren looking over at me.

"Were you texting James?" she asks.

I nod. I didn't want to say much about it because it's not fair to her.

She sighs. "You're lucky Everly. Never take him for granted."

I want to cry. "You're right. Thank you for reminding me. I won't."

She sits up in bed and turns the volume down on the tv. "You know, I always wanted to be a therapist. I wanted to help people with their problems and make them feel better. To make them not feel so alone in this world."

Is that how she's feeling? "Lauren, you're not alone. Ashley and I will always be here. You have your brother, too."

She gives a sad smile. "After high school, you guys are going off to college. You won't be around, and that's not your fault. I want you to have fun and a good life. I want you both to be with your true loves and concentrate on them. My life with Lorenzo is supposed to be me at home, being a wife and eventually a mother."

"That's not so terrible, though, is it? And I can go to college anywhere. Heck, if you want, I can take courses online in your living room while he's working. I'm here for you Lauren. I'm not going anywhere." I mean every word I say.

She laughs, but it isn't her normal laugh. "I could never ask you to stop living your life, Everly. You need to live it and enjoy every moment. Life is too short..." she pauses for a moment before continuing. "Can I tell you a secret?"

I nod.

"I've never wanted to be a mother. In fact, I hate children. Do you know he wants at least five kids? What would I do with five kids that I hate?" She sounds so serious.

"Lauren... you will not hate your kids. No one likes kids, especially at our age. They are sticky and annoying. But you will be a great mother and love your kids. I know you will," I say sincerely.

"Thank you for being here, Everly. You're such a good friend," she whispers.

She lays back down and rolls over on the bed. She looks so sad, and I hate this for her. I hate there is nothing I can do, so I do the only thing that I can. I curl up against her and hold her as she sleeps, and I drift off to sleep with her.

I wake up to my phone alarm going off and the sunlight coming through the cracks in the blinds. I roll over to find Lauren missing from the bed. I turn off the alarm and look at the time. It's nine in the morning, and I don't remember setting my alarm last night. I really have to pee, so I get out of bed and go toward her bathroom. I don't hear her in there, but I knock anyway. There's no answer.

I turn the doorknob, but it's locked. That's odd, she must not have heard me. I knock again and state loudly, "Lauren?"

Still no answer.

I knock harder. "Lauren? Are you in there?"

No answer.

I put my ear to the door to listen for any signs of her and there is nothing. Maybe she accidentally hit the lock on the way out of the bathroom, but for some reason, my heart starts racing. What if she's hurt?

I bang on the door this time. "Lauren! Are you in there? Are you okay?"

Nothing.

I begin to panic. What if she slipped after getting out of the shower? These locks are the same as the ones I have at home. It's like a little slit, so all I need is a coin. I dig through my purse and get a nickel out. I turn the lock and open the door.

I freeze when I see her lying on the floor, unconscious. I run to her and touch her forehead, hoping that will help her wake up. She doesn't move, and she is... cold... so cold... in fact; she doesn't look like herself. No.

"HELP!" I scream as loud as I can. "Please!! Someone help!!!"

I hear footsteps racing our way, and Brandon is in the doorway of the bathroom.

"What happened?" he asks as he races over toward his sister on the floor.

"I... I don't know... I found her like this. The door was locked," I say, trying to figure out what is happening. This doesn't feel real. I feel like I'm in a dream.

"Shit! Lauren! Lauren, wake up!" Brandon cradles her head on his lap.

I'm panicking and frozen. I don't know what to do. I should call for help. I tap the button on my watch three times. Declan will come and he will know what to do.

"Call 911 Everly!" Brandon says and his face is so pale and panicked. He looks like he is frozen too and doesn't know what to do.

I crawl out of the bathroom to the end table where my phone is. By the time I reach my phone, Declan and Lauren's mom are in the room. Declan looks panicked as he's searching for me.

When he lays eyes on me, he asks, "What's wrong?"

"I... need to call 911... Lauren..." I say, not able to get out my words. Why can't I get out my words? Why am I breathing so fast? This isn't real.

I hear a woman's scream. Was it my scream? No, I didn't scream. I look over toward the bathroom to find Mrs. Faucett on the floor, yelling Lauren's name. Declan grabs his phone and calls 911. I don't know what he tells them. I can't hear anything. My ears are ringing.

Declan pushes Mrs. Faucett out of the way and looks at Lauren. At this point, I crawl back to the bathroom and am sitting against the wall watching the scene unfold. My breathing is rapid. I can't do anything. I need to do something.

Declan starts CPR on her. No. That means she's not breathing. If you're doing CPR, then there's no pulse. This can't be happening. What happened? I look around the room and I don't see a puddle on the floor. There's no puddle. She must have just tripped then. But I don't see any blood. If she wasn't breathing and she tripped, wouldn't there be blood?

Mrs. Faucett's screams pull me back to reality. Why is she screaming like that? The ambulance will be here soon, and they will save her.

Some men in uniform push through the bathroom and kneel next to Lauren. Declan says something to them, but I can't understand him. It's like he's speaking a different language. There are two words that I understand, though that make me stop breathing. "She's gone."

The EMTs are working around her, and Declan's looking through the bathroom. He holds up a medicine bottle and looks at it. His face looks sad. He hands the bottle and a piece of paper that's on the counter to one of the EMTs, and they take it.

Declan kneels in front of me and says, "Everly, let's go downstairs and get out of their way."

I don't respond. I just stare straight ahead. At this point, I can't see Lauren's body. There are too many people surrounding her. Brandon's crying with his mother by the bathtub and the EMTs are surrounding her body. Why aren't they doing CPR anymore? Why aren't they trying to save her?

"Everly..." Declan says gently and touches my cheek. I look him in the eyes and that's when I know it's true. She's gone. Those words will haunt me for the rest of my life. They don't just mean she's gone. She's dead. Dead.

I still can't move, and I don't think I'm breathing. Declan lifts me up in his arms and brings me downstairs to sit on the couch. I can't move or say anything. He puts his arm around me and doesn't let me go. I don't move.

It feels like hours are passing by, but I'm pretty sure it all happens within minutes. I sit on the couch and watch them wheel out her body in one of those body bags. Her body is in that bag. She's being taken away from the house and she'll never come back.

I watch Mrs. Faucett race out after her, screaming, "My baby!"

Brandon is sobbing but trying to hold on to his mom to keep her from following them further. I can't watch anymore. A police officer takes a chair and sits in front of me. He asks me questions, but I can't understand what he's saying.

Declan grabs my face and puts his right in front of mine. "Everly, they need to ask you some questions. I need you to answer, okay?"

I nod. I'll try. Declan stands up for a moment and I want to reach out to tell him to stay, but I can't. I watch him take out his phone and make some phone calls.

"I need to know what happened. I need you to talk to me, okay?" The officer says with pity on his face. I don't like it when people look at me with pity. That means something horrible is going on in my life, but what could be worse than being dead? Lauren is dead.

"What is your name?" he asks.

I look over at Brandon, bringing his mother into the other room. I need to be strong for them. They need to know what happened.

"Everly," I say.

"Good. Everly, what happened?"

"I..." I shake my head. I need to get this out. "I woke up, and she wasn't in bed. I went to the bathroom, but it was locked. I unlocked it and..." I can't say the rest.

Apparently, I don't need to say the rest. "It's okay. You found her on the floor like that?"

I nod.

"Did she say anything to you before she went into the bathroom?" he asks.

"No. We fell asleep last night. She was sad, though. I was holding her," I reply.

"Why was she sad?" he asks.

Why is he asking me this? Isn't this just a horrible accident? She tripped and hit her head or broke her neck. Why does it matter why she was sad?

"She didn't want to get married this week," I respond.

He nods and continues writing in his notebook.

"Did you take any pills?" he asks.

"What?"

"Did you take any pills or medicine?" he asks again.

"No."

What is he talking about? Declan gave them a bottle of medicine in the bathroom. Does he think I took some? Why?

He looks like he is about to ask another question, but Declan comes back. "That's enough questions for today. I'm taking her home."

The officer stares at him and says, "I just have a few more..."

Declan interrupts, "No. You can ask her later when she's ready."

Declan grabs my hand and helps me up. This time, I stand up and walk with him. I walk out the front door and he opens the passenger door for me. He helps me in, and I sit down. I feel like a robot.

He gets in the driver's side and looks over at me. "Everly..."

I look at him and see the same pity. Why is everyone looking at me like that?

"I'm sorry," he says.

"Sorry for what?" I ask and he looks like he pities me even more.

"Say it!" I yell at him. Where did this anger come from?

"There was nothing you could do, Everly. She took too many," he says.

Took too many? Too many what? Oh, those pills? Why would she... No... No... It's all starting to make sense now. No... She wouldn't... She was sad, but she wouldn't...

"No..." I say, barely a whisper. "She wouldn't... Are you saying she killed herself?"

He doesn't respond, but he doesn't have to. His face says it all.

"But I... I told her... No..."

My breathing is fast again as my heart is racing out of my chest. Reality is slowly coming back to me, and it no longer feels like I'm in a fog. I'm in Hell.

I push open the door and start running. I don't know where I'm going to run to, but I need to run. I need to find her. She's alone right now. She's alone, and she's probably scared. I promised she wouldn't be alone.

I feel arms wrap around me and lift my feet off the ground.

"Put me down!!!" I scream and fight against him.

"No, Everly, let's go back home," Declan says in a soothing voice, like he isn't struggling to restrain me.

"No! I need to go to her! She's alone, and she's scared! I need to go to her!" I yell and feel the tears finally start pouring down my cheeks.

Declan doesn't say anything else; he just sits on the ground and pulls me with him. He lets me thrash against him. I'm screaming and I don't even know what I'm saying. I'm crying and I can't stop. I can't breathe.

I start to hyperventilate. I've never felt like this before. I can't breathe. Good. Lauren can't breathe either, so if I can't breathe, then she's not alone. You're not alone, Lauren. I promise.

I sit on the ground, trying to catch my breath. I see Declan sending off a text, but I don't care who it's to. I don't care what he has to say. I lay down on the sidewalk and close my eyes. I still can't breathe.

Declan is in my face again, saying, "Everly, you need to breathe. Concentrate."

I can't. I don't want to breathe. Clearly, I can't stop breathing though because I can't stop crying. I'm not angry anymore; I'm broken.

I lay on that sidewalk with my head in Declan's lap for what feels like an eternity. I see two familiar figures run up to us, but I close my eyes. I don't want to see anyone else. Who else is here? It's not fair that I have all these people around me, and yet Lauren is alone.

I feel familiar hands touch my face, but it isn't Declan. My head is still on Declan's lap.

"Everly... Everly, look at me." It's Jake. What is Jake doing here?

I open my eyes to see Jake's face right in front of me. I close them again quickly because he has the same look that everyone else has. Pity. Concern. I hate that fucking look.

"Everly, let's go home. James is on his way home," he says while rubbing my hair back behind my ears.

I don't have much of a fight in me anymore, so I nod. Jake puts his hands under my armpits and helps me up. I notice Ben come behind me and hold me steady at my waist. I don't look at Ben's face. I can't handle anyone else looking at me like that.

They all help me to the car like I'm hurt. I'm not the one that's hurt, Lauren is. They should be helping her.

Jake tries to let go of me, but I hold on to him. I don't want to be alone. I deserve to be alone because Lauren is alone, but I don't want to be alone. I'm selfish.

He slides into the passenger seat with me and puts me on his lap, so we both fit. It's like he knows exactly what I need without me having to say it. I bury my face in his chest and start sobbing again. Or had I never stopped? I'm not sure.

Jake carries me into the house, and I can hear Mrs. Crawford. "Put her on the couch. I'm getting her some tea."

Jake tries to set me down on the couch, but I have a death grip on him. I won't let him go. Instead of fighting it, he sits down and holds me in his lap. I'm not going to take my face away from his chest because then I'll be facing Mrs. Crawford too. I'll have to face reality.

I can hear voices in the other room. They must be talking about what happened. Why do they need to talk about what happened?

I feel a gentle hand rub my back. "Everly, honey. I need you to drink. I brought you some tea."

I don't respond.

"Please Everly. Let's get you sitting up," she says, but I still don't respond or move.

"I've got her," Jake says, but he sounds angry.

I don't hear a response, so I'm not sure what happened. I hear footsteps and Mrs. Crawford talking to someone, but everything fades away.

# Chapter Nineteen

I'm pretty sure days went by as I lay in Jake's arms. If it wasn't days, it sure feels like it. Occasionally, he whispers to me that he's here, and he's got me. How long is it acceptable to stay like this in his arms and not face reality?

I hear the door slam open and another familiar voice yell, "Where is she?"

Lots of footsteps follow behind the voice, and they stop near me. Go away. I don't want to be bothered.

"Everly..." James whispers in my ear.

Is James really here or am I imagining it? I feel like I'm in a dream again. Everything's so foggy.

"Everly... I'm here now. Baby, look at me," James says, trying to pull my face away from Jake's chest.

I need James. Where has he been? I lift my head to look and see if he is really here. He is. The moment I see him, I sob again and jump into his arms. He holds me and sits us on the couch. I feel Jake shift and get up.

I bury my head into James's chest now and he keeps whispering to me, "Baby, I'm here now. It's okay. I'm here."

After I stop crying, James is able to sit me upright. The room is full of people. I don't want the room to be full of people. Mrs. Crawford, Declan, Bash, Jake, Ben, and James are all in the room. Sitting and waiting. Waiting for what? For me to be okay? I'm not okay.

The doorbell rings, and Mrs. Crawford stands up to get it. She talks to the man for a moment and then leads him into the room. I've never seen him before, but he doesn't look at me like he pities me. I like him already.

Mrs. Crawford comes over to me and says, "Everly, this is Mr. Vance. He's great at listening and he's here for you to talk to him."

She hired a shrink to come talk to me? "I don't want to talk."

Mr. Vance pulls a chair up in front of me and sits down. "Everly, sometimes it's good to get out what you're thinking. I'm here to listen and help you process what happened."

I don't need to talk about what happened, and I don't need to process what happened. If I do... then it's real and I can't wake up from the dream.

Mrs. Crawford asks everyone to leave the room. I hold onto James because I don't want him to go. I hope he doesn't leave me.

"He can stay if you'd like," Mr. Vance says as he leans back in his chair.

I nod.

Everyone has left the room at this point except James and Mr. Vance.

"Do you want to tell me what happened, Everly?" he asks, like he doesn't know. I know he knows.

"I failed her," I say, but the words come out as a whisper.

"Tell me what happened," he says in such a calm voice, like someone isn't dead here.

"She killed herself," I say louder.

He nods. "Your friend Lauren. Right?"

I nod and he continues, "Tell me what happened from when you woke up this morning."

I know I need to tell someone what happened. They all deserve to know. "I... I woke up, and she wasn't in bed. I went to go to the bathroom, but the door was locked. I kept calling out for her but... she didn't answer. I unlocked the door with a coin and found her... she was... she was on the floor, not moving. I screamed for help and Brandon came in, but we didn't know what to do. I called for Declan, and he came. He called 911 and then tried to give her CPR. It didn't work. She was dead."

James tightens his hold around me as I cry again. I can hear his breathing getting harder, like he's holding back crying.

"Do you know how she died?" he asks, and I know he knows that too.

"They said she took pills. She killed herself," I say, like it was just a normal fact.

He nods again. Why does he keep nodding? "Did she ever indicate that she would take her own life?"

I just stare at him for a moment. Does he think she told me she'd kill herself and I didn't do anything about it? Of course I would've done something about it.

"She was sad, but I never thought... She was sad last night. She didn't want to get married. She kept saying how alone she'd be once we went to college without her. I told her I would do it online. I'd do my courses in her living room every day, but she didn't want that for me. She... She was so sad. Why didn't I see it?"

I'm questioning myself now. Why didn't I see it? Were there more signs that she was going to take her life? How could I not see it?

"Everly, it's not your fault. Sometimes there really are no signs and even if there are, it's still not your fault," he says.

Wasn't it though? "I was in the room though... How could I..." I can't even say any more. How could I not know she was in the bathroom a few feet away, taking pills to end her life?

Dr. Vance says a few more things, but I'm not paying attention anymore. I'm staring off past him. I'm pretty sure he asks some questions, and I just ignore him. Eventually, he must have given up because when I come to, he's gone. James is still holding me, though. He doesn't say anything.

Mrs. Crawford comes back into the room. "Everly, your father is flying back right now, and he will be here in the morning. But I don't want you alone tonight. Would you like to sleep in my room?"

I look at her, trying to comprehend what she is asking. "Um. No thanks."

She looks concerned with that answer.

James finally speaks up, "She'll sleep with me. I'm not letting her go or out of my sight."

Mrs. Crawford looks at James with a concerned look.

"Mom, I am not leaving her!" he says sternly.

I watch her nod and walk away.

James grabs my face in his hands to look at me again. "Hey. I'm here and I'm not leaving you, okay? Let's go to bed."

Is it bedtime already? I look out the window to see it's dark outside. How long have I been sitting here? Didn't I just wake up? Even if I did, I'm exhausted.

I nod and follow him up to my room. I just stand there as he goes through my dresser to get out my pajamas. He holds them out for me, but I don't take them. I can't move. Are we back to this again?

"Do you want to take a shower?" he asks, looking me over. I must look horrible. A shower does sound nice.

I nod again.

He goes into the bathroom and turns the shower on. He comes back out for me and walks me into the bathroom. He takes off my clothes and helps me in. He takes off his shirt and pants but leaves his boxers on as he steps in with me.

I stand there and don't move. He squirts some soap on my sponge and washes my body. Then he puts some shampoo in my hair and rinses it out. It feels nice being taken care of and the water is so warm.

He turns off the water and gets out. He wraps me in a towel and dries me off before putting on my pajamas. I feel like a robot. I'm just moving exactly how he tells me to, but I'm not doing anything myself.

He leads me to the bed and covers me up. He turns off the light and lays next to me, putting his arm around me, holding me. This is exactly how I was holding Lauren last night, and now she's gone. How can she be gone?

I start crying again. How many more tears do I have?

James sits up against the headboard and pulls me into him, stroking my hair. He still says nothing and just lets me cry.

When I begin calming down, he asks, "Do you want to talk about it?"

No. Yes. I don't know. Should I?

"I was holding her like that last night. The way you were holding me. She was upset. She didn't want to be alone. James... She's alone now and she must be so scared. She's in a body bag. I watched them wheel her out in a body bag. It must be so dark where she is. She didn't want to be alone. I left her alone," I sob again.

"No... Baby..." I can hear James crying. Why is he crying? "Baby... You didn't leave her alone. You were there for her. She wasn't alone when she died, and she's not alone now."

I don't believe him. "She was alone, James. She was in that bathroom alone when she took those pills. She was on the floor alone as she took her last breath. She was alone, and I left her alone. How could I do that?"

James doesn't say anything because he knows I'm right. I let her die, and I let her die alone. What is Ashley going to think? Oh my God. Ashley. Does she know?

I sit up quickly, and James asks, "What?"

"Ashley. I need to tell Ashley," I say, while throwing the covers off me.

James grabs my arm. "No, it's okay Everly. She knows. We told her you would talk tomorrow. You need to go to bed, okay? Get some sleep."

I lay back down because James is right. I shouldn't talk to Ashley tonight. She is probably hurting too, and she probably hates me. I don't think I can handle her hating me right now. I just need one night in James' arms. Even though I don't deserve it.

Lauren's would be wedding day, Christmas, came and went. New Year's Eve came and went. New Year's Day came and went. Finally, it's the day of Lauren's funeral. Because of the holidays, everything took longer to plan the funeral. Apparently, just because people die doesn't mean that people stop enjoying their life. They can't be bothered on a holiday, of course.

Everything has been a blur since the day I found Lauren dead. James hasn't left me alone, but at this point I wish he would. I've done nothing but cry and lash out at him. I'm angry, so angry. I'm mostly angry at myself because it's all my fault.

I have only talked to Ashley once since the day it happened, and I was right. She hates me. She blames me for what happened to Lauren. She kept asking me how I didn't know she was in the bathroom killing herself. How I didn't see the pills. How it took me so long to find her. Yeah, if I didn't already blame myself, I certainly would've after she was done yelling at me. She hasn't tried to talk to me since.

There wasn't a viewing for Lauren. Apparently, it was in her wishes that she didn't want one. She didn't want people to see her dead body. Her family respected everything she asked for. Why couldn't they have respected her wishes when she was alive? If they did, then none of this would've happened.

I stand in front of Lauren's grave with the casket lowered inside. Dirt was thrown in and flowers placed on top. Many who came to say their goodbyes have already left. I asked James for a moment alone, so he walked away in the distance, but not too far. Ashley didn't even look at me.

The service beforehand was nice. Everyone went up there telling stories about what an amazing person Lauren was. She was such a kind soul, and she died too young. It was all true. I didn't go up there to say anything because what could I say? They all said everything good about her and no one would want to hear from the person who let her die.

I look off in the distance to see four figures standing and staring toward the gravesite. They are all dressed in what look like the same black suits. Expensive suits. The man standing second to the right looks familiar. I continue to stare at him until I realize where I recognize him from. Lorenzo. Lauren had shown me pictures of him before and that's him. There's no doubt about it.

All the sadness built up inside me from today turns to pure rage at seeing him. Why is he here? He's the one that killed her! How dare he show up at her funeral! I can't stop myself from walking toward them. I stop directly in front of him and stare at him as he stares back. His face is emotionless, as though he doesn't feel a thing. How can you come to a funeral and not feel a thing, especially when your fiancé was just buried?!

Before I know what I'm doing, I slap him in the face. The other three men take steps toward me, but Lorenzo holds up his hand to stop them.

"You must be Everly," he says, again, with no emotion on his face or in his voice.

"And you must be Lorenzo," I try to say equally emotionless, but know I failed.

He nods. "I'm sorry for your loss."

I laugh. It's a deranged laugh. "You're sorry? You don't look very sorry and you're the one that drove her to kill herself!"

His eyes shift to another emotion that I can't read, but I don't care. I'm so angry at him and I'm losing control. I cry again and beat on his chest. He doesn't try to defend himself from my attack and his friends don't budge, either.

Through my tears, hits, and screams, I yell, "She didn't want to marry you! You took everything from her!" I pound two more times on his chest. "She had dreams and a full life planned for herself!" Pound three more times. "You made her kill herself! She was so fucking scared to live the life you were forcing on her!" Two more times. "Then you made me become the bad guy! I'm the one who was a few feet from where she killed herself! I'm the one that found her dead and couldn't save her! I'm the one to blame for letting this happen, but you're the one to blame for it happening in the first place!" I continue to pound on his chest until I feel arms wrap around me from behind, pinning my arms to my side. I keep yelling, "If only you at least pretended to love her! She just wanted to be loved!"

At this point, I give up fighting whoever is holding me back and sink to the ground, crying. I hear Lorenzo mutter, "I'm sorry" and turn to walk away. The other three men walk with him. Two of them have their hands on his back, like they are comforting him as they lead him away. Why does he deserve to be comforted?

I look back at who had me to find Declan was the one holding me back and James is now kneeling beside me.

"Let's go home, Everly," James says, standing up holding his hand out to me.

James has been there for me this whole time, trying to piece me back together, but I don't think I can be pieced back together. It's not fair that James has to keep doing this for me.

I ignore his hand and stand up. "Declan's going to take me home."

I walk away with Declan walking beside me. No one says anything as I get in the passenger seat of Declan's car. I look out the window to find all my friends and family watching as the car drives off. Even my father has been here for me and has taken off work. I've had too much pity from everyone, this needs to end today. It's finally over with. The funeral is done, and everyone is going to move on like she never existed. Isn't that how it always is?

"Everly..." Declan says, still staring at the road. He looks concerned.

"What Declan?" I snap at him.

He glances at me and then back at the road. "I need you to promise me you aren't going to talk to Lorenzo again."

I'm shocked and confused. It's not what I was expecting.

"Why?" I ask.

Declan taps his fingers for a moment on the steering wheel like he's trying to figure out how to word what he's going to say. "He's a dangerous man, and you just hit him... at least twenty times. He's not someone to be messed with unless you have a death wish."

I laugh. Is he serious? I look at his face and realize he's deathly serious. "What? Is he like in the mafia or something?" I joke.

Declan glances at me again. "Something like that."

Oh shit. Is he part of the mafia? Lauren kept saying over and over again that Lorenzo isn't a good man. He didn't look that scary, but I guess he and his friends did look intimidating. It would also explain why Lauren kept refusing to go into hiding. If he was in the mafia, then surely, he would have the means to find her. A shiver runs down my back as pieces are being put into place on why Lauren thought death was the best option.

# Chapter Twenty

I skipped the first week back to school and stayed in my bedroom most of the time reading. Reading has always been an escape for me, but it really isn't helping my current situation. I still hate myself for what happened with Lauren, but I have to move on for everyone else's sake.

James went back to college reluctantly. I have been keeping my distance from him mainly because I feel bad for dragging him down. He has been texting me every day, multiple times a day. He plans to come home tonight for the weekend, and I'm conflicted about how I feel. I need him so much that my heart hurts, but I don't want him here and miserable with me.

I lay in bed with the covers over my head until I hear my phone buzz with a text.

My heart stops and I can't breathe. I unblocked Adam when I called him on Thanksgiving and figured there was no point in blocking him again. Is his text saying what I think it's saying? Is he saying that he killed Lauren? No, she clearly committed suicide, so what is he saying?

> **What do you mean?**

Adam

> **Exactly what I said. One down, plenty more to go.**

I feel sick to my stomach. That's exactly what he's saying. Plenty more to go? Am I included in that? I don't care, but I need to make this end. He's trying to do this to hurt me. I can't have friends or else they are going to get hurt.

> **There is no one left. I don't have any friends or a boyfriend anymore. Leave me alone.**

That wasn't the truth, but I'm going to make it the truth. The more distance I put between all of us, the better. Maybe Adam will leave them all alone.

Adam

> Well that is a turn of events. I heard Ashley is no longer your friend but I didn't know about the others. Tell you what... you keep your distance from everyone, and I'll let them live. That means no more boyfriend and this is your last warning. You know what will happen if you tell anyone about me contacting you.

> Deal

I don't know if Adam is telling the truth, and he had anything to do with Lauren's death, but I'm not going to take the risk. I've been wanting something that I can do to keep my friends safe and that's exactly what he has given me, so I'm going to do it. I'll do anything to keep them safe and quite honestly, I deserve to be alone, anyway. If I couldn't save Lauren and she's alone, then I deserve it too.

I've been keeping my distance from everyone recently, so it shouldn't be that hard to continue doing so. I'm just going to have to ignore more text messages from my friends, which I hate to hurt them like that when they've been there for me, but I rather that than them be dead.

James got home an hour ago, and he immediately came to my room. I pretended I was asleep, and he didn't try to wake me. I needed a little more time to figure out how I'm going to break things off with him. I feel like my heart is breaking in two just thinking about losing him, but I don't have a choice.

I take a deep breath and send James a text before I chicken out.

I throw my phone on my bed and walk slower than I ever have before to his room. My stomach is in knots, and I feel nauseous. My heart is racing a mile a minute, and I want to turn and run the other way.

I knock on his door, and he immediately opens it. He pulls me inside and closes the door behind me.

James hugs me and says in my ear, "I've missed you. How are you doing?"

"I'm doing okay now," I say, trying to be convincing with a small smile on my face.

He leans down and kisses me. It's a gentle kiss, and I let it last longer than I should, but I want to savor it since it would be the last kiss we ever have.

I get the courage to pull away and put some distance between us. He looks at me, concerned, not hurt. He's always so concerned about me.

"James, we can't do this anymore," I say, trying to keep my emotions in check.

He furrows his eyebrows. "What do you mean?"

"I mean us. We can't be together anymore."

He takes a step toward me, and I step back. Now he looks hurt.

"I don't understand. Everly, I'm here for you and we can take things slow. I'm not going anywhere," he says, trying to reach for me again as I continue to pull back.

I can't let him touch me because if he does, I'm going to lose it. I don't think I'll be able to continue this charade if he touches me. I can literally feel my heart ripping in two right now. This is absolute torture. The man I love with my whole heart is standing in front of me and looks so torn and hurt. How do I leave him like this? It takes every effort not to jump into his arms and tell him I need him. I need him so badly it hurts, but it'll hurt even more if something happens to him because of me.

"James... I appreciate that, and I know you care about me. I care about you too, so that's why I'm doing this. It's better if we end this now. I don't want to be with you anymore. I'm sorry," I say the words, but they taste bitter on my tongue.

I twist the promise ring he gave me around my finger and contemplate taking it off to give it back to him. I don't know why, but I can't bring myself to do it. I place my fisted hands down at my sides.

He watches me and goes to say something, but I push past him and out the door. I hear him yell out my name, but I run as fast as I can down the stairs and to the workout room. I had put on some workout clothes, knowing that I would need a release after what I just did. I pull on some gloves and start slamming my fists into the punching bag. I'm pretty sure that the gloves aren't doing anything because my hands are hurting. That's okay, I need the pain. I deserve the pain.

I hear someone enter the room, but I don't take my attention away from the punching bag. I continue to hit the bag until I realize that whoever it is, isn't going to walk away without speaking to me. Turning, half expecting it to be James, I find Declan. I let out a sigh of relief and plop myself on the floor by the bag. I'm exhausted.

"Want to talk?" Declan asks, sitting cross-legged in front of me.

"Not really," I say, looking up at him.

The way he looks at me has changed drastically in the past week. After Lauren's death, Declan looked at me like everyone else, with pity. After the initial shock wore off, he now just looks determined. Determined to help me, fix me. Where everyone else is walking on eggshells around me, he's stomping all over them. I appreciate it.

"Want to train?" he asks while standing up and holding his hand out for me.

I take his hand and nod. "I broke up with James."

Declan looks shocked for a moment before asking, "What did he do?"

I laugh and I'm pretty sure that's the most genuine laugh I've had since Lauren's death.

"Nothing. It's the whole it's not you it's me thing," I shrug.

"You sure that's what you want?" he asks like he's my therapist. I mean, he's better than the therapist I currently have.

"No, but it's what I need."

He nods and moves to the side of the room, pulling out a red marker from the drawer. What does he need a marker for?

He walks back over toward me and says, "Take off your shirt."

Once again, I laugh. "Declan, are you trying to get me naked?"

He grins. "If I wanted to get you naked, you'd already be naked. I'm asking you to take off your shirt, that's all."

I shrug my shoulders and do what he said. I throw my shirt across the room, and it hits the wall before falling to the floor. I stand there in my short workout shorts and a sports bra. I trust Declan with my life, so taking my shirt off when he's requesting it isn't an issue for me. If he told me to get completely naked, I would do it knowing he had a good reason.

He uncaps the marker and hands it to me. "I know we haven't been training long with knives, but I want to show you what would happen if someone got your knife from you or had one themselves."

I'm not entirely sure why we are using a marker versus the training knives we have been using, but I'm down. We get into a position to have a knife fight with a marker. He lunges toward me, and I try to stab him exactly where he has shown me too many times. Before the marker can touch him, he grabs my arm and takes the marker easily from me, turning it around on me. He uses it to mark down my forearm and then he backs up.

I'm stunned for a moment, looking at my arm before he lunges again and hits me in the stomach with it. Apparently, we aren't going to stop and chat about this, so I try to defend myself and take the knife back. We go back and forth for only a minute, where I completely fail, and he keeps marking me up. Finally, he takes one last jab right over my heart.

I feel like being overly dramatic, so instead of continuing to fight, I put my hand over my heart and fall to my knees. I make a fake gurgling sound, saying "Oh no!" and plop to the floor with my tongue hanging out and eyes wide open.

Declan's caught off guard by the whole dramatics, but he lets out a deep laugh before holding his hand out to help me back up.

I continue the dramatics by saying, "I'm dead. I can't get up."

"If you were dead, you wouldn't be talking."

I take his hand and stand up. "Fair enough."

I stand in front of the large mirror in the room, and he shows me all the places the marker hit, which was pretty much my entire body. There are marks on my arms, legs, neck, face, stomach, and chest. I get what he was doing now, but I already knew that I wouldn't be any good in a knife fight yet. We've barely trained, and he is a master at fighting. Of course I was going to lose this one horribly.

We sit on the floor facing each other again before he speaks, "I'm not trying to make you feel bad, Everly. You're still new at fighting with a knife, and I want you to take that into consideration before you pull one. Clearly, I have a lot more training than you and would beat you in a fight. I need you to judge your opponent before pulling one out. If you think they could beat you in a knife fight, don't pull out your knife. You're just giving them another weapon to hurt you with. That also goes for killing your opponent. If you are not willing to use the knife on them and kill them, then don't pull it out. These are all situations where pulling a knife out will give your opponent an extra advantage. If they pull one first, then you can pull yours. Sometimes it may also be better to use it as a distraction technique, only if you think you can beat them in a knife fight. Pull your knife, kick them in the balls, then run."

I think about what he said for a moment before responding and it all makes sense. If the person is better than me, then they will most likely be able to take the knife and use it against me. If I'm not willing to kill the person, then they can take it from me easily as well. Using it as a distraction is a good idea, but I can see where that is only when absolutely necessary, and I'm still willing to use it if needed.

"I understand," I say.

Declan nods and we both stand. "Do you feel better?"

I give him a small smile and say, "I do. Thank you for every-thing, Declan."

He pulls me into a hug and holds me there for a few mo-ments. Declan and I have gotten close since I've been here at the Crawford's house and this past week, we've gotten even closer. I know he is my security guard, but I consider him one of my best friends. I just hope that Adam never finds out because I need someone in my life by my side.

# Chapter Twenty-One

It's been a week since I've broken things off with James and continued ignoring my friends as much as I can. It's been a horrible week for that reason and because I came back to school this week. The kids are whispering behind my back, or should I say, in front of it. Every day after I come home from school, I just want to call James and have him tell me everything's going to be okay, but I can't. Instead, I take things out in training with Declan. I try pulling out my little book with the fun memories from the summer, but that just makes me more depressed about what I'm missing out on. Ashley still hates me, and Lauren's still dead. It's becoming more and more difficult to stay positive.

I head to the bathroom after class. I hide out in one of the stalls when a couple of girls come in talking about me. It's not uncommon to be talked about after everything that happened with Lauren, but I'm not about to show my face to people who clearly have no respect for me. I thought I've heard it all, but this is new.

"Can you believe that she's actually still coming to school like nothing happened? I bet she gave her the drugs to kill herself. I heard they had her name on the prescription bottle," one girls says.

"Wow, really? So, she basically murdered her. I knew Lauren wasn't happy about the arranged marriage, but I never took her for the type to take her own life," the other girl states.

"Yeah, I also heard that she was going to kill herself with her but chickened out at the last minute. I have no idea how she can live with herself. Poor Lauren, this whole thing is tragic," a third girl chimes in.

I didn't realize I was holding my breath until I was getting dizzy. I slowly inhale and exhale, counting my breaths. I feel sick to my stomach. Where are they hearing these rumors and why are they spreading them? Or are they the ones making them up? I don't understand how people can be so hateful to someone they don't even know.

I wait until they leave the bathroom before coming out of the stall. I wash my hands and try to pull myself together when I hear the late bell ring for class. Great, now I'm late for class.

As I walk through the empty halls, I hear some guys talking and the sound of a locker being hit. I turn the corner to find three guys from the football team pinning Alex to the set of lockers behind him.

"We can't let a fag play on the team. You're going to quit, and we're never going to see your face around the stadium again.

You got it?" one of the players says. I think his name is Richard, which Dick is a fitting nickname for him.

I walk up behind them, and they don't even notice me. I clear my throat and ask, "What's going on?"

They all turn to look at me as Dick smirks. "This is none of your concern, Monroe. Head to class."

I look at Alex's face, and it's like he's pleading with me to leave. Yeah, no. I'm not leaving him here alone with three huge guys pinning him against the locker.

As if they think I'm going to walk away, they all turn back to Alex. One of the others asks, "So how long have you been screwing Tanner?"

I cringe at his question and look at Alex's defeated face. Before he can answer, I walk up beside them again and say, "Alex... I think it's time to let the secret go..."

Alex looks at me wide-eyed and I realize he probably thinks that I mean telling them about him and Tanner, so I continue quickly. "Alex isn't screwing Tanner, as you say. He is with me. We've been dating in secret for a while."

The three guys look back and forth at each other and then stare at me to see if I'm telling the truth. I keep my face straight so they can't see through the lie.

"Why would you hide that?" one of them asks.

I laugh, "Really? Well, to start, I was dating James and hadn't broken up with him yet. You know Ben's older brother? He would've killed Alex for the betrayal. Then when we did break things off, I'm not the most popular person around the school, as you know, so I didn't want to bring him down. I appreciate the lengths he went to keep our secret, but clearly, it's better for him if it's out. Now let him go."

Dickwad, yeah, I changed his name because that sounds even better for him. Dickwad let Alex go and asks, "Is that true?"

Alex looks at me and says, "Yeah, man."

Dickwad smirks and pats his back. "Alright, sorry about that. Let me know when you're sick of her. I could use a good screw." He looks me over and winks.

Alex looks like he's going to punch him, so I grab his arm and pull myself into him. The guys slowly walk away but keep their eyes on us. To make our story seem more real, I stand on my toes and kiss Alex on the mouth. He doesn't react at all.

Once the guys are gone, Alex pulls me into the maintenance closet and turns on the light. "What the hell are you thinking Everly?!"

I scoff. "What? I just saved you. You're welcome."

Alex runs his hand through his hair and looks up at the ceiling, taking a deep breath. "Your reputation is going to be crap now, and more guys are going to be coming after you, thinking you're an easy lay."

I laugh and say, "Really? My reputation is already crap and I can handle the guys. Plus, if we continue saying we're together, it'll at least deter half of the decent ones."

Alex puts his hands on my shoulders and stares into my eyes. "What happens when Ben and Jake find out? They're going to tell James."

My heart skips a beat for a moment, but I push the feelings back down. It's probably best if James does find out, then he can move on with someone else and not hold out hope that we're going to be together. I twist the ring on my finger, which has become a habit lately. I still haven't been able to take it off.

I shrug my shoulders. "It's fine, Alex. James and I are done. No need to worry. We only have a few more months to get through school, and we can finally be free of this awful place. Let's get through it together, okay?"

Alex pulls me into a hug and says quietly in my ear, "Thank you Everly. I owe you everything."

He releases me and places a kiss on my forehead. We leave the closet and get to class late. It just so happens this is the one class we have together, and we decide we don't care and walk in together. It looks bad, but it also helps our story that we are together.

"Do you two have a note for being tardy?" Mr. Delisle asks.

I shake my head. "No, I'm sorry it was my fault. I had a breakdown in the bathroom and Alex helped me out."

The whole school, teachers, students, and staff all know about what happened. A breakdown in the bathroom is a convenient excuse and a very believable one.

Mr. Delisle asks, "Do you want to go see the counselor?"

I shake my head again. "No thank you, I'm good now. I've missed enough classes, and I really need to be here."

He drops it and moves on. That's the good thing about being a sweet, good student. You can pretty much get away with anything as long as your lies are believable. Who expects the quiet girl who makes good grades to actually do something bad?

I try to avoid Jake's gaze as he looks between Alex and me. It won't be long before the rumors get around the school and, in return, get to Jake. I will give it until the next class. I also bet that Ben will know by lunchtime, too.

I was right. By the time lunch rolled around, the entire school knew. Man, those football players are worse than the gossipy girls in the school. It's for the best this way. Alex doesn't have to deal with a ruined reputation for being gay, and he can continue with the football team. There's no way those guys would have let him play and most likely would have beaten him up if needed to get him to leave.

"I've heard a rumor that I need clarification on," Ben says as he sits in front of Alex and me.

Ben is always kind, and he is never one to believe a rumor. I can tell in his eyes that he is hopeful the rumors aren't true, but I also can see some anger that they might be. I hate lying to my best friends, but if that's what Alex needs, then that is what I'm going to do. This isn't my secret to share. Plus, if they are mad at me, it makes it easier to keep my distance from them and, in return, keeps Adam away from them.

"What did you hear?" Alex asks, taking a bite of his sandwich while keeping his eyes trained on Ben.

"That you two are screwing and have been together for months," Ben states coldly.

Alex and I look at each other. I try to gauge what he's thinking, but I'm not sure. His eyes look like they are pleading with me to continue the ruse, but they are also sorry and conflicted. Alex takes too long to respond.

Ben slams his hand on the table. "Damn it, it's true, isn't it? How could you do this, Alex?"

Ben looks hurt. He's angry, but he's hurt. I hate this. As much as I want to come clean or crawl under the table, I continue with the lie.

"I'm sorry, Ben. We really don't have anything to say," I say, hoping he will just be angry enough to storm off and drop it.

Ben looks at me with pity, but also anger. I can tell he's conflicted about how to approach this with me. Before what happened with Lauren, he would have told me like it is. He probably would have yelled at me and told me I'm a horrible person for doing this to James. I'm horrible for betraying their trust. Yeah, I'm pretty sure that's what he's thinking right now. He's just not willing to say it out loud in my current delicate state.

His hands are clenched on the table as he asks, "How could you do this to him Everly? I thought you loved him?"

Ouch. It feels like a knife was just stabbed into my barely beating heart. I let out a low breath and barely whisper, "I do..." Then I quickly cough to cover up what I just said, hoping he didn't hear it.

"I don't know what to tell you Ben, it is what it is. We never meant to hurt anyone and there's nothing we can do about it now," I say, willing the tears in my eyes to stay where they are and not fall. It is so hard lying to my friends when I can see how much it hurts them.

Ben shakes his head and angrily stands up. "I wish the other rumors were true that you were gay. That I could handle. This... I'm done here." Ben leaves his food tray on the table as he walks off.

Yeah, I can't handle this either. I don't say anything to Alex as I pick up my backpack, walk out of the lunchroom, and right out the front door. Declan is out of the car before I even make it off the final step to the entrance.

When we reach each other, he asks, "What happened?"

"I'm ready to go home," I state, keeping my voice even and the tears at bay.

He doesn't argue and opens the car door for me. We drive home in silence, but the thoughts running around in my head are anything but silent.

The decisions I make are continuously hurting others. I think I'm doing the right thing, but it feels so wrong. Lauren is dead because of me. Ben is upset with me and Alex. The hurt look on his face kills me. I feel like that's not even going to be the worst of this. There's no way I can look at James because he's going to be even more hurt, and I can't handle seeing him hurt. Jake is going to be disappointed in me and probably not surprised, which will hurt too. Then there's Alex. Alex is feeling guilty. I know it. He's having to decide between hurting his best friend or hurting his boyfriend and losing his spot on the football team. Either way, he loses.

I continue to sit in the car even as we pull up to the house. Declan watches me for a moment before asking, "Do you want to talk about it?"

All I have to do is give him a look for him to know that I don't. I'm pretty sure he knows me better than anyone else. I suppose that's what happens when you basically watch someone 24/7.

"Can we train?" I ask.

"Yeah, sure. I'll meet you downstairs in fifteen," he says and walks around the car to open my door.

I get out and head upstairs to get some workout clothes on. I think I just need to punch some things and tire myself out again.

Declan and I go at it for over three hours. I punch the punching bags hundreds of times, and I spar with him. He lets me get in a good bit of punches, as if he knows I need it. I do and I hate myself for it because now I've hurt him too. Physically.

As I sit on the floor taking a break and drinking my water, I hear someone come through the door. I look over to see Ben walking toward me while holding his phone. My heart sinks, knowing exactly who's on the other end.

"I'm training right now Ben, I don't have time," I say, getting up off the floor and heading back toward the punching bag.

Ben grabs my arm and says, "Make time. You owe him an explanation."

I shake my head. "No."

Ben rounds me and stands directly in front of me with his hand still on my arm. "Yes, you do. Just talk to him for five minutes. He deserves that. You know he does."

My heart rate slowed during my break, but now it's back up like I've just run a marathon. Ben's right, he does deserve an explanation. If I were James, I'd expect one. I want to throw up at the thought that I'm going to have to sit here and lie to him. Lies that are going to hurt him.

"Fine, put it on speaker," I say.

Ben pushes a button on his phone and says, "You're on speaker, James."

"Everly, what's going on?" he asks. I can already hear the hurt in his voice and yet hopefulness that I'm going to tell him it's not true.

"I'm in the middle of training. What's up James?" I ask, like it's a normal conversation that's not about to destroy him.

"I heard you and Alex are together?" he asks.

I swallow the lump in my throat down and say, "Yep."

There's silence and I can see Ben studying me. I should have done this in private.

"When did that happen?" He clears his throat.

"A few months ago. Don't exactly remember when," I lie.

There's more silence, and I'm not going to be the first one to fill it.

"Was it before or after my birthday?" he asks, clearly hurt but trying to keep it together.

This time I clear my throat as I quickly wipe the one tear that escaped, hopefully before Ben could see. "I... After."

More silence.

"Do you love him?" he asks, and I hear the hitch in his voice.

Jesus James. I can't handle this. "James..."

"I need to know. Do you love him?" he asks again, sounding a little angry this time.

I take a deep breath and stare at the ceiling. What do I say? If I say no, then what does that mean? I don't even know. But if I say yes... then that's it right? And that's what I want. I want James to move on. This is killing me hurting him, but he needs to move on. He'll be taking my heart with him, but it must be done.

I made my decision. "Yes."

James ends the call.

"Damn it!" I yell and punch the punching bag as hard as I can, over and over again.

Ben doesn't say anything as he watches me for a few moments. I don't look back at him, but I eventually hear him walk out of the room.

Declan comes up beside me. "Everly, talk to me."

The tears I'm holding back come flooding down my face. There's no holding them back anymore. I throw my gloves and sit balled up in the middle of the floor, trying to control my sobs. Declan sits next to me silently until I stop crying.

"Everly... what are you doing?" he asks, concerned.

"I don't know..." I whisper.

He puts his arm around me. "You and Alex are not together. I've never seen you together outside of school this year, minus the summer. You don't meet up with him, and I bet if I looked at your phone you barely have any texts to him, never mind messages declaring your love for him. Why are you lying?"

Of course, Declan would know I'm lying and there's no use lying to him. This isn't something about my safety, so I know I can trust him.

"Alex is gay, and he doesn't want anyone to know. His teammates had a suspicion and had him pinned against his locker today, telling him he needs to quit the football team. I saw it and stepped in. I figured if I said we were dating, then they would leave him alone. We only have a few months left of school... We'll get through it," I say the last part more to convince myself.

"Everly... You can't keep doing things for others when you hurt yourself in the process."

"Declan, you can't tell anyone. I'm already committed to this, and the damage is done," I say, pleading with him.

"I won't tell anyone. I'm here for you, Kid," he says.

I give him a sad smile, and I love that he's always here for me.

When I get back to my room, I check my phone to find the text from Adam that I've been expecting.

Adam

**New boyfriend?**

I'm glad the news carried to you. I needed to get James to leave me alone and my friends mad at me to keep them away. I'm doing everything you want me to do. Alex is a means to an end.

Adam

I knew you were smart. I'll be watching.

Of course he will be, so that means I need to be extra careful not to spend too much time with Alex making it seem like it is for show, but then I need to make sure I spend enough time with him to make everyone believe I'm with him. My whole life is getting too complicated, and I can't keep up. I need to find someone to talk to and it's not a paid therapist. In the meantime, I pull out my hidden stash of drugs and forget my problems for the night.

# Chapter Twenty-Two

A month and a half passes quickly and my life feels like it's getting worse and worse. My friends all hate me, and I honestly am hating myself. I keep trying to convince myself that I'm doing the right thing, but I'm so miserable and everyone else is miserable around me. I can't have any friends because Adam will find out and go after them, so finding people to see every now and then so I don't feel completely alone has been my goal. My decision-making skills have been sorely lacking as well.

Meeting up with Brandon isn't unusual since Lauren died. I feel like it's a misery loves company thing because we really don't have anything in common other than Lauren's death and our use of drugs to get us through it. We also both blame his parents for her death, even though we still share the guilt.

I am currently sitting in a coffee shop waiting for Brandon. He texted me yesterday that he wanted to meet up to hang out today and since I have nothing better to do, I agreed. He walks in fifteen minutes late and looks awful. Brandon has always been handsome. That hasn't changed, but he doesn't look happy. His hair is shaggy and in desperate need of a haircut, and the bags under his eyes show he's not getting much sleep. It looks like he hasn't shaved in a few weeks, as there's much more than just a little stubble growing. I hate to see him like this, but I probably don't look much better.

I stand to give him a hug as he reaches the table. "How's it going?" I ask as we sit back down.

I already ordered his usual coffee for him, but it's probably cold by now. He takes a sip and doesn't seem to mind.

"It's going. What about you?" he asks.

"It's going," I repeat.

We both stare at each other. There's not much to say, and we both know we're barely surviving.

"I quit college," he says nonchalantly.

That's how most of our conversations go. We say things that probably should be a big deal, but we don't act like it. Our tones are usually monotone too. Sometimes I question how we got to this point and why we even bother talking to each other. We really don't help each other with advice or anything, but I suppose sometimes it's nice just to say what we're thinking without a grand reaction from the other person.

"What are you doing now?" I ask.

"I have a job, but my parents cut me off. I haven't talked to them since," he says, while taking another sip of his cold coffee.

"Are you able to afford a place to stay and everything?" I ask because I genuinely care. If he didn't, then I would help him out. I have more than enough money that I never use.

He nods. "Yeah, the job I have pays great. I don't need my parents' money."

"What do you do?"

He leans back in his chair and smirks. "I'm in sales."

The way he says that makes it seem like what he's doing is not a legal thing. In fact, knowing him, I'm fairly certain that means he's selling drugs. I hate that for him and hope he doesn't get caught, or worse. But with our type of friendship, I keep my mouth shut. He's smart, and he knows what he's getting himself into.

"Well, that sucks for your parents. It sounds like they've now lost both of their kids. You would think they'd learn," I say, putting the blame on them once again.

Brandon and I spend most of the time just sitting and enjoying each other's company without talking much. That's how this usually goes. We come to say what we needed to get off our chest and then move on with our day. While this seems to be somewhat of a one-sided therapy session, I like to think of it as a check in with each other too.

Brandon gets a text on his phone, reads it, and replies. While he does that, I check my phone and see a text from Alex.

Alex

I think we should come clean.

My heart skips a beat for a minute. Alex has been hinting he's not comfortable lying anymore. I think he really misses his best friend, but we don't have that much longer for school. Plus, I really don't want James to find out this is fake.







I'm positive Ben wouldn't tell anyone, and he would be okay with us pretending, for Alex's sake, but I feel like we're in too deep. I kind of wish we had told him from the beginning, but we both panicked. Neither of us expected any of this to happen. I don't get a chance to respond before Brandon pulls me from my thoughts.

"I have to go talk to my boss. Do you want to come with me and hang out for a bit? I have some stuff for you," he says, getting up out of his chair.

I look out the front door and see Declan's car still parked directly in front of the building. I convinced him to stay outside, but I know he can see inside.

"We need to go out the back," I nod toward Declan. "Let me go first and meet me there in a second. Make it seem like I went to the bathroom."

He nods and sits back down. I get up and walk toward the bathroom but make a turn toward the back door. We specifically picked this place for that reason. It's easy access to the back door and I can make a quick escape. Declan's going to be furious with me again, but I can't find it in me to care enough.

I lean against the brick wall outside and wait for Brandon to show up. He comes out a minute after me and we walk toward his car. I hop into the passenger seat, and he drives off. We go five minutes down the road and stop at a club. So, his boss is based out of this club, good to know.

We make our way inside, but since it's early in the day, there are few people here.

Brandon walks me over to a table and says, "Stay here and I'll be right back."

He walks toward the back, and I give him some space before I follow. Yeah, I'm not sitting in a club alone, plus I'm curious about who his boss is and what he's doing.

I watch Brandon walk around a corner and knock on a door. He enters and closes it behind him. I tiptoe up to it and put my ear to the door in hopes I can hear what's being said. It sounds like one other man inside with Brandon, but most of it is mumbling. These doors are too good at muting sounds.

I reposition myself with my ear to the door, hoping to hear better. I hear a few words like "the drop is at" and "midnight." Unfortunately, I couldn't hear a place or day with that. Not that I would really do anything with that information, anyway.

I jump as someone clears their throat behind me. Crap, I didn't hear anyone walk up. I turn around to face who it is and find myself eye level with a man's chest.

"What are you doing?" The deep voice asks.

I look up and realize I know exactly who this is, and I know that chest very well. I only hit it around twenty times on the day of Lauren's funeral... Lorenzo. What is Lorenzo doing here? And what is Brandon... No... Brandon cannot be working with him. For one, I feel like that's a huge betrayal to Lauren. How could he do this to her? And two... Didn't Declan say he was like Mafia or something? Oh, no... Brandon what did you get yourself into?

I guess I take too long to respond because he repeats himself, "What are you doing here?"

My heart is beating fast, as I suppose I do have some self-preservation instinct. "I'm here with a friend and waiting for him."

He looks toward the door that I clearly had my ear up against and furrows his eyebrows. He doesn't say anything else as he opens the door without knocking and lightly shoves me inside. He isn't rough, but I can tell that I'm not getting away if I want to.

A man sitting behind a desk glares at us as we enter, and Brandon spins around in his chair wide eyed.

Standing behind me with his hands on my shoulders, Lorenzo asks, "Does this belong to either of you?"

Brandon quickly stands up and says, "Yes, I asked her to stay out by the bar."

Brandon looks at me like he's frightened, but also betrayed. Sorry Brandon.

"Sit." Lorenzo says as he gently leads me over toward the chair next to Brandon.

He continues, "I found her eavesdropping outside the door."

"Is that so? Tell me, did you hear anything interesting?" the man asks.

He looks familiar, and I'm thinking that he was one of the men with Lorenzo at Lauren's funeral. Seriously, what is Brandon doing with these guys? I look around at his desk to find a nameplate with the name "Matteo" on it. So that must be him. Funny that some mafia people would have a nameplate on their desk. Then again, I suppose he works for this club, so he probably needs to keep up a professional appearance.

I shrug and answer truthfully, "Not really. The door is pretty good at being soundproof. I just heard a lot of mumbling and something about a drop at midnight. Couldn't hear the details as to where or when."

Matteo stares at me while I'm talking, and then his mouth turns into a wide grin. "Well, isn't that refreshing? Honesty. That's something we rarely see around here."

Lorenzo is standing next to Matteo with his arms folded and studying me with a neutral face. He doesn't seem impressed, like Matteo.

We are all silent for a moment until Lorenzo finally speaks, "Everly, right?"

Well, there goes the hope that he didn't recognize me. "Yep," is all I respond with.

"Why exactly are you here?" Lorenzo asks.

Brandon tries to answer for me, but Lorenzo puts his hand up before he even speaks. "Brandon, go wait outside."

Brandon looks over at me with those wide eyes again, like he's afraid for me. He hesitates, but eventually he stands and leaves the room, closing the door behind him. Well, I guess it's good to know I can't count on him to have my back.

I didn't realize I let out a little laugh at that until Matteo asks, "What's so funny?"

I keep the smile on my face as I answer, "Just thinking it's good to know where Brandon and I stand is all."

Lorenzo puts his hands on the desk in front of me and leans toward me. His face is only half a foot away from mine.

"I don't know what your relationship is with Brandon, but I suggest you end it. He's not someone you should be hanging around," he says seriously and as if he was concerned for me.

I tilt my head like I'm studying him. "Why is that?"

Lorenzo rounds the desk and takes the chair Brandon was sitting in. He moves it to face me and then moves my chair to be directly in front of his. We're so close our legs are touching, and I wouldn't be able to get up if I wanted to.

"This is not a world you want to be part of Everly. I suggest when you leave here you never return and you do the same with Brandon," he says again in a serious tone.

It's not a world I want to be part of? Well, if it's the mafia, then he's right. I don't want to be part of that, but I'm angry at his words. He was about to drag Lauren into this world. Dead center of it by marrying her. I feel like either I have no emotions or the emotions I have are in overdrive. At this moment, they are in overdrive, and I'm angry.

"And you were willing to drag Lauren into this world?" I spit back at him.

He doesn't flinch at my tone or words at all. "She was born into a family who made ties with this world, so there was no choice for her. It was unfortunate, but you have a choice and I suggest you make the right one."

It's unfortunate? Yeah, it is unfortunate that she's now dead. Is that where most people end up in this world? Knowing the little that I know, I understand more why Lauren ended her life. It was probably a better alternative to this one. As he said, there was no choice for her. My heart hurts for her all over again.

"Yeah, it's unfortunate all right. But you're not going to tell me who I can hang out with. Brandon is my best friend's brother, or was. I owe her to be there for him where I can," I say because it's the truth.

"Brandon is a big boy, and he's fine. We're looking out for him and will continue to for the rest of his life. We take care of our people. Go to college, Everly. Go live your life."

I don't know why, but his words make me snap. "Go live my life?! Screw you, Lorenzo!"

He leans forward and places both hands on each side of my chair. His face inches from mine again and he looks angry. "If you were anyone else right now, you would not be leaving this room."

He glares at me, and I continue to glare back at him. I know that was a threat, but I'm also wondering why he is treating me so differently from anyone else. Is it because he feels guilty about Lauren's death? He knows I was one of her best friends.

Matteo interrupts, "Are you not afraid, Everly?"

I break my staring contest with Lorenzo and look at Matteo, who has a serious face. Really? That's what he's concerned about right now?

"No," I say.

"Why?" He asks like I'm a puzzle he's trying to figure out.

"You can't be afraid if you don't care about what happens to you," I say and somewhat regret the words as they come out.

I've felt that way for a while now and it is true. Do I care about what happens to me? I'm pretty sure I don't. Maybe some may miss me for a little bit, but in the end they'd all be better off without me.

Lorenzo sighs and leans back again, shaking his head. I feel like there are some unspoken words here, but they are going to stay unspoken.

He's about to open his mouth, but the door flies open to reveal Declan stepping inside with his gun out, pointing at Lorenzo. Matteo quickly draws his gun, but Lorenzo holds up his hand like he did with Brandon earlier.

"No need for the gun. I suggest you put that down now. Everly was just leaving," he says without moving, waiting for Declan to put his gun down.

Declan looks at me to make sure I'm okay, and I nod. He lowers his gun, and Lorenzo scoots his chair back and stands up. I do too and walk over toward Declan, who wraps his arm around me and keeps his attention on Matteo and Lorenzo.

Right when we get to the door frame, Lorenzo says, "Everly, I hope you take my advice, and I hope I never see you again."

Declan stiffens, but we keep walking. Brandon is outside the door and gives me an apologetic look. We don't exchange any words, but we don't need to. I have a feeling this is going to be the last time I see Brandon.

Declan opens the passenger door for me and basically pushes me inside the car. He walks around to the driver's side and slams the door. He drives away without a word, and he looks so angry. His knuckles are white from gripping the steering wheel tightly. We drive in silence for a few minutes until he pulls off in front of a little park and parks the car.

He shifts in his seat to face me and yep; he is definitely angry.

"What the fuck Everly?!" Declan roars at me.

"What?" I ask innocently, like I don't know what he is talking about. I mean, I'm not entirely sure which part he's so mad about. Is he talking about leaving the coffee shop without notifying him? Is he talking about hanging out with Brandon? Is he talking about going to a club? Or is he talking about what happened with Lorenzo and Matteo? There are a lot of things he could be talking about.

Declan laughs, and not a good laugh. I don't recall the last time I've seen Declan this angry. Maybe never.

"What? Seriously? You fucking ditch me at the coffee shop and then somehow end up in a room with the mafia boss and his brother. What the hell are you thinking? Are you trying to get yourself killed?" he yells at me. Yep, yells. I've officially made him lose it.

I cringe at his words because did he just say mafia boss? "What do you mean mafia boss?"

Declan sighs and takes a deep breath like he can't breathe since he is so angry. "I told you Lorenzo was dangerous Everly and not to mess with him. Tell me what happened. Everything, now."

I shift in my seat and figure there's no reason to lie to him. "Brandon said he needed to meet with his boss for a minute and offered me to go with him and then we'd hang out. He told me to wait in the club, but I followed him to the back and tried to eavesdrop, but Lorenzo caught me at the door. They brought me in and kicked Brandon out. Lorenzo told me I need to stay away from Brandon and them because I don't belong in their world. Then you barged in."

Declan is looking at me like he is trying to figure out if I'm telling the truth or not. Whatever he's thinking or sees on my face makes him believe me. Declan laughs. "Shit Everly, you just had me point a gun at the mafia boss. I could've been killed. They should've shot me."

I didn't think about that. I could've gotten Declan killed and it would've been all my fault. Why do I keep doing things like this? All I am is a danger to everyone around me, and I keep hurting people.

I look Declan in the eyes, "I'm sorry Declan."

I can feel my eyes tearing up and Declan pulls me in for a hug. I let him hold me for a moment, but then push back, knowing I don't deserve comfort from him. Did I really just sit in with the mafia boss and his brother? How the heck am I still alive? And why did Brandon mix himself up in all that? I have so many questions that I know I probably will never get answers to.

# Chapter Twenty-Three

I walk into the building at the address Asher texted me. Declan, of course, walks ahead of me to make sure everything is safe. There's a hallway with doors leading to what I assume are little offices.

After Lauren's death, Asher offered me to talk to him whenever I needed. I had just finished telling him about how I hated the therapist my father hired. I also hated the idea of having to pay someone to listen to my problems because they only care about the money and not me. At first, I didn't take him up on his offer because I doubted my father or Declan would be okay with me frequenting a club weekly. Asher had a way around that too, taking me to one of the office buildings he owns. He owns so much that I don't even know what's not owned by him anymore.

It took me a while to accept his offer, but after almost getting Declan killed, I figured it was time. Even I know that using drugs and drinking alcohol isn't going to fix my problems. Plus, Brandon and I aren't talking anymore, so my supply has been dwindling and cut off. I'm sure I could find someone else to provide me with what I want, but I don't trust anyone.

Once we get to the office door, I knock. The voice inside tells us to come in and Declan goes first. He looks around the room and shakes hands with Asher. They act like they are business partners. Does he know him? That's a question for later.

Declan leaves us, closes the door, and I stand there until Asher speaks. "Come sit."

I follow him over to a seating area with two comfortable chairs and a couch. We each take a chair facing each other. Looking around the room, the walls are completely bare, and the tiled floors are ivory colored. He has a dark wood colored desk with barely anything on it and two chairs in front of it. It looks like a staged office that is never used.

"How are you doing?" he asks.

I study him as he leans back in his chair with one arm on the arm of the chair and his other arm casually across his lap. His right ankle is crossed over his left knee. He looks comfortable. I, on the other hand, sit leaning on my left elbow with my right knee bouncing up and down quickly.

"Not good," I say.

He leans forward a little. "Talk to me Everly. That's why I'm here."

I sigh. "I'm thankful that you're willing to listen to my insignificant problems, but I am curious why you're willing to."

He smiles. "I told you before Everly, I care about you."

"You don't even know me."

"I know enough," he replies, leaning back into his chair.

Yeah, I'm not sure what exactly he means by that, but maybe I should just be thankful for his odd friendship.

"Well, I appreciate it. So, I keep making mistakes and I don't know what to do anymore. I keep hurting my friends and everyone around me. I lied to James, Ben, and Jake that I'm dating Alex and have been for months. Ben and James won't talk to me anymore, which is probably for the best, but it still hurts knowing how much I hurt them. James thinks I love Alex. That's not even the worst mistake that I made. The other day, I sat in with a mafia boss and his brother. Declan came barging in with his gun pointing at them and could've gotten killed and it would've been my fault. I don't think things through anymore. I'm just stupid and keep hurting people," I say all this quickly and slouch down in my chair, trying to make myself as small as possible.

"Okay, wow. There's a lot to unpack there. I need to hear about this mafia story first," he says, leaning forward again like he needs to get close to hear me.

I give him the rundown on what happened when I met with Brandon and then ran into Lorenzo.

"So, it sounds to me like you didn't know who he was there to meet or that you would run into them. You can't really blame yourself for that part. The only thing you could control was who you were hanging out with and what you did. Do you think Brandon is someone you should hang out with?" he asks and talks exactly like a therapist would. Has he done this before?

"Probably not, and I don't think I'll be seeing him again. I wanted to make sure he was okay and protect him."

"Why do you feel like you need to protect him and make sure he's okay?"

I sigh. "Because we all know how I feel about Lauren's death. It's my fault, and now Brandon has to deal with her being gone. Lauren would've wanted me to take care of her brother."

Asher rubs his chin with his thumb, studying me for a moment. "I'm not going to keep telling you it's not your fault because you're going to believe what you want, but I will tell you it is not your responsibility to take care of Brandon. And as Lorenzo said, they will take care of him, and I believe that he's telling the truth. Lorenzo is considered a good man in his world, and he's true to his word."

Well, isn't that interesting? Asher knows Lorenzo. How? Never mind, I really don't want to know. I'm just going to assume that Asher knows everyone.

"Yeah, as much as I hate Lorenzo, I think you're right."

"So, tell me about what's going on with Alex and why you're lying that you're with him."

I let out a long sigh. I know I came to Asher to talk to someone and for some help, but I'm annoyed with answering all these questions. I slump back further in my seat, putting my elbow on the armrest and my head in my hand. Asher cocks an eyebrow, which I know he's wondering why I'm so annoyed.

"Alex is gay, and no one knows about it. Some boys on the football team got suspicious and were threatening him, so I jumped in and pretended to be his girlfriend. I figured I could save him and show James he needs to move on," I say, closing my eyes.

Even saying James' name destroys me on the inside. When I'm not with him, I feel like I can't breathe. I miss him so much it physically hurts. I find myself twisting the ring around my finger as I always seem to be doing lately. I still haven't been able to convince myself to take it off.

Asher tilts his head, watching me. "Interesting... Why is it that you feel like you need to save everyone?"

I laugh. "I don't think I need to save everyone. I just want to help my friends when they need me."

He nods. "That's not a bad quality to have, but you need to take care of yourself, too. You know how on planes they tell you to put on your oxygen mask before helping anyone else with theirs?"

I nod. "Yeah, yeah, I get it. I need to help myself first... but... what if I don't know how to help myself? What if I'm drowning and there's no way to save myself, but I can save everyone around me before I go down?"

Asher sits up in his seat. "So that's how you're feeling? Everly, you can't give up. If you're drowning, you need to concentrate on yourself and give your all to come up for air. You can't let everyone else push you down deeper in the water."

"They aren't pushing me down deeper," I snap.

Asher puts up his hands in front of him. "I don't mean any offense. Let's take out the metaphors. You're hurting right now because of Lauren's death and haven't let yourself completely grieve. You feel guilty for her death and then you think you know what is best for your friends. You are pushing everyone away, even James, and then you feel bad because you can see how much they are hurt. You're trying to save them, but in the meantime, you have more and more guilt weighing you down. So yes, I believe you are letting them push you down deeper."

Fine, he has a point.

"Well, it's too late now. I'm already too deep. There's no way back up," I say, feeling defeated.

"It's never too late."

I snap my head back up to look at him and feel the anger rise in me. "It is Asher. You don't understand. I've already committed to pushing them all away, and it's the only way to keep them safe."

He tilts his head again in question. "What do you mean to keep them safe?"

I sigh again and go into the story about Adam. I start at the very beginning and end with our last conversation. I don't miss a single detail and I'm pretty sure that took half of our session time, not that we really are timed since he's not a real therapist. I know that I'm not supposed to tell anyone about Adam, but there's no way that Asher knows him. This won't get back to him.

I can see the rage in Asher's eyes as he says, "Fuck Everly. I'm so sorry. You should have come to me sooner. I'm going to take care of this."

I was so surprised by him cursing that I didn't have time to comprehend he pulled out his phone and was texting someone. Who was he texting in the middle of our session after I just told him that? And what does he mean he's going to take care of it?

"No, don't Asher. You don't understand. He's untouchable and his family is powerful. Even my dad couldn't end this, and he thought he did. Please don't. I don't want you to get hurt, too," I say, pleading with him with my eyes.

Asher shakes his head. "It's too late. It'll be taken care of shortly. You won't be hearing from him again."

I gasp. "You don't even have his last name."

Asher smiles. "I don't need it."

I shake my head. "Please, leave it alone."

"Everly, it's already in motion. There's nothing I can do to stop it. Let's talk about Adam being out of the picture. If he is, then what about your friends? Will you talk with them again? And James?"

I look away from Asher and stare at the wall, thinking about his question. If Adam wasn't in the picture, then yeah, I would apologize to my friends and try to make amends. But James... I don't know.

"Yeah, I would try to talk to my friends again," I say, purposely leaving James out of that.

"And James?"

Ugh, I should've known he wouldn't drop it. "I don't know."

"Do you love James?"

I look down at my lap so I wouldn't give it away. Of course I love James. I love him so much it hurts, and I don't think I'll ever be able to love anyone the way I love him, but I can't tell him that. I shrug my shoulders.

"Everly, I need you to be honest with me."

I sigh again. "Yes, I love him."

Asher nods. "Let me ask you something. Are you afraid of loving him? Do you think that maybe you are afraid to lose someone else you love so much? You lost one of your best friends. Do you think that maybe you're afraid to lose James, so you are pushing him away before that happens?"

Holy crap, that was deep. Are we sure that Asher isn't a real therapist? Either way, he might be right. I don't think I've ever thought about that before, but it makes sense. Regardless, there's nothing I can do about it now.

"Maybe, but I'm already committed to keeping my distance from him, so I'm sticking to it," I say.

"Why are you being so stubborn?"

"I guess that's just the way I am. I don't want to talk about James and I'm pretty sure time is up," I say, standing up and grabbing my purse.

Asher stands too. "Alright. Do you want to get together again this time next week?"

I nod. "Thanks Asher."

"Anytime. If you need to talk about anything, you can text or call me. Anytime."

I walk out the door, feeling a little lighter than before I walked in. While I may have been somewhat closed off and snappy, I really think it helped to talk about everything with someone. Asher actually cares about me and wants to help me. I have no idea why, but he does, and that feels good. Now, if only Adam really could be dealt with and be out of my life forever. I'm trying to keep the panic at bay that Adam will know I told on him again. I mean, what are the odds that he will be able to find Adam when he knows nothing about him?

# CHAPTER TWENTY-FOUR

*You don't deserve to live. Go kill yourself and do the world a favor.*

*You should have been the one to die, not Lauren.*

*How can you live with yourself?*

*Slut.*

Someone snatches the notes out of my hand before I can read the rest of them. I look over to see Jake crumpling them up and tossing them into the trash. It's been a daily occurrence having these notes taped to my locker, and they just seem to be getting worse. I'm not sure why I come to my locker every day and torture myself, especially when I never use it.

"Everly, stop getting here early every day to read these retarded notes," Jake says while putting his arm around my shoulder and pulling me close.

I tried pushing Jake away the past couple of months like everyone else, but he wasn't having it. He gave me my space, but he's always been there for me. He even tries to get to school before me so he can take down the notes before I see them. Sometimes he's successful, but lately I've been getting here earlier. Why? I'm not sure. Like I said, I like to torture myself; I guess.

Asher and I have been talking two to three times a week. Sometimes I talk to him on the phone, and he's been an amazing listener. He has some good advice, but I'm stubborn and don't want to take it. The only advice I've taken recently is letting Jake back in. He told me to pick one friend to make amends with and start there. So far, it's been going well, and I'm happy to have him back in my life. Plus, it has gotten him to stop incessantly texting me individually and in the group with the boys.

Jake walks me to our class as he always does. "With Adam out of the picture now, I don't see why they are continuing to do this."

I shrug my shoulders because it doesn't make sense to me either. Whatever Asher did seemed to work. At least, for the meantime. Adam hasn't contacted me except to apologize and let me know that he won't be contacting me again. He said that he told his friends to leave me alone too, but clearly that didn't work, or it's just other stupid bullies at school unrelated to him. Though, whatever Asher did, it helped. I've never heard Adam sound like that before, and he's never apologized before. Regardless, I still keep my guard up.

Classes seem to drag on and this year is going by painfully slow. I really don't know how I'm going to survive a couple more months before graduation. Even though I missed a decent amount of school this semester and everyone would say I'm depressed, my grades are amazing. I haven't been doing much outside of school other than studying, training, and talking with Asher.

When I get to lunch, I expect Jake to sit with me as he has been for a couple of weeks now, but he's nowhere to be found. I sit at the end of my lonely table and watch Ben with his friends. Alex occasionally sits with me to ensure people think we're still together, but he has the excuse of sitting with his football buddies half the time. I suppose being alone isn't so bad. Alex told Ben about our lie and things are still tense between both of them. Ben is now mad that we lied, which I understand. I haven't heard from James, so I'm not sure if Ben told him or not.

A tray plops down hard in front of me, and I'm surprised when I look up to see who it is.

"Hey," Ashley says, sitting down across from me.

"Hey," I say back.

We sit in silence for a few moments as we eat our lunch. I barely eat any more than a few bites of meals. I've lost a good bit of weight, especially since I've been training more and eating less. Declan keeps trying to push me to eat more, but he's let up a little as long as I eat just enough.

I hear Ashley shift in her seat and sigh. "I shouldn't have said what I said to you after Lauren's death. It's not your fault, I'm sorry."

I look up at Ashley, and my heart tightens. I've missed my best friend these past few months, but she had every right to say what she did and to be angry with me. I don't blame her at all.

"Thanks, but you were right. No need to apologize," I say, shrugging my shoulders.

She looks at me with pity in her eyes. "No, I wasn't right. I won't argue about it with you because I'm still having trouble believing it's not my fault. I just... I think we both needed and still need time to heal. I've missed you, Everly."

I feel tears threatening to fall from my eyes. "I've missed you too," I whisper.

We mostly sit in silence for the rest of lunch, except for Ashley telling me her plans for college. She's been working with a therapist too and she decided to apply to colleges in Georgia and California. She thinks that a fresh start far away from here should help. I told her once she knows which college she's going to, I'll apply as well. College applications were already due, but with the amount of money my father has and my grades, I'm sure that they can be persuaded to let me in as a late admission. Starting fresh across the country sounds like a good idea. I'm not entirely sure what I want to go to college for, but I still have some time to figure it out. My father has been bothering me about it a lot lately, so I've just said I want to go into Graphic

Design. It's not really a lie because I am interested in it, but I don't think that's the career path I really want.

The bell for lunch ending will ring in a couple of minutes, so I decide to leave early and head to my locker. Whoever writes those notes tends to put them on before school and after lunch. Again, I like to torture myself by reading them.

When I get closer to my locker, I hear arguing and the sound of something hitting metal. I round the corner to see four large boys fighting with someone by my locker. My eyes widen when I realize it's Jake who is currently being pinned to the floor. One of the boys land a punch to his face. I run over to grab the arm of someone about to punch Jake again. I pull on his arm, but he pushes me off, making me fall to the floor. There's no way I can fight them off if Jake can't.

I yell for help, but of course there's no one around. Jake pushes his way free, rolls to the side, gets up, and punches the nose of the one that was holding him down. By the looks of it, there were multiple punches Jake must have landed before they got him pinned down.

Two of them get ahold of Jake again and pin him to the locker.

"Stop it!!" I yell and no one responds to me. I feel invisible.

The other two are hitting Jake's stomach, and he's gasping for air. I finally come to my senses and press my watch three times. Declan is out in his car and thankfully my locker is at the entrance of the school, but it would still take time for him to get here. Time Jake may not have.

I get the courage to run up and body slam into the one who has been pounding on Jake. To my surprise, we both go tumbling to the floor and another says, "What the fuck?"

It would have been a good distraction for Jake to take a shot, but he's also on the floor and looks like he's badly hurt and can't move. The one I knocked down twists my arm and rolls me onto my back, pinning me down. I whimper as the pain shoots through my arm and shoulder.

"You bitch!" he yells, lifting his hand to hit me.

I brace myself for the impact that never comes. When I open my eyes, I see Declan yanking him off me and throwing him against the lockers. The others run away, and the teachers finally come out to see what all the commotion was. Declan restrains himself from hurting him and lets him go. He also runs. Cowards.

I crawl over toward Jake, ignoring the pain in my shoulder.

I help him sit up against the lockers and place my hands on either side of his face. "Jake! Are you okay?"

Jake looks at me with a weak smile but doesn't say anything. He's clutching his arm against his chest and his face looks horrible. He has a bloody nose, cut lip, and a black eye that is swelling shut.

Declan puts his arm on my shoulder, looking me over. "Are you okay, Everly?"

I nod. "I'm fine, but Jake..."

"We have the ambulance coming for him. What happened?" he asks.

"I don't know. I found them beating him up. They can look at the cameras. I need to stay with Jake," I say, not wanting to leave him.

Declan nods and goes to talk with the teachers and administration for a moment, but never takes his eyes off me. When the EMTs arrive, they load Jake on the stretcher, and he looks awful. I follow them out and ride with him to the hospital. I tell them I'm not going to leave his side. Jake passed out sometime during the transfer.

Declan follows behind us in his car and sits in Jake's room with me. I explain what happened once I get there but didn't know what started it all. Declan makes the doctors check my arm, but I refuse x-rays. I know it's not broken. They put it in a sling and tell me to get it checked if it isn't feeling better in a few days.

Mrs. Hale shows up shortly after we arrive, and I have to explain everything again to her, as Jake still isn't awake. Why isn't he awake? They wheel him off for some x-rays and other tests. I feel nauseous thinking that he might not be okay. I watch Mrs. Hale pace around the room on her phone while Jake is gone, and I need something to do.

I text the boys' group.

> I'm with Jake at the hospital. He's in bad shape, getting tests done now. He's still unconscious. I don't know who beat him up or why. I'll give details asap.

Bash

> I'm driving there now.

Ben

> Fuck, that was Jake?! Why didn't you tell me? I'm coming now.

James

> I'm with Bash.

Ben will most likely be here in the next twenty minutes, but Bash and James will be another hour. I don't know how many people they allow in hospital rooms, but I hope they don't expect me to leave. I don't know why, but I feel responsible for this. I'm not leaving Jake's side.

The nurse brings Jake back into the room after the tests. It feels like forever until Ben arrives. Once he does, Declan steps out of the room. Ben looks over at Jake before he comes to sit next to me. He notices my arm.

"What happened to your arm?" he asks.

I don't take my eyes off Jake while I respond. "I tried to fight them off."

I feel Ben's hand on my good shoulder. "Everly…"

A knock sounds on the door as a doctor walks in. Mrs. Hale immediately hangs up her phone without even saying bye to whoever she's talking to.

The doctor asks a bunch of questions and then states some results from the tests he just did. There's a lot of confusing information in there and I honestly can't keep up. I only hear that he has a fractured rib, but thankfully, no internal bleeding. Something about a brain injury and we need to wait and see.

Mrs. Hale seems unusually calm as she excuses herself to step out of the room to make a phone call. If it were my son laying in a hospital bed like this, I feel like I'd be a mess. I'm a mess and he's just my friend.

I get off my chair and kneel beside Jake, putting my hand on his. I don't care that Ben is in the room with me. I start sobbing.

"Jake... Come on you have to wake up... The quicker you wake, the quicker you can recover from this. You can't let those jerks win." My voice is high pitched from crying while talking to him.

I'm kneeling on the floor beside his bed, holding his hand for what feels like hours. The door opens and Declan walks in. I know that look on his face. He has information.

I keep my hand on Jake's as I position myself to face Declan by the door. "What is it?"

Declan looks conflicted, which means he is debating what or how he should tell me something.

"Tell me everything, Declan. We don't do secrets," I say, reminding him sternly.

Ben sits in the chair quietly, intently watching Declan.

Declan clears his throat. "I saw the security footage. Jake was standing near your locker for about twenty minutes, waiting. They came up and started taping something to your locker and Jake confronted them... Some words were exchanged before Jake threw the first punch and it went from there. You joined in a few seconds later."

I stare at Declan the whole time he speaks, but when he finishes, I look at the floor, deep in my thoughts. Jake did this for me? He missed having lunch with me so he could see who was putting those notes on my locker? He confronted them and even started the fight for me? My stomach turns and I feel sick. I can't believe he is here in the hospital because of me.

While I'm trying to hold back being sick, James and Bash walk into the room. I keep my hand on Jake's and put my face into the side of the bed. I can't help but let out the occasional sob as I'm trying to contain every feeling and emotion inside.

I hear Ben telling them what happened, including what Declan just told us. Fine, it's fine. They should know that he is in here because of me. They should hate me even more.

I feel someone sit beside me and wrap me in their arms. I immediately know it's James. I try to push him off, but he won't let go.

"Everly... This wasn't your fault," James says.

I laugh out loud at his words before looking at him. "Really? How do you presume this isn't my fault?" My voice gets louder and angrier as I continue. "He waited twenty minutes by my locker for ME. He confronted them for ME. He's in here because of ME."

James places his head on my shoulder. "Come on, let's go get something to drink and take a minute."

I look James in the eye and say sternly, "I am not leaving Jake's side."

He nods and looks at Ben and Bash. They both leave the room, leaving me and James alone with an unconscious Jake.

James lifts me up in his arms and sits me in a chair. He moves the other one in front of me as he sits down and places his hands on either side of my face.

"Everly, look at me. You cannot control other people's actions. They choose what to do. This is not on you," he says sternly.

I want to believe him and logically what he says makes sense, but I can't help how I feel. I feel like I'm a common denominator here. Everyone around me keeps getting hurt... or worse. This is why I keep pushing everyone away. This is why I need to.

It's like James knows what I'm thinking because he wraps me in a big hug again and whispers in my ear, "I love you, Everly. I'm not going anywhere, even if you tell me to leave."

I shouldn't, but I let myself melt into James' chest. Everything feels so much better when I'm wrapped up in his arms. He has a way of making the world and all the pain in it disappear.

Jake wakes up that night and is already acting like nothing happened. He's making jokes and laughing. I apologize over a hundred times, but of course Jake keeps saying what everyone else did, that it wasn't my fault. Then he has the nerve to apologize to me and feel bad about my arm being hurt.

Ben, Bash, James, and I all stay the night uncomfortably in his room. We pay them off to ignore the visitor policy. The perks of having money. Mrs. Hale went home for the night and Mr. Hale hadn't arrived yet. Mrs. Crawford came a few times to check on Jake and the rest of us. She brought us everything we could need to stay the night. Again, if it were my son, I would be here the entire time. I don't understand his parents.

They want to keep Jake a couple more nights for observation due to his brain injury and other injuries. While everyone else came and went, I didn't leave his side once.

"Everly, you stink. Go home and shower," Jake says with a smile.

"I don't care. You haven't showered either, so we can stink together," I say, teasing back.

He sighs. "Seriously, I'm okay. You can go home and rest."

"Nope, not happening. I'll leave here when you do."

He groans. "So, you will go home when I'm released later today?"

"Well, I was thinking I would come stay in your room for a few nights..." I say. I'm joking, but if he asked me to, I would.

"Oh really? Are you trying to get into my bed again?"

"Your bed is a lot more comfortable than this chair," I tease.

"You know, all you have to do is just ask and you can sleep with me," Jake scoots over and pats the bed beside him.

I don't want to take up any space on his hospital bed, but he's about to be discharged soon, anyway. I lay down beside him and put my head on his shoulder. We lay there silently for a while.

"Everly..." Jake starts, but I interrupt.

"Shh." I shush him.

"But..."

I interrupt again. "No, don't say anything. I don't want to hear it. Let's just stay like this a little longer and pretend everything is okay in the world."

He doesn't argue and pulls me closer. I let him, even though I know his body is hurting.

# Chapter Twenty-Five

The decision I made that led me to the top of this roof wasn't made lightly. I sit thirty stories high, barely registering the city around me. There's a cool breeze that whips around like it could spin me in circles if I let it. Spinning in circles seems to be all I've done for the past few months. One poor decision led to another, and then another. I've come to terms with that is just who I am and it's time to end it. There's only one way to ensure no one else gets hurt.

I pull out the bubble mailer from inside my jacket to ensure it's there. I haven't sealed it yet because I wanted to double check everything is in order. I've gone through the names on each envelope inside and know it's everyone. I flip through each one, one more time. They are all there.

The thing about Lauren's death that got me the most is the guilt. Guilt eats you alive. I've come to terms with the fact that it'll never go away. The fact that I could have done something to save her before she attempted and while she attempted, is what gets me. If she had written me a letter telling me how much my friendship meant to her and that there was nothing I could've done that would have prevented her from taking her own life, I could've lived with that. I wouldn't have all this guilt on my conscience. Such a beautiful soul taken from this earth too soon. So many people said that about her and it's true.

That's why I wrote these letters. No one will really miss me. In fact, they will all be relieved once I'm gone. I'm nothing but a burden and I just hurt people. I'm not a beautiful soul like Lauren was. I use my pain as an excuse, and I know that it's never going to end. Someone else is going to end up dead if I don't do something about it. The bullies at school think they were being mean by telling me I should've been the one to die and I should go kill myself, but they were just giving me the best advice. Maybe they weren't even being mean, and they just saw the truth. Regardless, this decision is for the best for all involved.

I thumb through the letters one more time and my heart skips a beat when I realize that I have missed one. Asher. How did I forget about Asher? I look around as though a piece of paper and pen will appear out of nowhere, but of course it doesn't. Idiot. Exactly why this is the best decision.

I sigh and pull out my phone. I don't read the missed messages, especially the ones coming from Declan. By now, he has realized I'm gone and will most likely be heading this way. I can't waste any more time.

I pull up Asher's texts to type out what I should've written in an envelope for him. I thought about texting everyone before

I jumped, but there's too many people to text. That would give too much time for someone to find me. One text won't hurt and then I'll do it immediately after.

Sitting in the middle of the roof, I text Asher.

> Asher, thank you for being a friend when I needed it the most. You've made my life the most bearable that it could be, but nothing you could've said or done would change the outcome. Thank you and I hope you find true happiness wherever life takes you.

I would've liked to have said more to him, but I don't have the luxury of time, and my point would have gotten across to him. I put my phone in my back pocket and make sure the letters are secure inside my jacket. I have to make sure they won't fly out on the way down. I couldn't risk leaving them at home for someone to find before I made it here. I also made sure it was waterproof, so the blood doesn't seep through onto them. I've thought about it all. I care for my friends and family, but I can't seem to show it to them with my actions. So, I hope this one last action shows it to them and they won't have to suffer anymore because of me.

I let out the breath I was holding and walk to the edge. I peer over the wall and down to the ground. Yeah, there's no surviving that. Good. There are still so many lights on in the buildings around and cars going to wherever they are going. I pull myself up on the wall and look down once again. I thought maybe I would second guess myself once I got up here, but I'm not. I thought there would be fear and my body would be telling me I'm stupid and trying to force me to reconsider, but my heart is at a normal rate. I'm at peace with this decision.

I look up at the sky and I can see some stars tonight. I smile because it's so rare to be able to see them in the city. While looking at the beautiful night sky, I lift my right leg like I'm just taking another step on the roof, except there isn't anything below me. I fall forward and close my eyes as I feel the wind whip around me.

Instead of barreling down like I would expect from walking off a roof, I'm tugged backward onto the hard surface of the roof. That's not the concrete surface I thought I would be feeling. What happened? I open my eyes to see arms wrapped around me from behind. How?

I turn to see Asher staring at me with wide eyes. We both roll over to stand, but he doesn't let go of me.

"What the hell are you thinking Everly?!" he asks angrily. No. Not angrily. Pained.

Shouldn't I be feeling something right now? Like relief that I didn't just plunge to my death? Sorrow because of what I almost did to my friend, who is clearly hurt? Nope, not feeling anything. There's no reason to because we all know it really is the best decision.

"How did you get here so fast? I sent you that message less than three minutes ago," I ask, honestly intrigued by his answer.

Even if he was outside of this building, there was no way he would be able to make it all the way up here so quickly. It's thirty stories. There's no way.

Now he looks angry, and he doesn't even answer my question. "Everly, what are you doing? Are you really going to kill yourself?"

"Yes, and you shouldn't have stopped me. Trust me, everyone is going to be so much better off once I'm gone. You'll see," I say, trying to pull away and make my way back to the edge of the roof, but he won't let go.

"Everly! How can you say that? Everyone who loves you... Do you not remember what Lauren's death did to you? You really want to do that to everyone you love?" his voice starts off yelling, but slowly tones down to more of a whisper toward the end.

I pull out the envelope from my pocket and wave it at him. "I wrote everyone letters stating exactly what they need to hear so they won't feel that way. I am sorry I forgot to write you one, but I remembered right before I jumped and texted you."

He doesn't move and doesn't let me go. He just stares at me like he's trying to figure out if I'm crazy or not. Spoiler alert, I am. That's why I need to go.

"Everly... No letter is going to make anyone feel better about your death. Come on, let's go talk..."

I interrupt him, "No. I'm done Asher. I appreciate everything you've done for me, but no amount of talking is going to help. I keep hurting everyone and I... I just hurt. I can't do this anymore. I know I'll hurt everyone doing this, but at least it'll be the last time I ever hurt anyone."

Asher looks like he wants to say something else, but the door to the roof flies open, and Declan appears. He runs over to me faster than I've ever seen him run before, and he wraps me in his arms in a big hug. I'm stiff as a board against him. I don't curse that often... but... fuck!

"Declan, please let me go. You don't understand..." I hope that somehow, they will let me make this decision, but who am I kidding? They aren't going to let me walk off this building.

He pulls back, staring me in the face. "Everly... No. No! I can't believe... How could you?"

And that's when the numbness begins to fade. I've never seen Declan cry before and he's crying. Broken voice, tears, and all. My damn heart comes back to life, making me want to cry and feel pain. His pain.

No, I can't do this. I can't live like this anymore. There's no happiness, there's nothing. I need this to end!

I try to push him off, but he has a death grip on me. I scream, "Let me go! You don't understand! I need to! Declan! Let. Me. Go!!!"

I thrash, kick, and try to punch him. I start to hyperventilate and can't breathe. It wasn't supposed to happen this way. My legs lift off the ground as he continues to hold me in a bear hug and Asher comes up behind me. They say something, but I can't make out what they are saying because I'm not even me anymore. I can't survive this. I wasn't supposed to be alive right now. I can't do this!

Asher gently places his hand on my forehead and before it all goes black, I hear him say, "Everly, I'm sorry."

I open my eyes to see bright lights above me and hear a beeping sound coming from a machine beside me. I look down to find myself lying on a bed with an IV in my arm and a monitor attached to my index finger. Am I in a hospital?

I look over toward the chair beside my bed to see Declan staring at me. I'm not sure what he's thinking, but he's not happy.

"What happened?" I ask.

"You don't remember?" he asks, surprised.

I shake my head and stare at the bright lights on the ceiling for a moment. The last thing I remember... Oh... No... I do remember. I failed. I walked up on that roof to do one thing, and I failed. God, why am I such a failure? I should've never walked off that roof, at least the way I did. I was supposed to die tonight. Why am I not dead?

"You do remember." It's a statement, and his tone is harsh.

I nod, but I don't look at him or say anything. What could I say? I'm not sorry. I don't regret it. In fact, it needs to happen, and it will. I just have a feeling it'll be harder next time.

A knock comes on the door as a young male doctor walks in. He looks at Declan and then looks over at me. "Everly, I'm Dr. Marcatti, and I'll be taking care of you this evening. Do you want to tell me what happened tonight?"

I just glare at him. He's being nice, but he already knows. I don't need to say it.

"I'd like to hear from you what happened. Right now, we have given you some fluids, but they are almost done, and you'll be out of the hospital. Is there anything you can tell me about what happened tonight?" he continues to ask.

I stay silent.

"Did you take any drugs or drink alcohol?" he asks like it's the most normal question in the world.

I still don't answer him. There is no need because we all know they took blood work and would know what is in my system.

He sighs. "Everly... I'm going to ask this, and I need you to be honest. Did you try to take your life tonight?"

That's when I finally answer him. "Unsuccessfully, yes."

He nods. "You're going to be transferred to a facility once I release you from here. They can help you. I've talked to your father on the phone as he's out of the country. I do hope you take care, Everly."

With that, he walks out the door. Wow. So, I'm suicidal and you're just walking out the door and telling me to take care.

Sending me off to some facility. This is just great. I should be dead, not suffering more.

I continue staring at the ceiling and feel the tears stream down my face. I'm not going to cry, I'm done crying. The pain is going to end soon. I'll make sure of it.

"Everly..." Declan says as he scoots his chair right up against my bed and holds my hand. I let him.

"Talk to me Everly. Tell me how to fix this," he says like he's so defeated.

I stare him in the eyes and say, "Let me die."

# Chapter Twenty-Six

I'm starting to question if I did succeed at jumping off that building, killing myself, and landing in Hell. That's clearly what this place is... Hell.

Seriously though. After being released from the hospital, I was driven directly to the rehab facility, which is supposed to be the best in the state. Declan walked me in, and they buzzed me through a door where I waited in a little waiting area alone. Declan wasn't allowed to come back any further. A doctor or psychiatrist or whatever the person was, pulled me into a little office. The old man sat behind his desk while I sat in a chair in front of it.

So here I sit, while he asks me questions. Only three questions, to be exact. "Do you feel depressed? Have you thought about harming yourself? Have you thought about harming someone else?"

Yes. Yes. And Yes... I mean the last one I'd probably never act on, but those bullies at school and Adam? Yeah, I've thought about it. Was it dumb to answer yes to them all? Absolutely.

Would it have made a difference if I answered no to them all? Absolutely not.

With those three questions, he moves me along in the assembly line to the next person who is admitting me to the rehab center. I feel like a prisoner. They walk me through a metal detector, pat me down, and make me take off my shoes. They check everything to make sure I don't have anything on me.

I'm moved further along to the next person who brings me to my room. Inside are two beds. That's it. The walls are white, the sheets are white, the one pillow on each bed are... you guessed it. White. Everything is white. There's a very small window high up. Enough to let in a little light, but small enough my body wouldn't fit through it. Fantastic.

There's a bathroom attached to the room and would anyone like to take a guess on what color everything in it is? White! Never could have guessed that one. The shower is normal, with a bathtub and a shower head that isn't removable. The funny part about it having a bathtub is that it doesn't have a plug. Guess they don't want you taking a bath and drowning yourself. The toilet also doesn't have a lid on it. There's no mirror either.

"Your roommate will be back shortly, and they will come get you for lunch. Someone is bringing your stuff, but it'll take a while before we can bring it to your room. We need to check it to make sure there are no items that are restricted. Do you have any questions?" The lady isn't even pleasant. She acts like she's bored and ready to go home.

"Nope," I state back, equally unenthusiastically.

She leaves the room, and I'm alone. I sit on the bed and stare at the white wall. Is this what I'm supposed to be doing the entire time I'm here? Staring at a wall? I also never missed my phone so much. We're not allowed to have one and aren't allowed to make phone calls either unless it's to someone on our approved list and it has to be at a certain time. When? I have no idea. Who is on my approved list? Again, no idea.

The door opens and a girl around my age walks in. She has straight brown hair and tan skin. I notice the little holes all up her ears, the ones above her eyebrows, and on her nose. I assume she has a good bit of piercings, which makes sense they made her take them off. No jewelry is allowed. I'm surprised they let us keep our clothes on.

"I'm Katie," she says, holding her hand out for me to shake.

I shake it. "I'm Everly."

"First time?" she asks.

"Yep. You?" I ask and already assume the answer.

"My second, but it'll be my last." She sits down on her bed.

We are silent for a moment as she pulls her bag out from under her bed. She pulls out a notebook and pen and starts to write in it.

"So, what are you in for?" she asks and looks up from her notebook.

"Tried to walk off a roof and was pulled back," I say nonchalantly.

She smirks. "Ah, a failed suicide attempt. That's me too, though I tried to OD. The first time I didn't take enough. This second time I was caught in time, and they saved me. Won't be making that mistake again."

She's smiling. I'm so confused. "Does that mean you're not going to try to kill yourself again?"

She laughs. "No. That means that I'm not going to fail the third time."

I cock my eyebrow at her. "So, how are you going to get out of here if you're going to do it again?"

She laughs again. "Everly, I've learned to play the system. I'll let you in on a secret. They don't care. Smile and put on a good show. Tell them how much you regret what you did, and you are so thankful that you're alive. You're still sad about things, but you can't imagine leaving your friends behind blah blah. When they ask those three questions, answer no every time. You'll be out within a week."

She lays back on her bed and crosses her knee over the other, using her lap to write in her notebook. I wish I had a notebook.

I get up and go to the bathroom just so I can do something different. I sit on the toilet and look down at my underwear. No freaking way. If I thought it couldn't get any worse, it did. My period started. Yay me. And I have no pads or tampons.

I yell from the toilet, "So, what do we do if we started our period?"

"Wow, that's unlucky. Hang on, I'll go get something from them." I hear the door open and close.

Are we allowed to just walk in and out of here? I'm honestly surprised they didn't lock us in. It doesn't take long for her to return with some pads. I'm not a fan of pads, but I'll take what I can get.

I finished up in the bathroom just in time for a knock on the door and a voice saying, "It's lunchtime."

I follow Katie out of the room and follow her lead. They hand us some food on a plate, like in the school cafeteria. We walk around in a line and wait in another. I watch the person at the little window put something in her mouth and swallow it. She opens her mouth and shows the lady.

"What is that?" I ask Katie.

"That's where we go for our medicine. You have to take it in front of them and show them you swallowed it," she says, like it's the most normal thing in the world.

"I don't have any medicine," I say, wanting to get out of line. Well, I would have my birth control pills, but clearly, it's the week of the placebo pill, anyway.

She laughs again. She does that a lot. "Oh, you have medicine. Everyone has medicine."

When it's my turn at the window, I give her my name and date of birth and she scans the wristband they put on me earlier. She hands me two medium-sized pills in a little cup and some water.

"What are these?" I ask.

She answers with some crazy name that I've never heard of and then elaborates, "It's for your depression."

I shrug and take the pills. I figure I'm probably not getting out of taking them. What could they hurt?

I sit next to Katie, who seems to be friends with everyone at the table. I stay quiet and just listen in. It feels odd, like it's just a normal day eating lunch at school with friends. They talk about... normal stuff.

There's a poor girl at the end of the table getting yelled at by one of the workers here. The girl is super thin, like see your bones thin. She's leaning back in her chair with her arms crossed, ignoring the worker lady. The lady keeps pushing some gross shake looking thing toward her and her tray. She keeps saying if she doesn't eat, she's going to lose her privileges and something else that I don't understand. After a few minutes, the lady finally gives up and throws the girl's tray and the shake in the trashcan. She lifts her out of her seat by her arm and drags her out the door. I haven't been feeling much emotion lately, but that just looked awful, and I feel sorry for the poor girl.

After lunch, they lead us over to another room and have us sit in a circle in chairs. Katie told me this is group therapy. Fantastic. My personal hell. She says after group therapy, we can hang out and play games. If it's nice outside, they will let us go out in the little fenced area. I lean back in my chair to look out the back door. It really is a little fenced in area and that wooden fence has to be at least eight feet tall, if not taller. I doubt I'm scaling that thing.

The group therapy session is just as hellish as I thought it would be. We all have to explain what we are in for and what drove us to that point. This is some pretty serious stuff to be talking about with fifteen other people that you don't even know. I just keep to the basics, that I tried to kill myself because I'm depressed. Of course, they ask why I'm depressed so I just say my friend killed herself and I make everyone around me miserable. The therapist says something about that, but I'm not really listening.

Now what I am listening to is the legit crazy girl sitting three seats away from me. Now that chick needs to be in here and I need to be avoiding her. She talks about how she likes to blow up animals and buildings. Apparently, she burnt down her family's barn for the fun of it. She sees absolutely nothing wrong with destroying property or killing animals. She also wants to blow up some people at school. I definitely plan to stay far away from her.

There are a few people in here for eating disorders and trying to kill themselves like me. The girl from lunch is one of them with the eating disorder. I don't understand how yelling at her and taking away whatever privileges will help get her to eat, but I'm not a doctor. I could tell the girls that were just playing the game like Katie said and then the ones that either didn't know the game or didn't want to get out of here. Who wouldn't want to get out of here? Is it bedtime yet?

I wake up out of a dead sleep by screaming and banging. I sit up in bed to get my bearings and remember where I am. That's right, I'm in rehab. I look over toward Katie, who is just lying there with her eyes open, looking at me.

"It happens every night. You get used to it," she says, rolling over to face the wall.

Every night? What is this place? I lay back down in bed, trying to go back to sleep, but the screaming continues for a while longer. There's nothing more I can do but close my eyes and think about everything that led me to this point. My heart sinks as I think about James. I do my best to push it down, but every time I start to drift off, my brain decides to be stupid and reminds me how much I love and miss him. I decide to keep myself awake just so I can control my thoughts.

The next day is even weirder. When we get to breakfast, there are a couple of new girls that join us. Katie finishes her breakfast before me, and I'm one of the last at the table. That's my first mistake. One of the new girls comes over to me and stares at me. I try ignoring her, but she doesn't go away. I look her in the eyes and that is mistake number two. She lunges for me and starts strangling me. It catches me off guard, but all my training kicks in. I push off the table to stand up, grab onto her to steady myself, and knee her hard in the stomach. She lets go immediately and topples over. Two of the workers come over and grab her, pulling her screaming bloody murder out of the room. I half expect someone to come check on me, but no one ever does. Alright, then.

A few moments later, a group of girls come up behind me. The one in front sticks her hand out to me and says, "I'm Janicia."

I eye her hand for a moment and debate if I should take it. Is this another trick and I'm about to be attacked again? Or is she actually being nice?

I decide to take her hand and say, "I'm Everly."

She smiles and points to the two girls behind her. "Everly, this is Deanna, and this is Shauna. Us black girls stick together. Shauna has a black name, so she's one of us. With your fighting skills, you look like you're from the streets. We've got your back now if anyone messes with you and you'll have ours."

Um, okay sure. I'm a little confused and look down at my skin for a moment to see that it is still indeed, white. I'm not sure what skin color or being from the streets has to do with anything but okay. Also, I'm curious why we have to stick together? Is this being attacked thing common here? Regardless, they seem nice enough. It wouldn't hurt to form a couple of friendships to survive here.

A week passes and I'm still here. I now officially believe I did kill myself and am in hell. With that being the case, I'll be the first to say I made a mistake. The point of killing myself was to not ever feel anything again. I'm feeling.

Katie left two days ago, and I wonder how she's doing. She was adamant about offing herself the moment she got out. I wonder if she succeeded. I kind of hope she didn't though because she was nice. We got along well, and she seemed like a good person who was dealt the wrong hand, but if she's that miserable, then I hope she succeeds in what she decides she wants.

My new roommate, Martha, seems okay too. She's very timid. She's scared of everything and thinks our room is haunted. It doesn't make for a good night's sleep with her or the random screaming that happens every night. When I was allowed to use a razor, she tried her best to steal it from me. I don't really know what she planned to do with it if she got it, but I'm thinking I'm just going to be hairy from now on. I don't want to deal with her begging me for it again and then getting in trouble if she succeeds. I'm not sure exactly why she's in here, but my guess would be paranoia. In group, she talks about some weird things like people following her and breaking into her home. She talks about ghosts a lot and thinks everyone is out to get her. Hopefully, she doesn't think I am.

I talked to my dad once on the phone, but that was it. I didn't really have anything to say to him after that. He promised that he would be around more and that he'd come home to visit me in rehab if I wanted him to. I told him no, and it's fine. I really don't feel like seeing him, anyway.

I see the doctor every other day. He asks the same three questions every time and I answer them with no, like Katie suggested. I explain how I'm feeling much better, and I know I made a poor decision. I tell him the medicine is helping, which is a complete lie. I'm pretty sure those things are placebos because I feel absolutely nothing.

So, while I'm waiting to speak with him again this morning, I plan my speech about how well I'm doing and how I don't want to die. I'm ready to get out of here. While Janicia, Deanna, and Shauna have become good friends, I'm okay leaving them. No one has tried to strangle me again or bother them, so clearly, they had the right idea sticking together. They are all my age and seniors in high school, too. Everyone seems to be the same age, give or take a year. We're not allowed to leave this section or talk with the adults. We occasionally pass them in the hallways going somewhere, but we're forced to keep our mouths shut and eyes straight ahead.

The doctor opens his office door and calls my name. I enter and sit down in front of him. To my surprise, not, the questions are exactly the same. He looks so disinterested in what we are talking about, just like everyone else here. Does this place really help people? I feel like all it has done for me is teach me how to be a better liar and actor. And that no one really cares about you. Not that I needed that lesson, I already knew that.

"Well, Everly. If you feel good about it, then I think it's time you go home. I'll send a prescription to your pharmacy for your medicine, and we know you have a therapist already at home. We'd like you to see him at least once a week. What do you think?" he asks as if I'm going to say no, please keep me here.

"Sounds great! Thank you for your help," I say. I'm surprised I'm able to say it in an enthusiastic voice because I'm being sarcastic.

They bring me back to my room to pack up my things, and I wait in the gathering room where everyone is watching a movie. I'm not paying attention because I'm really excited to get out of here. I have to say it's the first time in a long time I've felt excited.

A woman calls my name and tells me it's time to go. My heart races from the excitement as I go to get my bag. I follow her out through a couple of doors until she finally leads me out the last door to the waiting area, where I see Declan waiting for me.

I smile and run to him, tackling him in a hug. I want to say it's all for show, but it isn't. I truly missed him and am happy to see him.

"It's good to see you too, Kid," he says, relaxing under my touch.

He takes my bag and leads me to the car. He doesn't say anything else to me until we start driving away and my stomach growls embarrassingly loud.

"Do you want to stop and get something to eat?" he asks.

"Yes! I'm starving. Maybe someplace with a good burger. I haven't had a burger in forever," I say, thinking about how a juicy burger really does sound amazing.

"A burger it is," he says as he continues driving.

We find a little restaurant that does have the best burgers. When it comes out, the burger is so big I don't think I can eat it all. I'm definitely going to try.

Declan watches me as I take a bite of the burger. "So... how are you feeling?"

I place the burger down and stare at him. I know what he's asking, and I know exactly how I'm supposed to answer.

So, I reply, "Good. I'm not going to try to kill myself again."

Which is a lie. I mean, I really haven't thought about it that much in rehab. I was thinking more about how to get myself out of there than what happens after, but nothing has changed. Everything is still the same and I don't foresee it changing. Katie was right, though; I can't go back. I'm going to have to do it right next time, and that might take some time. The best way to do this is to avoid everyone as much as possible. I don't want to hurt anyone again and the more I'm around people, the more I hurt them. I just can't help myself.

Declan is watching me carefully, trying to figure out if I'm telling the truth or not. He just nods. Which means he doesn't believe me. That's fine, I wouldn't believe me either.

"James misses you. He tried everything to be able to contact you and see you, but they wouldn't let him," Declan says.

"That's nice of him," I say, not knowing what to say to that.

I caught myself trying to play with the ring he gave me multiple times while there, to find that it wasn't on my finger since they took it. I put it on the moment they gave it back but tried not to think about why I wanted to wear it. If I'm being honest, I forced myself not to think about James while in there after the first night. I forced myself not to think of James while I was trying to kill myself. James has a way of making me... feel. I can't have that.

# Chapter Twenty-Seven

I finish my burger in silence as Declan stares at me. It should make me feel uncomfortable, but it doesn't. I know what Declan is thinking. He wants to know how it went in rehab, but he's not going to ask. He's also trying to figure out how much space he can give me without something happening. He's watching my every move.

"Can we make a couple more stops before heading home?" I ask getting into the passenger seat of the car.

"Where to?" he asks.

"First Lauren's grave and then to see Asher?"

Declan nods and drives to Lauren's grave. It's not too far, but it is far enough that I almost fall asleep on the way. I didn't sleep well this past week. Declan hasn't given me my phone back yet and honestly, I'm not sure that I want it. I kind of like having the peace and quiet, of not having to respond to anyone and being able to tune out the rest of the world.

When we pull up close to Lauren's grave, I see a figure sitting on the ground in front of it. It takes me a second to realize who it is.

"Let's come back later," Declan says, while putting the car in drive again.

"No. I need to do this now," I say, getting out of the car.

Declan opens his door like he's going to follow, but I say, "Declan, please. I'll be fine."

Declan looks conflicted for a moment, but he nods and sits back in the car. He leaves his door open though and sits with his legs outside of the car. The car isn't far from the grave, but it's far enough that he won't be able to hear what's being said.

I walk toward the grave, and Lorenzo raises his head to see who is intruding on his time. I plop down in front of him, cross-legged.

"I didn't expect to see you here, Lorenzo," I say evenly.

He leans back on his hands and studies me for a moment before speaking. "Did you know this was the day Lauren and I met?"

I didn't know that. I didn't know much about his relationship with Lauren other than she didn't want to marry him and her family was forcing the matter. I'm shocked to see him here, but even more shocked to know that he is here on the day they met. Maybe I judged him too harshly.

I shake my head, and he continues, "Her parents and my uncle came up with this arrangement. She was only sixteen at the time. When we first met, she was timid. She was beautiful, but a child. It was difficult to think at the time that we would be getting married and to treat her as my fiancé. She looked at me with so much hope in her eyes that first time I saw her."

I tilt my head, thinking about his words. "Hope?"

He shrugs. "Hope. Honestly, I don't know if it was hope that I would deny the arrangement or if it was hope that we could work out. Either way, as time passed by, I slowly watched that hope disappear..."

My heart squeezes at the way he's looking down at her grave. He feels guilty. I know that look and feeling too well.

I don't know what comes over me, but I put my hand on his and say, "It wasn't your fault, Lorenzo. I know that I blamed you and a lot of people did, but it wasn't your fault. I'm sorry for the way I treated you at her funeral. I was just... so angry. I needed someone to blame, and you were there..."

Lorenzo sits forward and stares me in the eyes. "We can't control the actions of others. What they do... what she did is on her. But the way I treated her didn't help in her decision to take her own life. I will forever share the blame in her circumstances, but I won't let her death be in vain."

We both sit silently for a few moments staring at her grave. The grass isn't fully grown over yet, but it is well maintained. There are fresh flowers, which I assume Lorenzo brought. He cared for Lauren, and I just wish she was here to see this side of him.

Lorenzo clears his throat. "I know what happened last week. I don't dare speculate why you did it, but you've seen the other side of this. If you're doing it for others, don't. That's not going to help them. Lauren did it for herself. She felt there was no way out and couldn't see a future ahead of her. I wish I would've done better for her, but I can't change that now. There's always a better future. Sometimes you have to push through all the bad, but it's there."

Lorenzo stands up and before walking to his car, says, "I'll be right back."

I stand up and watch him. When he comes back, he hands me an envelope. I look at it to find my name written on it.

"The night you attempted to kill yourself, I was about to meet with Declan to give him this. The police finally released a letter that Lauren wrote to me when she killed herself. In it, she told me where to find this and other letters to her friends. She wanted me to give you this." He nods toward the envelope.

I look at it and back up at him. "Did it help? The letter she wrote you, did it help?"

He shrugs his shoulders. "It helped me understand why she did it, but it doesn't help ease the pain."

I nod and feel tears forming in my eyes. I try to keep them at bay while Lorenzo is still here. I'll have to read this after he leaves.

As if he knows what I'm thinking, he pats me on the shoulder, and says, "I know I said I never wanted to see you again, but it was good seeing you, Everly. This world has a lot to offer you. Go find it. Get out of New York if you have to and find something good. You deserve it. Lauren wanted that for you."

I lean in and give him a hug. I never thought I would be hugging Lorenzo, but here I am. He's not the villain that I made him out to be. He may not be a good man in the eyes of society, but in his own way, he is good.

I pull away from him. "Thank you, Lorenzo. You deserve happiness, you know. I don't care what anyone says, you are a good man. I hope you find someone who sees you that way."

I see the side of his mouth twitch up for a split second before he turns to walk away. I plop myself down again in front of Lauren's grave and open the letter.

*Everly,*

*I'm sorry. I really am sorry that I left you this way. I want you to know that it's not your fault. I made this decision before I even met you. There is no future for me. At least, not one that I can live with. That's not the case for you, though. What you have with James is what true love is. Don't take the love you have for granted, whether it's with James or someone else in the future. Go to college and forget about me and your past. Major in what you want to do, not what others want you to be. I need you to move on and live your life to the fullest. I didn't have a choice in my future, but you do. Know that I'm watching out for you and rooting for you even if you think no one else is.*

*Love always,*
*Lauren*

I shove the letter in my pocket and laugh as the tears stream down my face. What the hell am I supposed to do with that? My sadness quickly turns to anger. Did she really think that letter would make me feel better? And how does she suppose I forget about her? You don't forget about someone like Lauren.

I lay on my back and watch the clouds slowly go by in the sky. I can't help but feel a little stupid myself. Here I was writing letters to everyone I loved, thinking that it would help them. I said if she had written me a letter, then I would've felt better about this. I don't. I kind of feel worse. Knowing she was sitting there thinking about me while she was suffering. Is that how my friends and family would have felt if I had succeeded?

I stand up and walk back to the car. Declan gets out and opens my door for me to get in. He always does that. He isn't my chauffeur, but he does it anyway. How would Declan have felt if I had killed myself and he read the note that I wrote for him? I shiver, thinking about it. I obviously wasn't thinking clearly enough back then.

Declan drives off when I say, "Declan."

He glances over at me, then back to the road quickly. "Yeah?"

"I'm sorry," I say and don't need more explanation than that.

He doesn't ask me for what. He already knows. "It's okay, Kid."

Was it, though? I guess maybe it is since I'm still here, but I don't feel like it's okay. I just want so much to stop hurting those around me.

We pull up to a tall building that I've never been to before. Declan pulls into an underground garage and parks the car.

"Where are we?" I ask.

"This is where Asher lives. He said we could meet him here," Declan replies.

We get out of the car and walk toward the elevator. Asher is standing against the wall with his arms crossed over his chest. When we approach, he straightens and walks toward me. I give him a small smile as he pulls me in for a hug.

We don't say anything as he leads us into the elevator and swipes his card over the reader pushing floor 48. Wow, does he really live in this building and on such a high level?

When the elevator opens, we walk into a small hallway where there's a door in front of us. Asher pulls out his key and opens the door. I'm in awe when I walk in. The place looks miraculous. The ceilings are tall with windows a couple of stories high. The furniture is modern, and everything looks so... clean. The kitchen is giant with a black island and countertops. When I walk over to the windows in the living room, I can see the city clear as day. It's a beautiful view.

"Asher, this is amazing," I say, spinning around taking it all in.

I spot some spiral stairs leading up and some leading down. "How many floors is this place?"

Asher watches me intently and says in a tone that all this is normal, "There's a floor above and below us."

"That's amazing. Thank you for inviting me here," I say, still walking around and enjoying the view.

Asher eventually leads me to his office further down a long hallway. I can't believe how big this place is. I don't even want to know how much money it cost. I have a feeling it's nothing short of two to three hundred million dollars. What exactly does this man do for a living?

Declan makes himself comfortable in the living room as I head into Asher's office. His office is just as extravagant. He has three bookshelves from floor to ceiling, full of books on each side of his desk. His desk is a mahogany color with some weird designs on it. There are also floor to ceiling windows here as well. I don't know how he gets any work done in here.

There's a couch on the right side of the room, along with two armchairs. Asher holds his arm out toward the couch for me to sit, so I do. He sits in the chair in front of me.

Asher stares at me and doesn't say a word. Is he waiting for me to say something? I suppose I'm the one that wanted to come visit him.

I tap my fingers on the chair as I say, "I'm sorry."

He raises his eyebrow at me, waiting for me to elaborate. He knows what I'm trying to say, but he wants me to say it.

I let out a breath. "I'm sorry I attempted to rid the world of myself and I'm especially sorry you were the one that had to stop me. I didn't mean to hurt you. In fact, it was quite the opposite."

Asher leans forward and says, "Ridding the world of yourself, as you put it, isn't going to help anyone. The fact you are apologizing makes me think something happened for you to realize that you were hurting the ones you love instead of helping?"

I nod as the lump in my throat catches.

"Do you still want to do it?" he asks in a serious tone.

I look past him outside at the city. Do I? I had every intention of doing so once I got out of that place. Do I still think everyone would be better off without me? Yeah, I do, but after talking with Lorenzo and getting the letter from Lauren... I don't know. My perspective on this has changed. I'm more confused than ever.

I must have taken too long to answer because Asher moves to the couch beside me, placing his hand on mine, and says, "Talk to me Everly."

I swallow that lump and clear my throat. "I may have a new perspective on things. I don't want to hurt anyone anymore, but I don't know if killing myself is the best way to do it. I don't know how I can stop hurting my friends, though."

Asher nods and leans back a little. "So, if your main concern is that you want to take yourself out of the lives of your friends to protect them, then why not do just that? You're about to be 18 and going off to college. You don't have many options to escape your life right now under the rule of adults, but you can do whatever you want once you graduate. Pick a college far away and start a new life, away from everyone."

Well, I feel pretty stupid because he makes it sound so easy and it probably is. He's right. I've only been thinking about the present. I haven't been thinking about the long term. I've been letting my emotions control me.

"Okay, but what about right now? I am still around them until I graduate. Who's to say I won't hurt them again before leaving for college?" I ask. It's a valid question. I mean, look at Jake ending up in the hospital because of me.

"I can promise you that everything has been taken care of when it comes to Adam and those who have bullied you at school. Go enjoy the last couple of months with your friends," Asher says.

"What if it's not?" I ask, not completely convinced after everything that's happened.

"If not, then you will come straight to me, and I'll get you out of here. I'll set you up wherever you want to go, new identification, money, and everything. I can make you disappear, and no one would be able to find you." Asher's face turns serious as he speaks.

Well, that... is a lot. The fact that he would do all of that for me if I asked him to. And that he has done so much already to take care of everything happening in my life. I want to know why he is so invested in helping me, but I know I'll never get a straight answer.

"Okay," is all I can say.

He smiles. "Is there anything else? Do you want to talk about what happened last week?"

I shake my head. "Not today. Maybe we can talk next time about it. But I do have one question."

"What?" he asks.

"How did you find and get to me so quickly?" It's been bothering me ever since he saved me. I swear there's no way he could've gotten there that quickly.

He clears his throat. "It's easy to track someone quickly, and I just happened to be... visiting a friend."

Visiting a friend in a commercial building? I mean, possible, but that's just too much of a coincidence. I'm not going to push it, though. I don't know what kind of answer I expected. That he teleported to me? Yeah, I would definitely believe the visiting a friend and tracking my phone quickly over that.

"Okay, well, I'm glad you were there," I say and mean it.

We both stand and he walks me to the door. He opens it and moves aside to let me go first. I pause in the doorway to give him a hug, and he hugs me back.

"Thank you for everything you have done for me. Thank you for everything you're willing to do. I don't deserve you, but thank you," I say as I let go and walk through the door back into the living room.

Declan and I finally set the course for home. My heart rate picks up thinking about having to face my family and friends. I'm nervous. Should I do what Asher said? Should I just try to enjoy the last couple of months and then leave for college far away and start a new life? It sounds so simple and yet the most difficult thing that I could do.

To get my mind off what I'm about to walk into, I ask Declan, "What do you know about Asher?"

He glances over at me before answering, "Why do you ask?"

I shrug. "I'm just curious. I don't really know much about him. What he does, how old he is, why he has become my friend and is so willing to help me…"

Declan laughs. "Do you really find it that hard to believe that people like you Everly? It's easy to become your friend and care about you. But to answer your other questions, I don't know how old he is, and he does a lot… He owns a lot. It's really a question of what he doesn't do. Did you know your high school is named after him?"

Well, that is news to me. Terion High School is named after him. Asher Terion. That makes sense… But why?

Declan answers my question without me having to ask it aloud. "He donated a lot of money to that school to make it what it is today. He's a good man, but he is mysterious. I won't lie, I did some digging into him and didn't find much. I trust him, though."

I don't have an issue with trust when it comes to Asher. I just want to know more about him. I guess I might have to stick around a little longer to see if I can figure him out and get to know him more. He's helped me so much and I don't even know how old he is.

When Declan parks the car in front of the house, I don't move. He comes around the car and opens the door for me and I still sit there staring at the house.

"No one is going to bother you tonight. You can go straight to your room, eat, shower, sleep, read, or do whatever you want. You can talk to everyone in the morning. And I'll give you your phone tomorrow, okay?"

I nod and finally get out of the car. Before walking toward the house, I turn to Declan and say, "Thank you."

I open the front door to find that it was just like Declan said. No one is here to bother me. I walk up the stairs and have an odd sensation as I walk toward my room. When I left this room, I thought I would never be coming back to it. I open the door and quickly close it behind me. I plop myself down on the bed and stare at the ceiling for far too long.

When I wake up the next morning, I feel a familiar body pressed against mine. I snuggle in closer for a moment and take a deep breath. I'll never get enough of the warmth and comfort that James holding me provides. I let out the breath that I took and push his arm off me to sit up. When I look around the room, I realize we aren't alone.

Ben sits in the chair close to my bed while Jake and Bash are sleeping on the floor on blankets and pillows as a makeshift bed. I can't help the tears that form in my eyes due to my heart squeezing at the sight of them. They're all here for me, even James and Bash. They're all skipping school and classes to be here for me. While I still feel like a burden to them, especially now, I can't help but feel a little bit lighter at this moment.

I lean against the headboard and just stay there, staring at everyone. I'm not moving from this spot until they wake up. I've made my decision. I'm taking Asher's advice and I'm going to enjoy the short amount of time that I have left in my senior year of high school. Then, I'm going to go to college as far away as possible and remove myself from their lives. It happens all the time anyway, right? Best friends go to college and lose touch with each other. My heart hurts a little thinking about it, but I know it's the best decision I can make for them.

# Chapter Twenty-Eight

I slam the car trunk closed with more force than I should have. I thought that all the luggage inside would be too much, and I'd have to sit on the trunk to even attempt getting it closed, but it all fit. My life and Ashley's life from New York all fit in one small trunk together.

Ashley is on one side of the car saying her goodbyes to her family and I'm on the other, staring at everyone who has come to see me off. While they may not know it now, this is going to be our final goodbye for most of them.

My father is the first to give me a hug and says a quick "I'll see you soon." He plans to come down to Georgia next week to ensure that Ashley and I are settled into the house he bought us. He has already made sure that it's fully furnished and each of our closets are filled with brand new clothes for the Georgia heat. By settled into, he means that security is top-notch and there's no way anything would happen to us. While Georgia Southern University requires first years to stay on campus, my father gave a hefty donation to bend that rule, along with another hefty donation to get me in late. The perks of having a rich father.

Mrs. Crawford is teary-eyed as she gives me an endless hug and, for the hundredth time, tells me to come back and visit. She requires at the very least a monthly phone call from me. After everything she has done for me my entire life, I can at least give her that. What she doesn't know yet is that I never intend to set foot back in this state again, which means I will never see this house again. Mr. Crawford gives me a quick hug and reminds me that if I ever need anything, I just need to ask.

Alex comes forward next and lifts me up in a hug. I laugh. Alex has made things official with Tanner, and everyone knows the truth. The best part about it was that on graduation day, he stood up on that stage during his valedictorian speech and announced he was gay. The gasps, whispers, and cheers were immense, and I couldn't have been happier for him. Of course, my friends all knew much sooner than that, which made things even better. I was thankful that I was coherent enough during his speech to witness all that. Ashley and I may have been high as a kite during graduation. Not much else was remembered from that day and plenty of other days before that.

I've been able to easily keep my emotions in check, but it's quickly coming to an end as I look over at the four boys who have been my family since I was little. I told myself I wouldn't think of anything as I said my goodbyes to them, but that quickly flew out the window as I hug each of them individually.

Jake... Jake pulls me into a hug and kisses my forehead before letting me go. I stare him in the eyes, and remember everything good in the world. My first real boyfriend and shortest-term boyfriend in the history of boyfriends. I love him. He's been one of my best friends since I was little and my partner in crime. So many antics we have gotten into, and so many pranks. Knowing that our time was ending soon, Jake and I played as many pranks as we could on every member of the family staying under this roof.

I'm fairly certain that everyone was living in fear and watching their backs every second of the day after the first couple of weeks I was home from rehab. Poor Declan was sporting blue hair for a few days. I'm surprised he didn't expect the hair dye in his shampoo bottle. He wanted to go get it fixed, but Jake and I kept him so busy with keeping an eye on me that he didn't have a second to himself to do so. I finally caved and let him take care of it. I swear that his hair still has a bit of a blue tint to it, but he'll deny it. I can't help but smile, thinking of all the craziness we got into.

Bash... Bash squeezes me tight, but he lets go quickly. I hear him clear his throat, which surprises me that he is the emotional one of the boys. I didn't get to see Bash much, considering he went back to college shortly after the night he spent in my room with the others, but I have to say he was the one to check in on me most often.

I'd wake up almost every morning to a sappy text from Bash, which I didn't know he had in him. He'd tell me how strong I was, how beautiful, how amazing, and every other compliment you could think of. He wanted to ensure I started every morning with a positive message, and he'd check in on me at the end of each night. I've been trying to convince him that he doesn't need to do that anymore, but he hasn't stopped yet.

Ben... Ben wraps his arms around my neck, hugging me. He pats my back and steps away. Ben definitely took on James' protective role once James went back to college. There was hardly a time when I was out of the house that I was alone. Ben made sure of it. He'd walk me to every class, and he'd help me carry my books. Even though the bullies stopped, I still didn't feel comfortable using my locker. Jake and Ben ate lunch with Ashley and me every day.

As much as Jake made me laugh, Ben's awkwardness made me laugh even more. He would get himself into situations that just didn't make sense. He used the help and don't ask questions rule the most of all of us. Just the other day, Declan and I had to pick him up down the street in only his boxers. I brought him clothes, but I may have tortured him a little before giving them to him.

Each of the boys had different roles and different ways to take care of me. I was covered in every fashion you could think of. It's another reason why this departure is so bittersweet. I've grown so attached to each of them, but I know it's for the best. They have been so concerned about me that with me gone, they can finally concentrate on their own lives.

And then there's James... James and I stare at each other as everyone else walks away to give us some space to be alone. Ashley is already in the backseat of the car waiting while Declan closes the driver's door and sits behind the wheel. James and I slowly make our way behind the tree next to us to give us a little more privacy.

James steps forward with the smallest amount of space between us. I can feel his breath on me. I inhale and hold my breath as he leans in for a hug. I close my eyes, hug him back, and finally let out the breath I was holding, which unfortunately a sob escapes with it. As we pull away, I quickly wipe away the tears that escaped.

"Everly..." him saying my name is all I need to hear. The way he says it tells me everything. He's not ready for this goodbye. He doesn't want it to be goodbye, knowing for me it's goodbye forever. If I'm being honest, I'm not ready either, but it's time.

James may not have been around as much as he wanted to be because of college, but he came home every chance he got. That included every weekend the moment he got out of his Friday class until he drove back for his Monday morning class. Every time he was home, I found myself in his bed, but only like when we were little. James never pushed it, not even once. He never asked for more. He never tried to kiss me or touch me other than to cuddle and comfort me.

I know where he stands and that he still loves me. As much as I tried not to show it, he knows that I still love him. That leaves us where we are right now. The hard moment where I make my choice and stick to it. No matter how difficult it is.

"James…" I whisper back.

"I know what you're planning to do, and I will always respect your choices. If this is truly what you want, then I'll let you get into that car, drive away, and never bother you again. But I need to know that you are 100 percent sure that it's what you want."

Damn it, why does James have to be so perfect? Of course, that's not what I want. I want to say no; I want you. I want to be with you forever, but I know I can't say that. Our lives are too complicated for that. James was right before we got together. Now that he's going to be a senior in college, every spare minute he has needs to be to concentrate on his father's business. He is already shadowing underneath him, and he won't have time for me. And with that, I know James. He will kill himself trying to finish college, please his father, and somehow find time for me. This isn't about me anymore; this is about him and everyone else. I made this plan, and I need to stick to it for them.

I open my mouth to speak, but James interrupts me by slamming his mouth to mine. I melt into the kiss. Our final kiss that I didn't expect to have. My heart sinks at the thought, and I feel wetness on my cheek. I've been so careful to hold in my emotions, I can't believe I'm letting it out right now of all times. I only need to last a few more minutes and then I can break down in the car once we drive off.

When I pull away from James, I realize that I'm not crying. The drop of wetness wasn't from me, it was from James. I look up at him to see him swipe at his eye, but if I hadn't seen him do that or felt the wetness on my cheek, then I would never have known he was crying. He looks so composed as always.

It takes so much effort to keep my voice even. "Thank you for everything, James. You were my first true love, and you are everything to me. I need you to enjoy life. Try not to let work take over your life. You have so much to live for and are amazing..." I take a breath, and it takes everything I have to get out the words that need to be said, "I'm 100 percent sure it's what I want."

I fiddle with the promise ring on my finger as I'm talking and finally pull it off. I've kept it on all this time, and I wasn't sure why until now. I needed it to have this moment for our final goodbye.

I hold the ring out to James, but he grabs my hands in his and puts it back on my finger.

"I made a promise that I intend to keep. I told you that I will love you forever, and I will," he says while still holding my hands in his to ensure I don't take the ring off again.

My voice cracks. "James... I... You can't..."

He interrupts me. "Everly, I need you to know that I'll wait for you. However long it takes, I'll be waiting. If it takes you ten months or ten years, I'll be here waiting. There's nothing you can say or do that will change my love for you."

I stare at him and have no words. He can't really mean that, can he? He's just saying that, so I'll change my mind, right? As much as I want to change my mind, I can't. It's for the best. For both of us. Why does it feel so wrong, though?

When I have no more words, James gives me one last hug and says in my ear, "Go now. Find yourself and then find your way back to me. Don't say anything. Don't look back. Go."

As he releases me from our hug, he turns me around and pushes me toward the car. I feel the tears streaming down my face and I know that my tears are mixing with his. I do exactly as he says. I walk to the car, get in, and don't look back as we drive off.

# ALSO BY

Is this really how James and Everly's story ends?! Of course not! Their story continues in fALLINg into You Again. Find out what happens to them six years later, from both of their POVs!

If you'd like the inside scoop of upcoming books and releases, join my Facebook group: www.facebook.com/groups/snchristensenreaders/

Follow me on TikTok
@authorsnchristensen

Preview of fALLINg into You Again
**Chapter 1- Everly**

New York. The place in the United States I vowed never to return to. The place where I'm currently sitting in a coffee shop questioning my life choices once again. The place that offered me a job when no one else would. Not only am I in the state that I desperately wanted to get away from, but I'm working at the high school I desperately never wanted to think about again. I've only been back in this state once since leaving for college. One time too many. Life surely has a sense of humor.

I sip my coffee as I watch Declan sit on a bench outside the coffee shop taking a phone call. I wonder who he is talking to, but I never ask anymore. The man has given up his life for me. I owe him everything. I have two security guards that have been with me since high school, but Declan is the one I'm closest to and who has never let me down.

I take my last sip of coffee and pack up my supplies on the table. It's time to head to work. It's been a full month since I've been back in New York and even with my very specific routines, it's not getting any easier. I throw my coffee away in the trash can and turn around, bumping into someone. Coffee splashes back onto the man's expensive suit, but he doesn't make a sound. I would have yelped if it had been my hot coffee splashing on me.

"I'm so sorry!" I say while reaching for the napkins right next to me.

I grab the napkins and start blotting his shirt, right over his rock-hard abs. I blush at what I'm doing. I can't believe I'm basically feeling up some stranger's abs. I throw the napkins away and go to apologize again, but the words get stuck in my throat when I finally look up at his face. James.

I've only been back in New York for one month and I've already run into him. In a coffee shop close to where I work and at least thirty minutes from his office. Why and how is he standing in front of me right now?

I continue to stare at his face as a slow smile grows on his lips. "Everly."

My name coming out of his mouth still makes my body react. I can't breathe and I feel goosebumps rising on my skin. Is it possible that he's gotten even hotter than the last time I was with him six years ago? Those piercing green eyes and that dirty blonde hair... It's gotten longer, but he keeps it professionally styled back. The urge to run my hands through it again still hasn't left me after all this time.

I look away and close my eyes for a split second. I take a deep breath to force myself to breathe and look back at him with a friendly smile. "Hey James, it's good to see you. How are you doing?"

He keeps his smile on his face as he says, "I'm doing good. You're back in town."

I'd be surprised if no one told him I was back here. "Yep. I'm surprised Jake didn't tell you."

He frowns. "Jake and I haven't spoken much in the past few years."

That's surprising, I didn't know that. "Oh."

Oh? Really? Is that all I could think of saying? I need to get out of here before I say something stupid. "Well, I don't want to be late for work. Sorry again about your shirt, but it was good to see you."

I don't wait for his response and start to walk by him. He grabs my arm and that little spark I always used to feel with him officially turned into a full-blown fire. I can feel his touch throughout my whole body. Once again, I hold my breath as I look toward him.

"You're back in town for good?" he asks, hopeful.

I nod, even though my brain is telling me to lie. I can't.

The smile reappears on his face as he says, "Let's catch up sometime. You still have my number?"

I nod again and realize how stupid I must look. "Yeah, sure. Sounds good. See you, James."

I quickly pull from his grasp and basically run out the door. I don't stop to look over at Declan as I walk down the street to work. Declan runs to catch up with me and puts his phone in his pocket.

"Hey, everything okay?" he asks when he catches up to my side.

"Yep," I reply.

He cocks an eyebrow and puts his hands in his pockets as he keeps the pace beside me. "What happened?"

I slow down and sigh. "I ran into James."

He nods, and he doesn't look surprised. Did he see James walk in? Of course he did. He sees everything, but why didn't he warn me? He knows I want to avoid him at all costs. We don't say a word the rest of the way to the high school.

I'm polite and say good morning to everyone in the front office as I make my way to my office and close the door. I'm fifteen minutes early and I need to get back into the right headspace if I'm going to be able to do my job.

In these situations, I instinctively reach for my notebook and do what I always do. I write a letter to my dead friend. I could easily text Ashley about what happened, but the best part about writing to dead friends is that they can't respond. Ashley could respond. And I have a feeling I know what she'd say. I'm not in the mood to deal with that right now.

*Dear Lauren,*

*It's been a month since I've been back in New York. A month since I've been back in this high school, which I promised never to return to. It's been almost seven years since you've died. I miss you, friend. Being back here makes me miss you even more, especially when I walk past your old locker. When I grab lunch from the cafeteria and when I walk by our old classrooms. I just... miss you.*

*You will never guess who I ran into today. James. Yeah, I know. I also know what you would have been saying to me these past six years that I haven't spoken to him. When I saw him, it felt like no time had passed at all, other than how handsome he has become. How can he be even more handsome? I still felt the same way I did when I was around him back in high school. I doubt he feels the same. Even so, I need to avoid him... right? Catching up would be a big mistake, especially since I know he can still make me feel that way. I can't deal with another broken heart. He's still probably with that girl, anyway. He didn't have a ring on, so I know he's not married. Why am I even considering seeing him? Of course I shouldn't! Thanks Lauren, you always know what to do. I love you. I miss you.*

I place my notebook back in my desk, feeling better about my decision. Pretending I never ran into James is for the best. A knock sounds on my door as I tell whoever it is to come in. My first student of the day enters my office and sits in front of me. She always looks so sad, as though she's just going through the motions of being here until she graduates. Is that what I used to look like in high school? I force a smile on my face and know this is why I'm here. While taking this job was not ideal, students like this show me exactly why I'm here. I'm going to do my best to help them. Not just to help them get through high school, but to be happy again. To find the joy in life and not go down the path that I did.

Today went by faster than I thought it would. When I walk out of the school, Declan is on the front steps waiting for me as he always is.

"How was your day?" he asks, just like he does every day.

"It was good. How about you? You getting bored yet waiting around staring at a bunch of teenagers all day?"

He laughs. "It can be quite entertaining, actually. I especially like seeing those skipping school to make out in their cars or to do drugs."

I laugh and shake my head. I don't know how he can handle this job. There's a lot of waiting around for me and being bored. Then, when he's not bored, I keep him on his toes. I'm thankful for him and I literally owe him my life.

"You know, if you see students doing drugs, you should really report them," I say seriously.

He smirks. "Just like I reported you?"

I roll my eyes. He's right, he never reported me. He probably should have, though.

While walking to the car, I overhear some seniors talking about homecoming.

"We need to find the perfect dresses! Since we're not going with dates, maybe we can get dates while there if we look hot enough," says one girl to her two friends.

"I don't care to find a date. I need to concentrate on my grades this year," one of her friends replies.

The other friend rolls her eyes. "You're never any fun. We're seniors. We're going to do this right!"

They all giggle and get into one car, driving off. I can't help but smile at remembering this time when I was a senior here. Most of my memories are bad, but not all of them.

# ACKNOWLEDGMENTS

There are so many who I want to thank for the success of writing and getting my books out into the world. First, and foremost, to my Lord and Savior Jesus Christ who died for my sins so I may have eternal life.

To my biggest supporter since I was little, Aunt Karen. Not only have you always been supportive of my writing and every dream I've had, but you also spent countless hours editing my books and listening to my story ideas. These books would hardly be readable without you.

To my husband, who read my stories as I wrote them, listened to every crazy idea that I had, and bounced back ideas. For taking care of the kids and allowing me to dedicate time to writing. For being understanding and taking on whatever role was needed when I was exhausted and stressed.

To Kelli, who was my first reader of these books and for being invested in the story and my characters. For understanding me and my anxiety by being there for me and texting as many times as I needed to support me.

To all my friends including Ashley, Wes, Sydney, Wendi, Jordin, and Kelly for believing in me and being excited for me to write these books. For continuing to support me through my writing journey and allowing me to share my excitement with you.

To my children, who have been patient with me and never once making me feel bad for spending time writing instead of time with you. To Amara, who constantly asked me how my book was coming along and being proud of me for being a writer. To Aiden, who graciously allowed me to go write and made me smile every time I finished for the day by being excited to see me again.

To my mother and father, who both believed in me from day one when I said I wanted to write a book. For always encouraging me to write the moment I said I wanted to be an author when I was little. For being excited and proud of me for my accomplishments.

And finally, to all my readers. I wrote these books because it was something that I'm passionate about. When I put them out there, I never expected anyone to actually read them. So, thank you for taking the time to read my stories and for getting invested in my characters. I can't wait to continue the stories of the characters and see where they take us.

S. N. Christensen

# ABOUT THE AUTHOR

S. N. Christensen lives in a town outside of Atlanta, Georgia. She holds a BA in English and MA in Secondary Education. From a young age, she has dreamed of being a writer. She loves writing in the fantasy, thriller, and romance genres.

When she is not writing or reading, she can be found teaching at her church preschool and serving at her church. When she is at home, she loves to spend time with her husband and two children playing games and crafting.